THE
ETRUSCAN

Linda Lappin, born in Tennessee in 1953, has lived in Italy since 1978, where she teaches English language and translation at the University of the Tuscia, in Viterbo. Originally a poet, she received an MFA in poetry from the Writers' Workshop of the University of Iowa, and is the author of a volume of poetry, *Wintering with the Abominable Snowman*, published by Kayak Press. Her essays, poetry, short fiction, and reviews have appeared in prestigious literary journals in the US, including *Agni, the Cimarron Review, the Literary Review, the Seneca Review, the Southwest Review, StoryQuarterly* and are forthcoming in *Frank* and *Prairie Schooner*. Her essays have been nominated for the Pushcart Prize, and her short fiction has been broadcast by the BBC World Service Radio. She is currently at work on a book of essays concerning women writers and artists in the 1920s and on a second novel based on the lives of Katherine Mansfield and her circle. Active as a literary translator, she has received two NEA grants in translation from the US government and the Renato Poggioli Award for Translation from PEN.

THE ETRUSCAN

LINDA LAPPIN

**Wynkin
deWorde**

2004

Published in 2004
by

Wynkin deWorde

Wynkin deWorde Ltd.,
PO Box 257, Galway, Ireland.
info@deworde.com

A CIP catalogue record for this book is available from the British Library

ISBN: 1-904893-00-7

Typeset by Patricia Hope, Skerries, Co. Dublin, Ireland
Credit for Harriet's map on page 203: Sergio Baldassarre
Cover Illustration by Roger Derham
Cover Design Supervision: Design Direct, Galway, Ireland
Printed by Betaprint, Dublin, Ireland

ACKNOWLEDGEMENTS

This book was born of many years' exploration in Italy. I would first like to thank Cipriana Scelba and the Fulbright Foundation for bringing me to Italy in the first place. I thank Helen Ampt for introducing me to the rustic ways of peasant culture; Lido of Stigliano for information about dowsing; Umberto di Grazia for encouraging me to investigate Etruscan ruins and medieval sword traditions. Books which inspired me while researching this novel include Prof. Mirella Billi's exhaustive and fascinating study of the gothic novel: *Il gotico inglese*, published by Il Mulino, 1986; Giovanni Feo's intriguing enquiry into Etruscan religion *Misteri Etruschi: Magia, Sacralità, e Mito*, published by Stampa Alternativa; and, of course, D.H. Lawrence's *Etruscan Places*. The Etruscan sites in this novel are all real and may be visited with any good guidebook, and here I would like to express my gratitude to the spirits of those places: Barbarano Romano, Norchia, Castel D'Asso. Special thanks also to Casa Capati in Vitorchiano, where I lived while writing this novel.

I'd especially like to thank Thomas Wilhelmus for his support, criticism, and willingness to read chapter after chapter these long years and Thomas E. Kennedy without whose help this book would never have seen print. Many thanks are also due to Valerie Shortland, my editor, and Roger Derham, my publisher, for believing in this project.

Lastly, I would like to thank my parents, Virginia and Gerald Lappin, who, of course have always believed in me, and my husband, Sergio, companion of all my Etruscan adventures.

TO SERGIO

CHAPTER ONE

Stephen Hampton sat on the sofa of his sitting room, reading a letter, a blanket thrown over his crossed legs. It was a chilly October evening, and he and his wife, Sarah, had just finished their tea. The dark red damask curtains had not yet been drawn, and a deep indigo twilight coated the tall windows as the street lamps came on across Russell Square. There was an ordered stillness in the room, as often reigns in childless households; the stillness required by men like Stephen who dedicate their lives to scholarly pursuits, and who must not be disturbed by children, women, or servants. One could almost feel the silence sifting down with the dust motes and settling on all the polished surfaces of teak and rosewood, bronze and brass, in this house where Stephen had lived all his life. The electric lamps with their green and gold shades illumined a sitting room recently cleared of much of the ancestral clutter that Stephen's family had accumulated for generations, and refurbished by his American wife in a more modern style, with a handsome new sofa and a clock above the mantelpiece, both made in Berlin. Yet some remnants of empire remained: the rich red Bokhara and Beluchi carpets, the many

1

statues of Buddha and Shiva and Kali brought back by Stephen's deceased father, James Hampton, from his journeys to the East, with the exotic botanical specimens of lush palms and ferns which flourished miraculously in this room in Bloomsbury, thanks to the tireless ministrations of Mrs Parsons, the Hamptons' housekeeper.

Outside, the gates to the public garden in the square had clanged shut for the night.

The clatter of omnibuses and vans gradually thinned, replaced by the tinkling drone of motorcars and taxicabs, vaguely reminding Stephen that they would be staying at home again that evening. Earlier in the afternoon he had forbidden his wife to accept an invitation to the theatre that night, and they had quarreled. But Sarah had only just recovered from influenza and he did not want to expose her to the evening damp. Perhaps later, after she went up to her room, he might step out to his club, for a smoke and a game of chess.

The gas fire leapt behind the burnished copper grate, casting dancing spots of light across the surface of his spectacles as he skimmed, lips pursed, through the letter. Stephen was a small but agile man, just short of 50, sharp-featured with pinkish cheeks and a moustache so immaculately groomed it looked as though it had been painted on. The canny grey eyes behind the steel-rimmed spectacles were bloodshot from eye strain, for his work as assistant curator of Chinese antiquities at the British Museum overtaxed his vision in his zeal to identify frauds and forgeries. He turned this same grave scrutiny upon the letter in his hands, as if examining it for signs of counterfeit – though more from habit than from interest, and stifled a yawn for he found the letter boring. It was, in truth, addressed to Sarah and not to him, and had been written by his cousin Harriet, who had been his wife's dearest childhood friend. It was not his habit to read his cousin's letters to Sarah, and indeed Harriet kept up a steady tide of correspondence with his wife, especially while traveling – which seemed to be always – and nothing delighted Sarah more than receiving a letter from her. Stephen did not quite approve of Harriet, who had been born in America and who styled herself as

2

an independent lady traveler and photographer. She wandered about the world, carrying a camera and dressed in a pair of trousers, the latter a habit, thank goodness, Sarah had not adopted. Nor had she followed Harriet out into the streets to parade for women's suffrage, another of the many causes to which Harriet had devoted her energies in the past.

Alas, Sarah had, however, imitated his brazen cousin by cutting off her hair in a deplorable new fashion, which, she had informed him, in America was called the Flapper style. Like many American women of good family, Stephen's wife was a piquant mix of the modern and the traditionally feminine. She scorned corsets but swathed herself at bedtime in yards of expensive French lace, rouged her lips, noosed her neck with ropes of pearls, and on occasion, he was convinced, smoked cigarettes, though never in his presence. Smoking was another habit she must have picked up from Harriet, although all the ladies seemed to be doing it these days, now that the war had ended.

Prim and composed, Sarah Hampton sat across from her husband, embroidering by the light from a lamp, dressed in a midnight-blue velvet frock buttoned snugly about her bosom, and a paisley shawl draped around her shoulders. The flickering flame of the gas fire had brought a bluish gleam to her dark hair and a rosy tint to her full face. She was waiting, he knew, to learn his reaction to his cousin's letter. Harriet had written from Italy, where she had gone to photograph Etruscan tombs and her letter somewhat clumsily attempted to capture the reader's admiration with its overblown descriptions of abandoned ruins immersed in an ivy jungle. By this trite means, Stephen supposed, Harriet hoped to convince his wife to join her in Italy later on in the winter, a journey he would not allow Sarah to make alone, given her delicate constitution. Nor did he wish to accompany her, for he had seen enough of Harriet in the last few months when she had come from America for the reading of his father's will. When she had finally left for Italy in September after an overly long stay at their home, he had been relieved to have her out of their lives again, for he could barely tolerate the friendship that had bound his cousin and his wife since their schooldays in Chicago. Still, if Sarah insisted, he knew they would be forced to accept Harriet's invitation, otherwise his wife might be bold enough to set out for Italy on her own.

The clock above the mantelpiece struck 6.00, and his housekeeper, Mrs Ethel Parsons appeared in the sitting room doorway to announce an unexpected visitor. Stephen looked up from his letter, and Sarah paused, needle in mid-air, as George Wimbly came bumbling into the room. An old family friend, Wimbly was a tall, brawny fellow, balding and angular, with a perpetually rumpled but winsome look about him. He was a great favorite of Sarah's, and seeing him, she gave a cry of surprised delight. Stephen too was pleased and he rose, tossing the letter aside and hastened forward to greet his friend. Wimbly was looking older at 53, a bit yellowish and not quite well,

"I had no idea you were back from India," said Stephen. Aside from a brief exchange of telegrams after his father died, Stephen had not been in contact with Wimbly for several months.

"No, don't get up," said Wimbly to Sarah, bending down to kiss the cheek which she turned eagerly to his lips. "Forgive me for barging in like this." Then addressing Stephen, he lay his large hairy hand on his shoulder. "So sad about your father's death. Hope it was a peaceful end."

Stephen averted his face. Though eight months had elapsed since his father had passed away that spring, the rankle of grief had not abated. "Thank you," he said hoarsely, his smile tightened to a grimace, "and yes, yes it was."

"You must have a cup of tea, George," said Sarah, setting aside her embroidery, and rescuing her husband from further distressing explanations about his father's demise.

"Indeed," said Stephen. His control regained, he rang for the maid and barked, "More tea, Parsons," and ordered her to draw the curtains.

"And could you please, Mrs Parsons," said Sarah, smoothing over her husband's curt manner with a gracious smile, "bring us some more of that lovely lemon tart?"

Mrs Parsons stepped to the window to close the curtains, then took the tea tray away to replenish it, while Stephen returned to his place on the sofa and Wimbly settled himself comfortably in a chair by the window.

"What brings you to London?" asked Sarah.

"Came back a bit earlier than expected. Wanted a bit of fresh air." When in the company of old friends, Wimbly sometimes spoke a telegraphic language, often omitting pronouns and sometimes verbs. He saved all his intellectual energies for his business ventures, at which he was particularly successful. Wimbly was a tea merchant.

"I can't say London is the right place for that, George, but we are delighted to see you," she said.

"Thinking of going to Cornwall, but have some business to tend to," Wimbly paused and cleared his throat. "Reason why I am here."

"Oh," said Sarah, arching an eyebrow and glancing at her husband. She had a hunch why Wimbly had come. Years ago, before his marriage to the daughter of an Anglo-Indian colonel, he had been Harriet's most ardent suitor. His wife had died three years ago, and he had not remarried. Wimbly must have heard that Harriet had come from America for the reading of the will. He had probably expected to find her still in London.

Mrs Parsons arrived with the tea tray. Sarah dismissed her with a smile, then rose to pour the tea. Wimbly drank his cup abstractedly, his eyes darting around the Hamptons' sitting room, which had been redecorated since his last visit. His gaze finally came to rest on a life-size statue of a Javanese Buddha, glinting darkly in a corner from behind the thick, trailing fronds of an Amazonian fern. Wimbly had always found that sculpture rather disturbing, like a silent and unwanted guest. He wondered that Sarah had not convinced her husband to pack it off to some charitable bazaar. Rattling the cup in his saucer as he set it down, he cleared his throat again and shot Stephen a meaningful look. "Hoped to see Harriet here!"

"Harriet is in Italy," said Stephen, in a neutral, yet potentially menacing tone, his eyes fixed on a spot on the wallpaper, "where she is photographing ancient ruins."

"Oh?" said Wimbly, with undisguised disappointment in his

voice. "Didn't say in her recent letter was planning a journey to the continent."

"It was unexpected," said Stephen.

"I see. Well." Wimbly sighed, lifted his hands in the air and let them fall heavily on the arm rests of the chair in a gesture of resigned determination. "Must be going."

"Don't be silly, George," said Sarah, smiling at her old friend's restlessness. "You have only just arrived. I won't let you go yet."

"Was there any particular reason you wished to see my cousin?" asked Stephen.

Wimbly quite openly replied, knowing that Stephen and Sarah were his greatest allies in the project that had brought him to London. "Wanted to propose marriage."

Stephen sighed. He too had guessed as much. "You have heard, I suppose, of her unhappy liaison with Peter Cranshaw?"

"Gossip travels to the darkest jungles."

"I never liked that fellow," spluttered Stephen, welcoming an opportunity to express feelings long brooded over in silence. "It was obvious he was only interested in her connection with my family. And then when he learned that her inheritance from my father had not been as much as he had hoped . . ."

"Was it not?" asked Wimbly, with a quaver of concern. Stephen's father, an art history scholar of international renown, had been inordinately fond of Harriet, and everyone had imagined she would receive a generous endowment from him when he died.

Stephen nodded. "Yes, but never fear, suitable provisions were made for my cousin. She will be well-looked after in all circumstances. My father did see to that, fearing she might end up like her mother."

"Stephen, please, don't start in again." It pained Sarah to hear Stephen deprecate Harriet's mother, an unfortunate woman who had run off to America with a fellow – against the family wishes – and then had been left penniless at his sudden death. Estranged for many years from the Hamptons and stricken by illness, she committed suicide shortly after her reconciliation with her brother, Stephen's father, who had then assumed financial responsibility for Harriet. Harriet had continued living in Chicago where she had been educated in exclusive women's schools. Sarah had met her at boarding school, and they had been inseparable companions throughout their youth, although she was four years younger than Harriet. While traveling together in Europe one summer, she met her husband, Harriet's cousin, Stephen. In recent years, Harriet often traveled, but she always kept in touch with Sarah by letter, and from time to time, she would pass through London to visit them when her itinerary allowed. On her last visit, Stephen had been grievously shocked when his cousin became involved with a younger man, Peter Cranshaw, a hanger-on of literary circles, without a penny to his name.

Sarah now appealed to Wimbly. "I don't believe that Peter was only interested in her money. I think he was truly fond of her. And of course, there was never any talk of engagement. You know how adamant Harriet is on the subject of women's independence."

"Independence!" snorted Stephen. "If it wasn't for my father's money, she would be spending her life as an impoverished school teacher in some backward American cattle town, rather than gadding about the world. She owes her independence to us. To my family."

"It's her family, too, you know. Do you think that justified your interfering with her happiness?" She addressed Wimbly, "You see, George, it was Stephen who had a little talk with Peter and insisted that it would be to his advantage to leave Harriet alone." Turning to Stephen she said, "And he dutifully followed your instructions."

"I didn't want people laughing at her, laughing at us, at our family, at me! Friendship between men and women must be conducted with . . . a certain amount of decorum. She was making a fool of herself, with a man like that, fifteen years younger."

"You are exaggerating the age difference! It wasn't fifteen but ten. And does age really matter?"

"It matters greatly."

"And the difference in our ages? Are you not nearly ten years older than I?"

"You know it's not the same thing. It's fitting and natural when the man is older than the woman."

"Why?"

Wimbly, who had been following this argument with embarrassed dismay, coughed and intervened in their bickering. "Not surprised that a younger man like Cranshaw succumbed to her charms. Hard-headed, but so very lovely. Still. At 39 –"

"42," Stephen snapped, "And old enough to know better."

"42?" said Wimbly, slightly taken aback, "How the time passes."

"A shame she didn't accept your first proposal, years ago," said Stephen.

"Wouldn't have me. 'You need a wife who knits you scarves and tells you which end to eat your egg from.' That's what she said, when I asked her."

Sarah laughed out loud and hid her mouth with the fringe of her shawl.

Stephen glared at her. "That sounds *exactly* like something Harriet would say."

"Oh, wasn't offended. She was right. I have always been insensitive to everything around me, never noticed anything, what I was eating, if my socks matched."

"So now you are thinking of remarrying?" asked Sarah.

"Have been a widower sufficiently long enough to consider it. Doubt if Harriet will accept, but I wanted to offer comfort in our mature years. Not the dashing suitor she may still be waiting for."

Stephen sniffed, rose from the sofa, and approached the gas fire, rubbing his hands to warm them before the flames. He stood in silence, contemplating a row of Tibetan lions on the mantelpiece.

Sarah picked up her embroidery and smoothed it across her knee. She was embroidering a cushion for Harriet, who had copied the design for her from the floor of a mosque she had visited on one of her trips to Cairo. "Harriet's very much the modern woman," she said, "I don't think she would ever marry, unless for love, and perhaps not even for that." As she stitched, her needle pricked the fabric with precision and control, then abruptly jabbed a thumb. Stifling a cry, she sucked a drop of blood away unnoticed by the others.

Still standing at the grate, Stephen wheeled round with sudden impetus to face Wimbly.

"Your quest is quite hopeless, my friend," he sneered. "My cousin doubtless intends to elope with an Etruscan."

Sarah burst out laughing again despite herself, and shook her head.

"Heavens man! Whatever do you mean?" said Wimbly, alarmed.

"Come, Stephen," Sarah coaxed, "I cannot bear to see you in such an ill-humor." To Wimbly she said, "That's just Stephen's silly idea of a joke. Harriet's gone to Italy to photograph Etruscan tombs."

"Last I heard she was studying Sanscrit. That at least put her interests in my quarter of the globe," muttered Wimbly.

"Well," said Stephen, "she seems to have given up on Sanscrit, at least for the moment. I believe she will be documenting the current state of archaeological research on the Etruscan tombs, and compiling a catalogue of artefacts for a society of table-rappers."

"Harriet's patron is a distinguished member of the Theosophical Society," corrected Sarah. She hated the way her husband always belittled Harriet's projects and the people with whom she associated.

Wimbly sighed. "But a project like that could take years. I may be more decrepit than the ancient mariner by the time she returns."

"Well, you know Harriet. Once she gets it into her head to do something like this, she throws herself into it, and then drops it the moment she grows tired of it."

"Her main project is to photograph some tombs that have never been photographed before. I think it is fascinating. I admire her greatly, and you should too," said Sarah.

"Of course I do. And I am fond of her, whatever you may think," her husband rejoined.

"How did Harriet become interested in the Etruscans?" asked Wimbly.

"She had a vision," said Stephen with sardonic emphasis, toying with the lions on the mantelpiece.

Sarah frowned and explained to Wimbly, "Harriet discovered an intriguing Etruscan statue at the Museum, and decided that she would like to know more about the Etruscans."

"And then," Stephen broke in, "at a seance an Etruscan rapped on the table and commanded her to go to Italy. To Viterbo, as a matter of fact."

"Good God!" cried Wimbly. "Didn't know Harriet frequented seances. Is she quite well? Perhaps this Cranshaw business has affected her nerves?"

"I assure you that Harriet doesn't believe in table rapping. She was just amused by the coincidence you see," said Sarah. "She went along to that seance because she was a bit depressed about Peter, and needed some distraction. Then she met a gentleman from the Theosophical Society who offered some funds for her research. It's all very logical, really."

"I see," said Wimbly, dubiously. "Viterbo. Isn't that somewhere near Florence?"

"I believe it is a sort of farming town somewhere between Florence and Rome," said Sarah.

"Harriet has just invited us to spend the Christmas holidays with her in Italy," said Stephen, picking up the letter from the sofa. "Sarah is determined to go and visit her, and has been threatening to go off on her own if I don't come along. You might come with us, George?"

"Harriet might not want me to come."

"I'm sure Harriet would love to see you," said Sarah.

"You can always lodge at a pension. We might have to do that ourselves," said Stephen. "We have been invited to stay in the farmhouse she is renting in the country, but conditions sound a bit primitive. Have a look for yourself," and he handed Wimbly Harriet's letter.

"The two of you may indeed lodge at a pension if you desire," said Sarah, as Wimbly glanced through the letter, "but I will stay with Harriet. Her description of the house is so charming. 'A house where time is not,' she says, full of huge old gilt mirrors and stone masks of Etruscan gods. It sounds like such an adventure, a quaint old house and those unexplored tombs all carved in a canyon. I am resolved to go even if I must go alone and drive there in a mule cart."

"Indeed we may have to do that," said Stephen, "It would seem to be a rather backward place."

Wimbly folded the letter thoughtfully and handed it back to Stephen.

"Well? What do you think?" asked Stephen.

"Curious," said Wimbly, "curious indeed."

Sarah could not persuade Wimbly to stay for dinner as he felt rather unwell and wanted to retire early. Around 7.00, he said good bye, and let himself out through the gate. A light drizzle had begun to fall. Directing his steps toward Gower Street he surveyed the high houses along the way, checkered with yellow windows in the gloom. A taxi rattled past and pulled up to the kerb a few yards ahead. He watched the passenger alight: A tall woman in a cloak, carrying a bouquet of yellow chrysanthemums, on her way to a party perhaps. The hooded figure, the graceful stride reminded him of Harriet, although he knew of course it could not be her – but then she was unpredictable. Could she have returned from Italy without telling anyone? He hastened his step behind the woman. Just as she was slipping through the gate of a small garden, she turned to look sharply at him, alarmed, perhaps, by the sound of his advancing footsteps. In the dim light of a lamp hanging by the gate, a haggard and elderly face glared at him from beneath the hood. He halted and made an appropriate grimace of apology as the gate banged shut in his face. The woman scurried up the steps of a dark house and disappeared through the front door. A diamond of yellow light appeared in the window, casting a bright lozenge upon the steps, and then flickered out again.

This is what I have been reduced to, he thought, buttoning the top button of his greatcoat against the London chill – frightening elderly ladies on deserted streets. He took out his pipe, paused beneath a street lamp to light it, then continued on his way, sidestepping puddles on the pavement.

He had come a long way for nothing. Not that he had dared hope to convince Harriet to return to India with him. He had armed himself ahead of time against disappointment. Putting his hand in his pocket, he touched the leather pouch containing the lapis lazuli necklace he had brought her as a gift and brooded a moment on the uniqueness of his feelings for Harriet, and for the uniqueness of her person. He had never met anyone like her. Harriet was all of one piece, simply herself. Why was that so appealing in a woman? Stephen couldn't understand it, he supposed. Stephen liked his women plump and rosy and submissive. Wimbly first met Harriet, over 23 years ago when she came, accompanied by Sarah, to spend a summer with the Hamptons and her wildness, her strong-boned frame, her sinewy limbs, had excited him as no woman had ever done before. He had indulged in sexual fantasies of Harriet riding him in the tall grass, her face hidden behind a mass of tangled blonde hair. For an entire summer he pursued her, but she would never have him. He was too tame.

He had gone out to India then, partly to show Harriet he was not afraid of the adventurous life. What it had cost him, at first! He had ridden elephants, shot at tigers; he had even taken a servant girl with a silver ring in her navel, not quite by force, no – she had been willing enough. But Harriet had not been impressed with his adventures. In the end, he married Dorothy and produced two strapping sons, both of whom followed in the footsteps of their maternal grandfather in choosing a military career. With one son stationed in Burma and the other in South Africa, Wimbly rarely saw either of them. He was a free man, so to speak, and financially in excellent stead, for over the years, he had doubled the family fortune in the tea trade. But Harriet could not care less about money.

Harriet was one of those people who believe there is a secret to life, a secret that perpetually eludes them. This, he supposed, was the key to her restlessness, to her travels to remote places, to her obsession for photographing temples or tombs. Her poetic description of her Italian sojourn was characteristic: lonely canyons carved with ruins, a house full of mysterious mirrors, 'where time is not'. He too had once stood in awe before the great bronze Buddhas ablaze in the glow of a thousand guttering lamps, wondering if there was a secret he had missed, buried deep in some cellar or locked away in a mouldy chest at the top of a mountain. But life had taught him that most secrets are sordid, or at least, not really worth knowing and that the answers to existential questions are to be sought in the practical details of daily life. When Dorothy was dying he kept asking himself what the sense of all that suffering was. Then after she had gone, he had felt her near him, at first, as a sort of presence, but that sensation, so strong, so unbearably poignant, had faded after a few weeks. Now instead there was just the blank space of her absence, filled with the empty sleeves of the fine silk dresses she had become too portly to wear in later years, packed into closets he now dared not open – an absence filled with the dusty china cups in the cupboard alongside the hideous Japanese dolls she adored, and a silence that boomed in his ears when from some obscene error he called her name aloud. Harriet with her bold movements and loud laughter might have changed all that somehow, or so he had hoped.

He would go with Stephen and Sarah to Italy at Christmas, as he had some business to tend to in the South of Italy in the New Year. January might be a suitable season for a southern journey, after the holidays. Perhaps Harriet might accompany him to the land where the lemon trees grow. In such a romantic setting, she might find his arguments more convincing.

Coming out onto Tottenham Court Road, he hailed a taxi and was soon delivered to his rooms in Pond Street. Before falling asleep that night, he remembered Sarah's mention of the Etruscan statue, and resolved next day to make a visit to the British Museum and acquaint himself with Etruscan funerary art.

CHAPTER TWO

Harriet's intriguing description of her house and its Etruscan setting had aroused Sarah's curiosity, and as the autumn progressed, she was keen to set out for Italy to join her friend.

But at the beginning of November, a letter from Harriet arrived, begging the Hamptons to put off their visit until late spring, claiming that the roof of her house needed repair and that the place wasn't yet comfortable or warm enough for guests, especially given Sarah's delicate health. The influenza epidemic remained a threat in the damp and insalubrious Italian countryside. Moreover, there were no pensions or hotels or even suitable houses to let in the vicinity. It wasn't like Harriet to make such excuses, and Sarah wondered what this cooling of enthusiasm might signify. Harriet had always been her closest friend and confidante. They had no secrets from each other, or so Sarah had always imagined.

By happy coincidence, shortly afterwards Stephen was called to Paris for a consultation concerning the authenticity of a few Chinese antiques that the wife of Sir William Petrie, an old friend, wished to acquire from a French antiquarian. The pieces turned out to be nowhere near worth the quoted price and Sir William was so pleased, not only at seeing Stephen again, but at being spared unnecessary expenditures, that he invited the Hamptons to join him and Lady Brigitte in Italy at their villa in Fiesole near Florence for the New Year.

When Lady Brigitte learned that Harriet, whom she had never met, but about whom she had heard many intriguing tales, was spending the winter in Italy, she demanded that Stephen extend the invitation to his cousin as well, and when Stephen mentioned that they had originally hoped to make a trip in the company of their friend George Wimbly, he too was generously included in the group of guests.

Sarah wrote to Harriet informing her of these plans, and requesting that she join them in Fiesole, but it took ages for her reply to reach them. During this time Sarah felt uneasy; she sensed that Harriet did not want to see them and could not understand why. She knew of course that relations between Stephen and his cousin had always been rather strained, but this had never been an obstacle in the two women's friendship. Perhaps now though, after Stephen's recent meddling in Harriet's affair with Peter Cranshaw, Harriet had begun to resent her cousin's interference and might even suspect that Sarah herself had had a hand in distancing Peter from her. She hoped that Harriet did not think this, as it was most decidedly untrue. She had firmly disagreed with her husband's intervention in Harriet's personal affairs, but she had been unable to dissuade him.

Harriet's answer to her letter arrived just a few days before their departure for the continent in December. It was a brief note, this too uncharacteristic for Harriet generally consumed reams of paper for her letters to Sarah. This time her letter succinctly stated that she would arrive shortly after New Year and depart a week later, for she was very much absorbed in her Etruscan projects which she could not leave untended. This too was not a good sign and only confirmed Sarah's suspicions that Harriet wished to avoid them, or perhaps George Wimbly.

Harriet made a dramatic entrance at Sir William's villa on the evening of her arrival. A light snow was falling, very unusual weather for Fiesole. She was driven up to the door in an open cart, hired at the station. Wrapped in a brown hooded cape dusted with snow, and carrying a basket of cabbages and pumpkins, she might have been a visitation from a fairytale or a rustic winter goddess of abundance. She was followed into the villa by a small gnome-like man bearing a trunk of photographic equipment. Lady Brigitte, who adored handsome, eccentric women, found her charming and was overjoyed to see that Harriet had brought her camera and equipment. She made Harriet promise that before her departure she would immortalize them all in a series of portraits.

Sarah watched Harriet closely that night at dinner. She was dressed in her usual formal dining costume, Turkish trousers of heavy silk jersey – Harriet never wore skirts and often favored male disguise while traveling – a padded Chinese silk jacket, and a string of Tibetan baubles, heavy coral and turquoise, around her neck. Lady Brigitte expressed sincere admiration for Harriet's outfit and immediately announced to her husband that she intended to have several pairs of trousers sewn for herself. Sarah certainly had never seen Harriet look so lovely. Not a hint of frost in her blonde hair, hardly a wrinkle in her soft pink face. The country food and air had done wonders for her, and now with her face flushed and her hazel eyes aglow from the wine, she radiated a new power of seduction that was not lost on either the men or women at table.

Was it seeing Wimbly again that had brought out this new, more feminine Harriet? Sarah noticed how George leaned towards her from his chair, how she too seemed to be leaning towards him, imperceptibly, as though drawn by a magnet in her shoulder. Could it be that Harriet's feelings for George might have deepened after her recent debacle with Peter Cranshaw? Perhaps Harriet, now getting a bit too old to dream of romance and thinking of her need for companionship, might just accept George for her lover or even for her husband. Sarah knew Wimbly had come with them to Italy to propose to her, and nothing would have pleased Sarah or Stephen more if she accepted. Wimbly could give Harriet a comfortable life in an exotic setting, which would no doubt fulfill her cravings for adventure. Moreover, they were all such old friends that the union of Harriet and George Wimbly would merely be the consolidation of a long established fact, a way of keeping everything in the family.

Then, as Harriet was lifting her glass in a toast, Sarah noted a ring on her finger: a gold ring with a ruddy stone. Where had that come from she wondered? Harriet never wore rings, she said they interfered with her work. As soon as she managed to be alone with Harriet for a moment, she decided she must enquire about the mysterious ring – a Roman antique, from the looks of it, and if so, quite valuable – but Lady Brigitte chattered to Harriet all evening and Sarah had no opportunity to speak to her alone.

It snowed the next day too. The garden with its maze of laurel and boxwood hedges, lichen-stained statues and towering cypress trees, was quite transformed under the muted white. Lady Brigitte was so impressed by the magical effect that she asked Harriet to take their portraits in the garden. A *limonaia* stood at the back of the garden, a low-ceilinged structure of grey marble resembling a decrepit wedding cake, with a row of tall arched windows of frosted glass. Here Sir William stored his lemon trees in giant clay vats on wheels, which were rolled out again into the garden in spring. Lady Brigitte used the place as a painting studio in summer, and a small stage-like platform where her models posed had been built in a corner. Behind the stage an arched window of clear glass looked out over a gravel path leading straight to the fountain in the center of the maze. Glimpsed through the window, the trees hung with glittering ice, the stone masks with their frozen spurts of water offered a stunning background. Harriet asked if they could put a couple of braziers inside to keep them warm while working. An early luncheon was planned, after which they would have nearly three hours' light to work in.

None of the men wished to sit for portraits, which Lady

Brigitte had decreed must be in fancy dress. Wimbly accompanied Sir William on a tour of his *cantine*, while Stephen begged leave to spend some time in the library, examining a few rare manuscripts in his host's collection. Scorning the men for their disinterest, Lady Brigitte and Sarah went off in a huff to Lady Brigitte's dressing room, where several trunks of costumes and rich fabrics had been hauled out from a closet. Opening the old trunks, they pulled out shimmering silks and transparent gauzes – crimson, gold, and turquoise, paste diamond tiaras and burlap dominoes. With the help of her maid, Lady Brigitte proceeded to prepare costumes for Sarah and herself, fitting Sarah out as a winter nymph of Botticellian inspiration. Her own costume, however, was to be a surprise.

Meanwhile Harriet was in the *limonaia* setting up her equipment. The servants had brought in three copper braziers which would soon warm the room sufficiently. A row of squat lemon trees, studded with small fragrant fruit, was pushed against the back wall beneath a skylight, and in the warm, dampish air, the trees gave off an inebriating, pungent sweetness. In a corner, Harriet had found a box of props and curios used by Lady Brigitte for her paintings. Rummaging through it, she selected a few things: some dusty maroon velvet drapery, a tarnished brass vase, a Roman bust of Janus, a broken white-marble column. Breaking off a lemon branch, she arranged it in the vase, then assembled all these things on Lady Brigitte's modeling platform.

Just as she had finished preparing the scene, Sarah stepped into the *limonaia,* her face flushed with excitement. She could hardly wait to show Harriet her costume. Sarah wanted Harriet to be dazzled by her beauty, for she knew she was still almost as lovely as she had been in her youth, her breasts still high and firm, her waist modernly slim and her haunches, not too full, yet softly rounded. Climbing onto the platform, she slipped off her boots and tossed off her fur to reveal her costume: a pink dancer's singlet and stockings, gauzy green veils, holly girding her waist, her neck and shoulders quite bare. Beside the platform, just out of sight of the camera, stood a brazier full of blazing coals, but Sarah was so delighted by the fun of posing, she hardly needed it.

This was the sort of game Sarah and Harriet had enjoyed as girls, dressing up in costumes illustrating figures from paintings or books. Later, when Harriet had her first camera, she had photographed these scenes. Fleshing out the shadows of the imagination, she called it. Once in London they had seen an exhibition of photographs purporting to portray real fairies, little dolls with tulle wings peeping out from behind bean pods and snapdragons. Sarah was fascinated by the exhibition and suggested Harriet do some similar experiments, but Harriet had only laughed. If one really examined any photograph closely, she had claimed, one would see not only fairies, but demons, as well as the very souls of things themselves, hidden in our midst.

Harriet studied Sarah's costume gravely, without a hint of appreciation or approval, and her cool reception was an unexpected disappointment for Sarah. She whirled round once, spreading her veils above her head like Salome, then performed a low curtsey. Still Harriet remained unimpressed and did not smile.

"Don't you like my costume?"

Harriet seemed puzzled by this question. "Of course I do. You look lovely, and I am sure Lady Brigitte will be quite pleased with your portrait."

Harriet's response did not satisfy Sarah. Harriet had been thinking of something, or perhaps, *someone* else.

Peering through the camera, Harriet ordered Sarah to strike a pose, then stepped forward again to change the inclination of Sarah's chin, rearrange her veils, move aside a fold of drapery. After many readjustments, at last she was ready. "There, hold that pose. It's absolutely perfect."

Sarah giggled, "Stephen won't like it. I can tell you!"

"Hush. Don't move. Look up, over there in the corner. Not at the camera."

There was a bright flash of magnesium. As Harriet slipped out the plate and slid a new one in its place, Sarah noticed Harriet's ring again and now seized the chance to ask her about it.

"This?" Harriet said and frowned, twisting the ring on impulse. "A Roman lover?"

Harriet made a wry face. "Not exactly." She studied Sarah again through the eye of the camera. "Put your weight on your left foot and point your right toe. There now."

This reluctance was not like Harriet. "Harriet, are you keeping something from me?"

Harriet sighed. "I suppose I must tell someone. If I keep these feelings bottled up any longer, I am likely to explode." Sarah waited to hear more, but Harriet only said, "Lift your arm over your head and arch your back slightly."

Sarah obeyed. For a moment, she wondered if Harriet was referring to George Wimbly, but felt sure that could not possibly be the case. In confirmation, Harriet added, "I've met a man in Italy. Can you believe, Sarah, that at my age I have fallen in love?"

At these words, Sarah felt as though she had received a blow in the pit of her stomach. It was not just that the word 'love' had never been part of Harriet's vocabulary. In the past Harriet had preferred 'affection', 'friendship', 'fondness', even 'attraction', and it was with such terms she had once described to Sarah her liaison with Peter Cranshaw. It was not only her choice of term, but rather the passion in Harriet's voice that alarmed Sarah. She had never known Harriet to feel real passion for any man.

Sarah had always presumed that *she* was the only person Harriet had ever really loved or could ever love, and even though Sarah was married, she continued to think of Harriet as *hers* alone, in a special bond dating back to their girlhood. For it was to her that Harriet addressed her marvelous letters describing her journeys around the world; it was to her Harriet returned in between those journeys. This thought had always given Sarah a selfish pleasure, for Harriet was her link to her own past, to a time when she had lived and breathed as her own person, without Stephen's guidance. To lose Harriet to some stranger would now mean losing herself, in a way.

"An Italian?" she asked, spreading the veil over her face and pursing her lips in a kiss.

"He's a count, not that it matters. An archaeologist of sorts. Reach out with that holly bough as though you were offering it to someone. Move that veil aside. And do smile, Sarah. It's not the end of the world."

The magnesium flared again like a torch.

"But it's an impossible affair, I'm afraid," said Harriet, turning briefly away from Sarah to adjust the tripod.

"Is your love not returned?" Sarah asked softly with cruel intention.

Harriet wheeled back round. Sarah was amazed to see her friend nearly in tears.

"It is! And deeply, too," Harriet said hotly, "But you see, he is not free."

"Oh Harriet, not a married man?"

Harriet sighed again. "Not exactly. I mean I don't know."

The door burst open and Stephen appeared. Sarah shrieked half in jest, but she could see her husband was truly angry to find her there in such a scanty costume. His face was livid.

"What on earth are you doing in here, Sarah, in this state of undress ?" he stormed, "I had no idea you intended to pose half-naked. And you have just recovered from influenza!"

He wrestled off his overcoat, rushed to his wife, and bundled it around her.

"I suppose this was your idea," he growled to Harriet.

"Stephen darling, please be calm," Sarah coaxed. "First, we are only trying to please our hostess. Secondly, if you haven't noticed, it is quite warm in here from the brazier, even warmer than in the villa. And it wasn't influenza, only a head cold. You always exaggerate my weaknesses. People will think that I am an invalid."

"Believe me, you'll catch your death of cold in here. I want you to do as I say, put your clothes on, go back inside, and climb into a boiling hot bath." He glared at Harriet. "I can't have Sarah falling ill while we are on holiday."

Harriet just shrugged and said, "It's all right, Stephen, we have finished. Sarah, you may tell Lady Brigitte I am ready for her portrait."

"You see, Lady Brigitte is going to have her portrait taken in costume, too."

"It may be all right for Lady Brigitte who has the tough hide of a buffalo. Come away this instant."

"Stephen! Don't be rude."

A crescent of ivory horns bobbed by in the window and a few moments later Lady Brigitte stepped into the *limonaia* and dropped her fur from her broad shoulders. The matronly form beneath had been squeezed into a Wagnerian opera costume, complete with metallic brassiere. It was clear to all that she had overheard Stephen's remark for she eyed him with cold disdain. Begging him for an opinion of her costume, she pivoted slowly on her plump legs so that he could take in the effect. There was nothing for him to do now but grumble a polite compliment and retrench. Coatless, he slunk out of the *limonaia* and padded through the snowy garden, leaving the women to continue their work. As he headed up the path to the villa, he heard them cackling behind him.

Later Sarah lay in the tub, glad for a moment's solitude to brood over Harriet's extraordinary revelation. She could not quite believe that Harriet was in love with a man, for Sarah was convinced that Harriet preferred women, but could not admit this fact to herself. Sarah had always supposed that was why Harriet felt attracted to gentle, effeminate men like Peter Cranshaw. They were male versions of Sarah herself. Although the idea of Harriet marrying George Wimbly quite pleased Sarah, for he was as familiar to her as a comfortable, well-worn armchair, the thought of any other person coming between them was intolerable.

Sarah had never told her husband about her girlhood intimacy with Harriet. Men didn't understand that sort of thing between women. It made them uneasy. As a girl she had loved and admired Harriet totally, passionately, but it was not the love she felt now for her husband. Her passion for Harriet had been a passing phase. She no longer felt such compulsions, yet she was convinced that the impossibility of carrying into adult life the tenderness they had indulged in as girls had somehow thwarted Harriet's emotional life forever. She had remained fixated, an adolescent, always running after dreams. Sarah's love for Stephen, despite his many faults – he could be testy, priggish and despotic, although underneath he was really a good and honest man – was her *all*. A love chastened and deepened by the loss of their only child through an early miscarriage, and her inability to bear any further children. She wasn't like Harriet with a strong vocation and a sense of individual purpose. Sarah had no interest other than pleasing her husband and making a home for him. That was why Harriet with her journeys and photographs had remained her beacon, daring to live and know and seek alone in the world on her own, in a way that Sarah could not imagine herself doing. So now hearing Harriet use this word 'love' so fervently in connection with any other human being, but particularly someone of the male sex, struck her to the quick. It relegated Harriet to a whole new planet of feeling Sarah had never suspected her friend would ever even remotely understand.

After Sarah had bathed and dressed, she had a cup of tea alone in the library. A large leather-bound volume on Etruscan art lay on the great oak table by the window. Harriet must have been consulting it earlier. Sarah studied the page: there was a photograph of an Etruscan tomb sculpture showing a half-reclining figure holding up an egg. The caption read 'found near Vitorchiano'. Wasn't that the name of the village where Harriet was renting a house, not far from the town of Viterbo? She turned the glossy pages of the heavy tome filled with photographs of tombs, sarcophagi, frescoed banquets of the dead lifting their goblets of wine from fruit-laden tables, while naked dancers whirled by in a frenzy. One tomb sculpture was particularly touching: a young girl lay with eyes closed, at her side crouched a fawn, or perhaps it was a hound, lapping water from a vessel in her hand. The dead girl giving water to the fawn conveyed a sense of tender repose, yet the sculpture in the photograph on the next page was truly terrifying: a demon with a huge hammer was striking the head of a man. Sarah pushed the book away. What did these arcane symbols mean? Harriet's interest in tombs was really quite macabre. There was no understanding it.

Outside, a deep-blue twilight had descended over the garden. The snow-shrouded cypress trees looked eerie against the dusk, like huge frozen flames. The fountain in the center of the boxwood maze was still a mass of ice. From the window, Sarah could see Harriet in her cloak walking arm and arm in the garden with George Wimbly. George shuffled like an old man through the snow, leaving a trail of deep footprints as he balanced an umbrella over their heads to keep off the snow drifting down from the tree tops. To Sarah he looked exactly like a trained bear in a circus act. A flash of anger swept through her. She was furious with Wimbly for being so ineffectual, with Stephen for being so overbearing, with the unknown intruder who was about to spirit Harriet away, and above all with Harriet herself. How could she desert her, and keep such secrets from her?

Entering the library, Stephen acknowledged his wife's presence with a peremptory clearing of his throat. Sarah colored and did not turn round, still annoyed with him for his behavior earlier. Even with her back to him, she was aware of her husband's every movement. He went to a shelf, took down a book at random and leafed through it, waiting, as always for her to be the first one to smooth over their quarrel. She knew he couldn't bear being in conflict with her for more than a few hours.

Sighing, she allowed herself to be conciliatory. "It wasn't that cold you know. With the brazier it was quite warm enough." She stared out the window as she spoke, one hand tugging at the velvet curtain, as if for support.

His back was turned to her. "I just didn't want you to take cold, that's all," he said, pretending to peruse a few pages of the book in his hands. He glanced back at her over his shoulder. "Looking at the crows out in the snow?"

"Not exactly, at George and Harriet walking in the garden."

"Oh?" said Stephen, returning to his book. "They seem to have been enjoying each other's company, those two old chickens. Do you suppose he has asked her yet?"

"I wouldn't be surprised if that's what's happening out there at this very moment."

Stephen snapped his book shut, and joined his wife by the window. Half concealing his face behind the curtain, he peered out at Harriet and George. They were now at the bottom of the garden near the *limonaia*. Harriet was leaning on George's arm. They seemed to be laughing at something.

"She looks like a medieval nun in that ridiculous cloak." Stephen remarked dryly.

"But it's not ridiculous," Sarah said, "It's very practical for traveling, and it suits her perfectly." Then after a pause she said, "Why are you always criticizing her? One would think you detested Harriet."

"Don't be silly. You know how fond I am of her. It's just that I feel responsible for her, for her happiness, for her future."

"You speak as though Harriet were a child and you were her tutor."

"Well, I am in a way. In addition to the generous £300 a year left to her by my father, you know that I am bound by his dying wish to provide for her in the event that she ever find herself in distressful circumstances. This means that if she should ever become ill, like her mother was, I am to consider myself responsible for her. And you should know Harriet well enough to realize that she is rather a child. She needs guidance. She's so impractical, so foolish with her money, all these journeys and projects of hers. And when £300 a year isn't enough, she'll come to me, to us for more! I've tried to make her aware of practical concerns. Not only money. People's opinions of one are important. One's reputation. I've tried to protect her from people seeking to take advantage of her. If she marries Wimbly in the end, it will be a great relief to me. I mean, all this business of Etruscans and seances. Next thing, she'll be wanting to photograph ghosts in haunted castles. These are no doubt signs of mental instability and a diseased imagination. And I'll be the one who will have to see Harriet is looked after when she finally cracks. I'll have to pay the bills."

"How can you say such a thing! Harriet is not ill and she is certainly not mentally unstable. Nor, I believe, was her mother until Harriet's father died. Given her mother's situation, disinherited by your family and all the rest, one can understand why she became so."

"My aunt was not disinherited by her family, despite her unfortunate marriage. It is true that there were a few years of misunderstanding, but Harriet and her mother were reunited to the bosom of our family shortly before her mother died, so you cannot blame my family for her suicide. And as you know, my father was extremely fond of his sister, and of Harriet. He would not be pleased to see what Harriet has done with her life and the fine education he paid for her to have."

"Harriet is first and foremost an artist, and recognized as such by persons more knowledgeable about such things than you." Sarah regretted these words the moment they were out of her mouth. She knew what Stephen thought of modern art and especially, of women artists.

"My dear," he sneered, "you do have an odd idea of art. Is that what you were doing just now in the *limonaia*? Creating art? Tell me, was the idea for that ridiculous costume yours or Harriet's?"

"It was Lady Brigitte's but I believe she got it from Botticelli."

Stephen groaned and looked at his wife, who at 38, was still remarkably beautiful. For a moment he swallowed his anger. If she hadn't cut off her hair in that hideous modern fashion, she *might* have modeled for Botticelli. Lady Brigitte wasn't wrong there. There was no point in dragging this out any further, when what he really wanted was to feel her body close to him and stop this bickering. Above all he wanted her to return to *reason*. He wanted to bring her round so that she could see that he was right, as he was right about so many things she sometimes disagreed with. He would have to use patience, of the sort one uses with wilful children.

He relented, "I am sorry darling for spoiling your fun. But it was in your best interests. I can't have you ill, now can I, while we're on holiday abroad?" He put his arm around her. Sarah, also tired of arguing, stiffly accepted this intimacy, neither encouraging him nor squirming out of his grasp.

"So you thought the costume was ridiculous?" she asked sharply.

"A bathing suit isn't really the thing for weather like this, is it darling?" He put his hands on her shoulders and began to massage them. "I'll bet you took cold there in that draughty room. I know just what you need."

At the touch of those expert fingers, Sarah relaxed, despite herself. She dropped her head, yielding to the warmth of his hands. Her tone softened.

"It wasn't a bathing suit. It was a dancer's singlet made of cashmere and lovely and warm."

"Darling, why don't we stop quarreling?"

She leaned against him, inhaled his clean scent, and tilted her head back against his chest. A thought flickered through her mind and she grew wooden again. "You're not jealous, are you, Stephen?"

He dislodged himself slightly, and asked, confused, "Jealous? How do you mean?"

"Of Harriet and me. Of our friendship."

"Jealous of you and Harriet? What an extraordinary idea. Of course not."

"Or perhaps you didn't like the idea of my being photographed, like that, in such a revealing costume."

He dropped his hands to his sides. This time Sarah was not coming round. He frowned. "It did strike me that it wasn't something I would hang over my desk at the Museum."

"And why not?"

"I don't know why. It just struck me as tawdry. It would be different if it were a painting, or a sculpture, an idealized, abstracted form. But a photograph is so brutally realistic. That sort of posing from pictures in costume seems to me rather silly, really. A bit infantile."

"You would think that."

Stephen sighed and turned away from her. Her eyes returned to the window.

George and Harriet had rounded the corner of the boxwood

hedge and had disappeared. It had begun snowing again, and their tracks through the snow were quickly filling in with white. The electric lights had come on in the garden, and the stark branches of shrubs and trees cast curious lattice-work shadows against the shining snow. The garden was now quite deserted, but a lamp was lit in the window of the *limonaia*. Sarah wondered if Harriet and George had stepped inside there.

Stephen peered out over Sarah's shoulder. "Do you think she'll have him?" Stephen's breath clouded the glass.

"No," she said, almost glad to displease him. "I know she won't."

"And why not? Wimbly is her dear friend. He adores her and has a good income. I hope you didn't say anything to her about it."

Sarah shook her head. "There's someone else."

"She's not still in love with Peter Cranshaw!"

"No! An Italian count."

"An Italian! That's all we need now is for Harriet to elope with a penniless count with fifteen children and a mustachioed wife, and who sings *O Sole Mio* to her under her window."

"It's no joke, Stephen, I believe she's serious."

"Perhaps I should have a talk with her."

"No, please, don't intervene again. I shall try to find out more."

Neither Harriet nor Wimbly appeared at tea time, and they were not to be found anywhere in the villa. Their absence sparked off a bit of speculation and Lady Brigitte jokingly suggested a search party, but no one took her seriously. Discreetly Sarah mentioned to no one that they might be in the *limonaia*, where the lantern had long since guttered out. Fortunately, the truants reappeared separately, right before dinner. Harriet looked preoccupied; Wimbly was uncharacteristically irritable and abrupt at the dinner table, where he and Harriet all but ignored each other. The others imagined this behavior was the effect of a lovers' quarrel that would soon be put to rights.

Instead, a new strained formality sprang up between these

once fond friends. Wimbly remained with the Petries for the full length of his proposed stay. Throughout that time, Harriet maintained a cool distance from him. Then right after New Year, he set off for Palermo on business, sailing from the port of Civitavecchia. As Sir William's motorcar rumbled down the drive with Wimbly waving from the back window, Sarah wondered if they would ever see him again. Neither Wimbly nor Harriet had said a word to her to explain their frosty behavior.

A few days later Sarah and Stephen left for Paris. Their attempts to convince Harriet to come with them were to no avail, she was anxious to return to Vitorchiano and her Etruscan researches, and no doubt, to her count. They parted at the train station in Florence where Sarah and Stephen boarded the express train for Paris. Harriet's own train, a battered local, transporting peasants and farm laborers back to the country, was scheduled to leave later in the evening. Harriet accompanied Sarah to her carriage, while Stephen dallied somewhere with the porter and their trunks on a last minute errand. The two women embraced on the platform. They were an odd pair: the sleek, petite London lady of fashion in her dark blue suit and little cloche hat, and Harriet, who looked even taller in her brown nun's cloak, with rubber boots sticking out beneath it, her blonde hair ruffled by the sharp January wind. Sarah climbed aboard, and was shown to her compartment. Through the open window, she reached her hand down to Harriet. Harriet clutched Sarah's small gloved hand with her strong fingers, now chapped and reddened by country life.

"You've told me nothing more about your count. I wonder if he knows how lucky he is to have conquered your affections?" Sarah said, seizing this last opportunity, for Harriet had told her nothing more about the man with whom she claimed to be in love.

Harriet dropped Sarah's hand, made a wry face, and looked away at the crowd milling on the platform.

"He's an unusual person," she said, "One in a million."

"He must be very handsome?" Sarah asked coyly.

Harriet stared at her as if not quite comprehending. "You

know I never really thought about it. I suppose he is, in his own way, if you consider a bear or a boar or a porcupine handsome. You might say he's a bit of all three," and she smiled faintly as if at a private joke.

Stephen appeared now at the end of the platform with a porter, who was trotting as fast as he could go, wheeling a cart piled with their luggage down along the line of carriages. It struck Sarah that even with a whip, Stephen couldn't have made the porter go any faster. Her husband waved to them with his hat. He looked hot and flustered.

Harriet, her face set in an unusually earnest expression, looked back up at Sarah. "I suppose you probably don't know what to think of all this. I don't even know myself. I've disappointed George terribly, as well as you and Stephen, I know, but it couldn't be helped."

"You have told me so little but I sincerely hope for you that it will all work out for the best. I do so want you to be happy."

"Happy or not makes no difference. He is *necessary* to me. Quite simply, to me he's like the sun. A secret sun no one knows but me."

Sarah was amazed by this extraordinary confession, but had no time to react. Stephen had now reached them, and was blustering about, giving orders to the porter who had begun to load their luggage onto the train.

"We're all ready now," said Stephen to Harriet, "I'm sorry you won't be coming with us."

"But you and Sarah must come visit in the spring. I'm counting on it."

"Yes, of course."

The train man blew the whistle and the carriage attendants urged the passengers to climb aboard. The carriage doors slammed all along the train.

"Better go," said Harriet, briefly embracing Stephen, brushing her cheek lightly against his before he hopped on board. She reached up to take Sarah's outstretched hand again through the window and held on tightly until the train began to move, forcing their hands apart. Sarah stayed at the window gazing back at Harriet for several long minutes. Then the train veered onto another track and she lost sight of her.

"I do hope she's going to be all right," she said, more to herself than to Stephen.

Later that evening, going through the Alps, Sarah could not sleep as the rough vibrations of the train kept jarring her awake. Lifting the window-shade an inch, she glimpsed a bright star above those shadowy peaks. A faint light filtered in. Her husband, lying in the lower berth cleared his throat to signal that he was awake, too. She lowered the shade. "I have been lying here thinking about Harriet," she said softly to the darkness, "I think she has been bewitched."

"Bewitched! That's a strong term. You women love to exaggerate."

"I've never seen her so . . . *taken* by anyone. I only hope that it won't be a bitter disappointment. She has already mentioned an obstacle of some sort."

Stephen made no reply to this remark. Instead he said, "I'm thinking of sending Parsons out to Harriet for a few months. She needs looking after. Someone who knows her ways and her language could only be a beneficial presence."

"But Harriet speaks Italian fluently, and she seems quite satisfied with her domestic help. Mrs Parsons on the contrary doesn't speak a word of Italian, and I would imagine having to adapt to foreign circumstances would be rather a strain on her, especially at her age."

"I tell you, Harriet needs looking after."

"Do you mean to spy on her, Stephen?"

"I assure you that is not my intention. I will send Parsons out for Harriet's own good. We'll have to engage another housekeeper for the time being. I shall arrange for a substitute as soon as we're back in London."

CHAPTER THREE

The door to the carriage burst open after much insistence and an older woman in a broad-brimmed hat peered out. A kerosene lantern hanging from a post dimly illuminated a sign over the entrance to the station across the tracks: ORTE. A portly figure in grey gabardine, clutching an umbrella, climbed down from a first-class carriage. At this late hour Mrs Ethel Parsons was the only person getting off here. She felt uneasy as she surveyed the deserted platform: she had expected to find someone waiting for her, but there wasn't a soul in sight. Not that she was expecting Miss Harriet to come in person, but surely Miss Harriet must have arranged for someone to fetch her from the train. Then again, Mrs Parsons hadn't counted on arriving past midnight. There had been a delay of several hours at the border between Italy and France.

The lights were burning in the building and through the windows she could see a few men milling around. She would have to go inside and see if someone was waiting for her there, but first she needed to find out what they had done with her trunk.

The train was still standing at the station. She looked towards the rear, down along the line of sleeping cars with lowered blinds, searching for the baggage car. Just then, the door to one of the cars banged open and several large bundles, crates, and sundry objects were hurled out onto the platform, and among these she recognized her trunk. As she hurried down the platform, a lantern waved, a whistle blew, and the train chugged out. A gust of black smoke descended upon her, enveloping her in a cloud of soot. She grabbed a handkerchief, brought it to her mouth and eyes, and when the cloud cleared she saw three men climbing over the tracks towards the pile of baggage on her platform. One of them reached for her trunk.

"Wait a minute if you please!" she shouted and trotted towards them. The men turned to stare in amazement as she came huffing out of the darkness from the other end of the platform.

She caught her breath, her bosom heaving, and appraised the situation. They looked to her like a pack of cutthroats, all ragged and unshaven, stinking of sour wine. With unwavering authority, she pointed her umbrella at the man who had seized her trunk and commanded, "That is mine and I'll thank you to carry it into the station, but no further," and then pointed at the station with the tip of her umbrella. The fellow seemed to understand these gestures well enough, although she doubted he knew a word of English. She followed the men, clambering right over the tracks and into the station.

Her heart sank as she stepped into the building. Among the crowd of idlers and beggars thronging the main hall, there was not a single respectable-looking person who might have been sent by Miss Harriet. She began to doubt that Miss Harriet had received Mr Hampton's telegram telling of her arrival. Luckily, in her purse, she had Miss Harriet's address and some Italian money Mr Hampton had given her.

A thick crowd of oglers quickly formed around her, gaping and laughing at her, and saying indecent things, no doubt. Soon they began to quarrel with the filthy little man carrying her trunk. Refusing to be intimidated, her porter defended himself verbally as best he could. Then one of the cut throats gave him a little poke, followed by a push. To her dismay, the man dropped her trunk and challenged his aggressor. A brawl was about to ensue, with her trunk and person right in the middle. To prevent further damage, she brandished her umbrella above her head and began to call loudly for help.

A guard roused by all the noise ambled over to see what was happening. He was astonished to find this stout old lady at the center of the commotion, whacking at the air with her umbrella. Taking her rudely by the arm, he conducted her to the station-master.

Mrs Parsons sat in the station-master's office where the wall clock had stopped at 8.45. Patting her flushed face and throat with her sooty handkerchief, she tried to explain to the station-master who she was and what she was doing there. The poor man knew no English and only stared blankly at her through his red-rimmed eyes and scratched the bald dome of his head as she concluded her story. But when she showed him the slip of paper where the words – *Miss Harriet Sacket. Vitorchiano Via Manzoni* – were printed in clear black letters, his face lit up with relief. He led her out to the square in front of the station where a milk cart stood hitched to a scrawny white mule. He motioned to Mrs Parsons to wait there and went to find the driver, who was dozing under an old blanket on a bench inside the station.

The porter, who had been following her about, now appeared with her trunk, loaded it onto the cart and stretched out his palm for a tip. She fumbled in a pocket, pulled out an unfamiliar coin and dropped it into his hand. The man frowned, muttered something, spat on the ground and shook his fist at her. Before she had time to reply properly to his insults, the driver arrived, and hoisted her bodily onto the cart. Off they rattled into a spring night, damp with many stars.

They crept along for what seemed like hours down lonely roads through the countryside, where there was hardly a tree or a farmhouse. At last the road petered out into a muddy track where the cart got stuck, and Mrs Parsons had to get down and help the driver push the wheels out of the muck, smearing red clay on her new traveling outfit and ruining her best pair of shoes. Then, after the driver had shamelessly relieved himself behind the cart, in full view, he hoisted her back on, jumped up, and off they went again.

The driver was a lanky, taciturn young man with a well-clipped moustache and a pipe clenched between his teeth. He hummed tunelessly under his breath as they drove along, glancing over at her from time to time in undisguised curiosity. She squinted back at him and clutched her umbrella, trying to fathom his intentions. She doubted that the station-master would have given her into the hands of a known murderer or rapist, but when he finally pulled up outside an abandoned-looking farmhouse along a dirt road, she began to have serious doubts.

He hopped down and came round to help her descend. She looked up at the house in apprehension. Not a light burning and all shut up for the night. The yard out front was untidy with chicken pens and rusted tools. Surely Miss Harriet could not be living in such a place. She shook her head. Perhaps he intended to leave her here and make off with her trunk. Or perhaps he had even more evil ideas. She gripped the edge of the cart and said very firmly, "I am not getting off until I am sure that this is the right place." He started talking to her then, pointing at the house, nodding his head, urging her, by dint of gestures, to climb down but Mrs Parsons refused. Exasperated he unloaded her trunk and put it by the steps. Then he jangled a sort of sheep bell hanging on a string by the entrance, and when no one answered, he rapped the knocker loudly and pounded furiously on the door.

It didn't look good to her at all. But what could she do? She couldn't go back to the station, and she couldn't very well stay out in the damp until morning. The house looked quite empty, or even possibly haunted and she began to get the uneasy feeling in her stomach that she sometimes got after a bad dream. At last a pale gleam, too dim to be a lamp, more like a candle, filtered through the slats of the shutter above the door. The window opened just a crack and a small, dry voice, like the voice of a sick child, whined something in Italian. The driver launched into a long harangue not one word of which Mrs Parsons could understand. Anxiously, she tottered down from the cart, approached the window, and beating on the door with her umbrella said as clearly as she could, "I am Mrs Ethel Parsons, the housekeeper of Mr and Mrs Stephen Hampton of Russell Square and I would be obliged if you would tell miss Harriet Sackett that I am here."

The window swung open. A face appeared briefly, then was gone. There was a slight stirring noise inside, like mice in a nest, then a creak of hinges. The door opened, and there stood a thin, hunched figure in a dirty nightdress, holding a dripping candle stub. It was Harriet, but she was so changed Mrs Parsons hardly recognized her.

"Parsons," said the figure stumbling forward and collapsing into the driver's arms. The candle stub dropped from her hand almost setting the poor man's jacket ablaze. A spattering of burning wax scorched Mrs Parsons' wrist as she stooped to retrieve the candle, still alight. While the driver held Harriet propped up like a rag doll, Mrs Parsons lifted the candle to her face. Harriet's skin looked yellow in the candlelight. Her nightdress was stained with bile and old blood.

"We must get her back to bed," she cried, and putting Harriet's arm around her shoulder, she helped the driver carry her upstairs.

The house was cold and dark, full of dust and cobwebs. No one else was living there, and as far as Mrs Parsons could see, Harriet had no servants. They found a bedroom and laid her in bed, covering her with some blankets smelling of mildew and old dogs.

The man went back down to get Mrs Parsons' trunk and brought it upstairs. He wanted to be paid immediately, but Mrs Parsons shook her head, pointed at Harriet in the bedroom, and repeated the word 'doctor' several times, gesturing that the man should go away and return again. The driver shook his head to say he didn't understand. Then she pulled a large bank note out of her purse, flaunted it before him and repeated her message again. This time he understood, and as he reached to snatch the money, she slipped it into her bosom. He muttered what must have been a frightful curse, but then ran down the stairs, and drove off as fast as the poor mule could manage, cracking his whip in the night as the cart jogged away.

Mrs Parsons had a look through the house, but could find no oil for the lamps, only a few candle stubs that mice had been chewing on. There was hardly any wood to build a fire, but she managed to light a small fire in the sitting room with pieces of an old crate, some newspapers, and a charred log salvaged from a previous fire in the fireplace. The kitchen was a large, dark, draughty room, smelling of smoke, ash, and mould, where a huge fireplace dominated one entire wall. It was furnished with an ancient cast-iron stove equipped with several voluminous cast-iron cauldrons, a rough stone sink, and a marble-topped table, gelid to the touch and long enough to lay a corpse out on. There were a few cupboards, but upon investigating them, Mrs Parsons found they contained little but bags of stale bread and a single egg, god knows how old. Then in one of the cupboards, she found a row of glass jars. Lifting a candle to the shelf, she was perplexed to discover that the jars contained mushrooms – which really looked to her more like toadstools – orange and purple, floating in dark green oil. On the hearth was a flask of wine, so she poured herself a glass and drank it down in one gulp, finding it delicious. She went into Harriet's room and sat on the edge of the bed, with her face in her hands, waiting for the doctor while Miss Harriet moaned and tossed in her sleep.

Two hours later the driver returned with the doctor, a thin, sallow man, with a patchy beard and a worn top hat, who, mercifully, spoke a few words of English. He seemed surprised to find Mrs Parsons there. Mrs Parsons also noted that he must have been familiar with the house for he went straight to Harriet's bedroom without having to enquire where it was. Demanding to be left alone with the patient, he shut the door firmly. A few moments later, he stuck his head out, asked for boiling water and closed the door again. The alarm in his face and voice upset Mrs Parsons who wondered uneasily what he intended to do to poor

Miss Harriet – but she obeyed. She found a tarnished copper kettle and trivet in the kitchen and boiled the water over the fire in the sitting room, then carried the steaming kettle straight into the bedroom, without bothering to knock. Concerned, she saw Harriet's nightdress was now drenched in bright red blood. She would have stayed to offer assistance, but the doctor shooed her out again, and locked the door behind her, so she waited in the sitting room, standing by the fireplace, wringing her hands as Harriet's screams echoed through the empty house.

At last the screams subsided, the key turned in the lock, and the doctor emerged from Harriet's room, looking somewhat relieved but exhausted. Mopping his brow with a grubby handkerchief, he explained, in what English he knew, that the patient's condition was delicate, but that with rest and care she should be all right. Then he invited Mrs Parsons to follow him into the room. She tiptoed over to the bed where Harriet lay unconscious covered by a torn strip of sheet. Blood-soaked bedclothes were heaped in a corner. Mrs Parsons surmised that Harriet must have had a miscarriage, and that the doctor had assisted a process which had probably begun before his arrival. Poor Miss Harriet was lucky to be alive, after losing so much blood. Mrs Parsons gathered up the red-stained bedclothes and carried them out of the room. The next morning she would burn them, and then proceed with a thorough cleaning of that filthy house.

The doctor left a few phials of medicine for his patient and promised to return within the next two days. Mrs Parsons offered him a banknote, but he refused to take it. Dawn was breaking as she accompanied him out to the mule cart, still waiting in the damp outside the front door, with the driver huddled asleep. She roused the driver with a poke and handed him his pay, then, after the doctor had climbed aboard, she enquired of him where she might find a post office. He pointed down the road towards an old stone gateway, about half a mile away.

At 8.00 that morning, in mud-stained shoes and splattered overcoat, she walked to the village, found the post office and sent a telegram to her employer in London.

'Miss Harriet gravely ill. Please advise.'

She then visited a shop in the village and managed to buy fresh bread, fruit, cheese, tea, oil for the lamps, and a bit of meat to make Miss Harriet some broth. Counting her coins on her way home, she was sure she had been cheated. Later that day, she built a fire in the garden and burned Miss Harriet's bloody sheets.

Mr Hampton's reply came sooner than expected. A boy on a bicycle brought a telegram to the house that very evening, as she stood battling to light the huge old-fashioned stove to boil some water for tea. Tearing it open, she was relieved to read that he and Mrs Hampton would set out immediately for Italy, and she should expect them by the end of the coming week. She did not want to be alone there for much longer if Harriet's condition should worsen, and to her mind things didn't look good at all. Harriet's fever had soared that afternoon, and Mrs Parsons feared infection might have set in. She had seen women in Harriet's condition before, done in by some careless doctor with a dirty button hook, but she didn't intend to tell the Hamptons about the operation she suspected the doctor had performed on Harriet the previous night. It would be much too dreadful a blow to Mrs Hampton. Better keep mum than be the bearer of distressing news, especially if Harriet should not recover. If Miss Harriet did pull through, there was no need for them to know this nasty detail, and if she didn't, surely it wasn't her place to tell them. That should be the doctor's duty. The only thing she could do now was to nurse Miss Harriet as conscientiously as she could, and pray that she recovered.

The next morning, while going through Harriet's dresser drawers in search of clean linens and nightdresses, she discovered a small, green, leather-bound book of ruled note paper.

It was a diary of sorts, presumably written by Miss Harriet. The first page bore the heading *Autumn 1922,* – which must have been when Miss Harriet had first come out to Italy. A hundred pages or so of dense script followed. Then came a blank section, and another heading *Winter 1922,* and then *Spring 1923.* In the latter pages of the third section, the handwriting had deteriorated into an almost illegible scrawl. Mrs Parsons took it to bed with her that night in order to examine it more closely, thinking it might be important, and considering Miss Harriet's dire state, she felt circumstances demanded that she delve deeper. Propped up on her pillows with her spectacles perched at the end of her nose, she opened the volume to the first page and began to read in the dancing flame of an oil lamp.

The Notebook of Harriet Sackett
Autumn 1922

1

The road to the tombs skirted a field of shriveled sunflowers, an army of nodding heads on stalks, bowed and blackened, awaiting harvest. There were no houses out this way, only wide expanses of tawny stubble, alternating with strips of freshly ploughed clay. Here and there on a hilltop, a dead oak or cypress punctuated the empty sky where hungry crows swooped low.

Grazing in the quiet meadows were flocks of dirty sheep. Their bells tinkled as they turned their heads to stare at me. A solitary traveler on the road, an alien by local standards: a tallish woman, no longer young, wearing a pair of moleskin trousers and rubber boots; a rucksack swinging on my shoulders. The black felt hat pulled low over my forehead concealed my cropped blonde hair. When working or traveling, I always dress in men's clothes. To those placid sheep I probably looked like a walking scarecrow.

In the distance, beyond the brown hills, I could just see the tip of a square tower where the owner of all this land lived – a reclusive count who also owned the farmhouse I rented nearby, on the outskirts of the village of Vitorchiano. The tombs I was going to visit that day were part of the tower estate, and I had been told that I should apply there to request official permission to photograph them and arrange for a guide. I had come to this remote corner of Italy to research Etruscan sites.

The Count had never answered the three requests I sent asking for permission. I was irritated by his failure to reply and wondered why he hadn't bothered. Was it laziness, inefficiency, or, as I suspected, haughty dismissal of my project, so typical of European men who never take women seriously. I had encountered such attitudes many times before.

After waiting a couple of weeks for an answer, I decided to dispense with formalities and just go along by myself to have a look at the tombs, even though I had been warned this might not be advisable for a woman alone, as it was a steep trek down through snake-infested terrain. That did not frighten me in the least. My rubber boots were sturdy. Besides, I couldn't afford to waste any more time.

Nor was I concerned about the Count's reaction to my unauthorized visit. I didn't even know the man. I had been his tenant now for nearly a month and I hadn't yet glimpsed him even from afar. I had heard that he was an amateur archaeologist of some repute and an expert on the Etruscans. That made me curious about him, I admit, but I wasn't going to go out of my way to make his acquaintance, seeing that he was too busy to acknowledge my letters. He'd never need to know that I had gone trespassing on his property. Anyway, he might be away on a journey, or bedridden, or even dead, for all I knew. Maybe that's why he never answered his mail.

Now the road climbed a hill where neat rows of grapevines lined the slopes in perfect parallels. The *vendemmia* had ended weeks ago, but a few yellow leaves and brown clusters still clung to the vines, rustling in the light wind. Beyond the vineyards lay another stretch of meadow. I had seen from the map that the meadow ended on the edge of a small canyon where a trail led down to Norchia: a sprawling city of tombs carved by the Etruscans over 2000 years ago along the cliffs of a gorge. No photographs of this site had yet been published in England or America and I had been sent here by the London Theosophical Society to prepare a report on the area. I wasn't planning to take any photographs of Norchia that day, so I hadn't brought my camera and equipment. I only wanted to explore the place beforehand, to see how much was visible amid the encroaching vegetation.

My boots crunched along the gravel as I gazed up at the drifting clouds. Except for the sporadic circling of crows, that lonely road seemed unnaturally still. Then as I rounded a bend, a dog began to bark and I almost jumped when I saw a huge black Belgian sheepdog standing in the vineyard up ahead where two peasants were pruning the vines. I halted in alarm but the dog kept barking, tail down, teeth bared. The men looked to see what was wrong. Noticing me, they put down their tools and stared. One of them grabbed the dog by its collar. The animal strained forward growling, ears, eyes, and nose alert to my every move.

In my career as a traveling photographer I have run into a few scrapes, and have developed a sixth sense about risky situations. I must admit I felt a bit nervous this time, out there in the middle of nowhere, but I was used to looking after myself. I told myself that those men were peasants, not brigands, and would probably return to their work as soon as I passed by. I was also fairly certain they would not let the dog attack me. I wondered whether I should take off my hat. I had read that dogs are sometimes frightened of people in hats, and yet I was reluctant to reveal my hair to these uncouth fellows. In such a backward country, a woman in trousers with bobbed hair might be considered an outright provocation. And indeed, I didn't like the way they were leering at me. I averted my gaze, hunched my shoulders, and tucked my chin into my collar so they couldn't get a good look at my face – then, feigning more confidence than I really felt, approached at a steady pace.

While one of the men kept the dog at bay, the other sauntered down to the road, and stood hands on hips in a menacing pose. It was obvious he wanted to bar the way. He was an older fellow with grey hair, somewhat stout, wearing a mud-smeared jacket. There was no way to avoid him unless I took off through the fields, which I thought unwise, given the circumstances. A confrontation between us seemed inevitable.

I thought I had better do something to ease the tension, so I nodded to them and said in a low voice, "Buona Sera," – in Italian, which I speak well enough, despite my marked Yankee accent. They were, perhaps, too amazed to reply, for they said nothing and just gawked. As I strode by, the dog snapped its white teeth. The peasant holding it let go – intentionally or not I do not know, and the animal lunged down the slope toward me. I cried out and stumbled back as the shaggy black form pounced through the air, missing me by a few inches. Just as the dog was about to spring again, the older peasant roared out a command, and the beast dropped instantly to its haunches in the road, peering at me with intense yellow eyes, its tail beating the ground. More furious than frightened, I glared at my would-be attackers, though I must say, that dog was well-trained. It occurred to me that this might have been the peasants' idea of a joke.

The dog's master stepped forward and mumbled an apology, "Signora," he said, with unexpected gentility, stressing that word *Signora* as if to show he had seen clean through my mannish disguise, "Don't be afraid. His bark is worse than his bite." To my astonishment, the dog trotted over, sniffed me between the legs, as dogs do, and licked my hand.

At that, the other man snickered strangely, and I turned to look at him, as I had not yet observed him closely. He couldn't have been more than eighteen, and was sickly thin. He seemed to be affected by some spastic disorder, for one shoulder twitched continually and his head lolled from side to side as he gaped at me. I felt a stab of pity for the young man. Many poor countryfolk, I knew, suffered from muscular and mental diseases which might have found alleviation in another social environment.

The two peasants, and even the dog, stared at me as if expecting me to speak up, offering some explanation for my presence there. Clearly they considered me quite an odd creature, if not an intruder. But I saw no reason to comply, after all it was a public road. Now that the dog had been subdued, they seemed less threatening. I wanted no further contact with any of them, so I nodded a curt reply to the peasant's apology and hurried on.

Just beyond the vineyard, the road divided. The road to the right circled back to the village, the one to the left led on to the tombs, and I headed now in that direction, but I had gone only a few paces when a voice rang out behind me. "Signora! Madame! Mees! Mees!" the older peasant was bellowing, in an attempt to produce an English sound, 'Miss,' perhaps the only one he knew. Glancing back I saw him following me. The young man and the dog trailed behind – I noticed then that the boy limped as he walked. Seeing that he had caught my attention, the older fellow waved and hastened his step. "You must be lost!" he blathered, "That's not the way to the village!"

Annoyed, I simply ignored him and broke into a fast trot. With that belly on him, I doubted he could run very fast. Still, I wanted to be free of him, so I kept running until I reached the brink of the gorge, where a giant oak tree stretched its branches across the canyon. Chest heaving, I leaned against the tree and caught my breath.

The view from here was stunning. The gorge spanned at least 300 yards across, its steep walls thickly covered with scrub oaks whose ochre and russet leaves shivered in the wind.

There was a drop of 100 yards to the bottom, where I could hear the swift gurgling of a stream concealed in the tangled undergrowth. I looked about for the trail, and then spotted a narrow groove carved in the cliff wall, leading downward. Alongside the groove, a series of hand holds had been bored. This, I surmised, was the only way down. Could I still manage such a climb? Now in my 40s I wasn't as limber as I once was. I took another deep breath, pushed up my sleeves and started down.

I had just placed my right foot firmly in the first notch of the groove and was about to lower myself down, when the peasant came huffing through the grass. As I slipped over the rim of the gorge, he shouted, "Signora, stop! You cannot go down there. It's dangerous," and began to run towards me.

"I want to see the tombs," was my chilly response and I lowered my foot to the next notch.

"You'll fall and break your neck!" he called, sticking his head over the edge and scowling at me. He reached out his arm to help me back up again.

Paying no attention to the brown fingers groping a few inches from my nose, I surveyed the drop below. It was much steeper than I had imagined and the groove in the rock too narrow in spots for my boots to maneuver comfortably in. Those Etruscans must have had smaller feet than my own size nine. It had rained recently and the groove was choked with slick, decaying leaves. But by grabbing hold of a root protruding from the cliff wall, I slid down to a ledge rather easily, where I breathed a sigh of relief and congratulated myself for being more athletic than I usually gave myself credit for.

"Don't worry," I called back, "I am perfectly all right," then added, as an afterthought, "Thank you all the same for your concern," and dismissed him with a wave of my hand.

At this the man muttered something indecent, pulled his arm back, and left me alone. Glad to be free of this nuisance, I looked to see where I was. I was standing on a sort of shelf extending along the cliff for quite a distance. It was not a sheer drop to the bottom, as it had appeared from above, for from this point on, the cliffs tumbled down in a series of giant steps or levels. There must have been three or four levels before you reached bottom and on each level a row of tombs was carved, half hidden by brambles and bushes.

I turned and discovered my first tomb, gaping right before me. Yellow lichen covered the facade, glittering in the sun. The immense doorway cut in a T shape, symbol of the Etruscan religion, led into a dark chamber where a thick growth of ferns sprouted at the mouth, and long scraggly vines trailed from the cliffs above. In the murky puddle of rainwater collected just inside the entrance, I spied my own reflection: a dark, hatted figure against a pewter sky.

Peering in, I could see that this entryway led to several other chambers hollowed in the cliff. The wall was blackened on one side and the charred remains of a camp fire lay piled near the entrance. A rusted iron grille leaned upright against the tomb wall, evidence that the place offered refuge to hunters, or shepherds, perhaps, who came here to cook their dinner at night, while their sheep grazed in the meadow above. The tombs were not as unfrequented, then, as I had thought. I did not venture very far inside, however, as I had not brought a lantern or any candles. My intention was to familiarize myself with the whole area before exploring the interior of the tombs.

About a dozen tombs were located along this shelf. Some had huge doors with stately decoration, others were mere grottoes, or just rough holes. I wandered along, cursorily inspecting them from the outside, making a mental note of the ones I would like to photograph. I was eager to see more.

A stairway in the rock led down from the shelf where I stood to the next level. But where the stairs ended there was a ten-foot drop. Here too, hand holds had been bored in the rock face. I knew it would be difficult, but not impossible, for me to scramble up again, and after a moment's hesitation, encouraged by my unexpected dexterity at rock climbing, decided to proceed. But first, I looked up at the sky where livid clouds had gathered. We might be in for a drizzle. This did not worry me too much, as I was wearing rubber boots and my faithful fedora, quite waterproof. I glanced at my watch, which I wore on a long chain around my neck. There wasn't much light left, as it was nearly 4.00 in the afternoon. Yet I was too fascinated to turn back before exploring a little further. I didn't intend to remain much longer. I would just take a quick look at the lower level, climb back up, and head for home.

The drop was even steeper than the previous one, but feeling intrepid, I seized a branch and plunged down. I have no memory of the flight or impact, no memory of pain or even recognition of what was happening. All I remember is the sharp cracking of the branch as it broke off in my hand. I do not know how long I lay there in the rain but I woke to see not the sky overhead, but a brown ceiling carved in stone. I smelled smoke and tallow, and turning my head slightly I saw the sputtering flare of a small torch fastened to the wall. I could hear the sound of heavy rain pummeling the ground. Although still groggy, I realized that I had been carried into one of the tombs where I now lay on a cold, lichen-spotted bed of stone vacated at an unknown time in the past by a dead Etruscan.

A broad face appeared from the shadows above me, hovering a few inches from my own. Its breath was warm and fetid; I recoiled from the strong smell of liquor and garlic. As my eyes focused on its features more sharply, I recognized the grizzle-haired peasant. He murmured something incomprehensible, then tipped a flask into my mouth. Brandy stung my lips and throat. I coughed, stirred, and felt an excruciating pain in my left ankle.

"So you've come round," he said.

I tried to sit up, but he held me down with a powerful arm.

"Don't try to move," he said, "You may be hurt."

My wet trousers clung to my legs, but looking down I could see that the clothes on the upper part of my body: jacket, shirt, undershirt, and even brassiere, had been removed and lay in a soaking pile beside me. In their place I was wearing a rough, woollen shirt which chafed the bare skin of my breasts. My boots and wet socks had also been removed. I must have slipped and lost consciousness, and lain there under the rain until I had been discovered and brought into the tomb where presumably this man had partially undressed me. I stared at the peasant standing next to me, eyeing me with a mix of suspicion and concern. Thick tufts of grey chest hair poked through the gaps between the tarnished buttons of the jacket – several sizes too small – fastened to his chin. Apparently he had taken off his own shirt to give me something dry to put on.

"I warned you," he said. "You might have been killed." He tried to give me another sip of brandy, but I pushed the flask away.

"No more," I said. "I am fine now."

My head was spinning, perhaps from the fall, and I wondered how much he had made me drink. I was grateful at being rescued and dressed in something partly warm and dry, but not at all pleased by the thought that he had stripped me half-naked and ogled me there in the tomb. As my wits returned, I understood what sort of situation I was in, alone, with him, like this, and I began to feel uncomfortable. I wanted to have a look at my watch so that I could see how late it was, and perhaps gauge how long I had been lying there. I felt a searing pain in my shoulder as I reached into my bosom to pull out my watch. Feeling under the shirt for the chain, I found it was gone. My first thought was that he had stolen it.

"Looking for this?" he smiled and dangled the watch chain in front of my eyes. The face was smashed. "No good now," he said. "You'll have to have it fixed." He slipped the chain around my neck and glass shards tinkled to the ground.

I didn't like his smirking manner at all. "We must go now," I said, "They'll be looking for me."

He glanced outside at the rain, still falling heavily. "Not yet, we must wait for it to stop."

"No," I said firmly, "I must go now. Surely I can't get any more soaked than I am already."

He said nothing and just stared at me. His eyes looked uncanny in the torchlight, piercing green, with iridescent flecks of yellow, like the frozen eyes of a stuffed parrot.

It was impossible to tell how old he was. An unkempt bush of silvery hair gleamed above a face as smooth and ageless as a bronze mask.

Once again he offered me the flask of brandy, but I shook my head. He took a sip himself, and then, stepping over to the foot of the slab where I lay, poured a few drops into the hollow of his hand and began to massage my ankles.

"This," he said, "should help get you back on your feet again."

I was about to protest at being handled in this manner, but at his touch, the pain in my ankle dulled to a tolerable ache. The sensation of warmth emanating from his hands was extraordinary, and in the cold damp of the tomb, extremely comforting. I put it down to the effect of the brandy I had drunk as well as the tingle of alcohol against my clammy skin.

49

I should have realized that this man with red clay caking off his sleeves, plying me with such solicitous attentions, was no boorish peasant. Firstly, he did not have the harsh, aspirated accent of the local peasants. His hands were smooth, with long tapered fingers, and he wore a gold ring set with a cornelian. These details made sense to me later, after I had learned the identity of my rescuer, which only a fool could have failed to guess. But at the time, I was hardly able to reflect, for as he stroked my feet and ankles, I was filled by the strangest feeling of warmth and vigor, so overpowering that I had to close my eyes. My whole body was invaded by luminous washes of color. Then a deep-blue light engulfed me and I lost consciousness again, perhaps not for very long, for suddenly there I was sitting on the edge of the stone slab, my own jacket buttoned over the shirt he had given me, my bare feet stuck in my wet boots.

He was standing next to me, one arm around my shoulder, trying to help me rise.

"You fainted again," he said. "It's starting to let up. We can go. Lean on me."

I don't know how I managed to climb back to the top again, although I was no longer in acute pain. My ankle was only sprained, not broken and the ache momentarily deadened, perhaps by all the brandy I had drunk on an empty stomach. Evidently the man was very familiar with the way up from the tombs, for he led me along a trail not quite as arduous as the one I had descended alone. The rain beat down on us relentlessly at first, and the water gushed in furious rivulets along the grooves and stairways as we scrambled up. I felt stunned, my body sluggish. I tried to command it to move more quickly, but it would not.

Sometimes I limped along, leaning on his shoulder, sometimes he led, pulling me up a crevice. Occasionally he pushed me from behind, feeling no qualms at all about where he put his hands to help me up with a rude little shove. I did not know what had become of my hat, or my rucksack, or the clothes he had removed from me. He had tied a kerchief around my head, while he went

50

bare-headed under the driving rain. But by the time we reached the top, the rain had stopped.

There in the meadow, sheltered beneath an overturned ox-cart, crouched the lame young man, and the dog. They must have been waiting there for hours in the rain. Now they pounced upon us, the dog barking and the boy shrieking, "Papa! Papa," at the top of his lungs. Seeing me now hatless and in the company of its master, the dog seemed reassured. It sniffed at me circumspectly then convinced at last that I was friend, not foe, licked my hand again and wagged its tail.

As we continued on our way, I leaned on the peasant's arm, hobbling through the mud that clung in great globs to the soles of my boots. The road had turned into a river; in drier spots, a bed of ooze. The dog trotted along briskly beside me, leaving deep paw prints in the thick red mud, the black plume of its tail high in the air. The boy dragged behind, happily enough, singing to himself, skipping through the puddles, splashing muddy water in all directions.

At last we reached the crossroads, marked by a tall iron cross fixed in a pile of rocks. The road to the right led to the village of Vitorchiano. My own house was down that road, a couple of miles before you come to the village. The one to the left led through a thicket, past a small cemetery and on to the tower where the Count lived. The peasant wanted to take me to the tower claiming that it was closer than the village, but I was too exhausted to go a step more. The anaesthetic effect of the brandy had worn off, and my ankle was now swelling in my boot. Shooting pains traveled up my leg and raw, stinging blisters had formed on my feet where the rubber chafed my skin. I collapsed on a stone by the roadside and begged him to hurry to the tower, and to arrange for some vehicle to fetch me and take me home. I promised the man a sizable reward in return for what he had done for me, and told him that I would be willing to pay the Count generously for the loan of his driver and carriage or motorcar, whichever he had at his disposal.

The man needed no further encouragement, and set off down

the road to the tower, with his son loping behind. The dog instead stayed to keep me company, and sat composedly beside me, licking my fingers as I toyed with the wet fur of his ruff. My clothes were drenched and the autumn air was chill. I waited a long time, it seemed, staring down the road towards the tower, then towards the village, thinking that my maid, Maria, might have missed me and sent out someone to search for me. From where I sat shivering, the only lights visible were a few red lamps twinkling in the cemetery, not a comforting sight. It occurred to me that I might easily catch pneumonia or even something worse.

With relief I heard the pounding of hooves along the road, the spinning of wheels on gravel. A horse-drawn cart rattled up and the driver, a burly man in a black suit, jumped down, rolled me in a blanket, and shoved me into the back. Then he climbed back onto the cart and seized the reins. With a shout and a crack of his whip, the wheels jolted forward and we sped like hell down the village road, while the dog scampered off towards the tower. The driver had obviously received instructions as to where to take me, for soon enough, he pulled up beside the old mulberry tree outside my house, leapt down, and ran to the door, knocking loudly, and bellowing for the maid.

Maria, still in her kerchief and apron despite the late hour, rushed out shrieking to the cart and the two of them carried me upstairs and into my bedroom. The driver then departed before I could tell my maid to pay him for his trouble. Muttering alternately curses and prayers, Maria sliced my boot open with a kitchen knife, stripped me of my wet clothing, and wrapped me in a layer of sheepskins. Then I waited in a sort of swoon by the fire as she brewed a bubbling hot bath for me in the zinc tub. By this time my teeth were chattering and the chills rippled through me in waves. After a long soak, I was rubbed vigorously all over with grappa, given hot milk with brandy, bundled up again, and laid in my bed on a mound of goose-down pillows where I plunged into a dreamless sleep.

It was early morning when I woke. Pale grey light filtered in through the slats of the shutters. My pillows and nightdress smelled rank and my face and hair were dampish with sweat. Turning my head on the pillow, I noticed my rubber boots, all the mud removed, neatly placed in a corner by the bed. One stood upright, intact. The other, split all the way down from top to toe, leaned against the wall. Vaguely I remembered Maria cutting it open to extract my swollen foot. I managed now to wiggle my toes, but my ankle was still painfully swollen and the blisters still raw. Otherwise I felt quite rested and cheerful. I reached out to ring the bell on the bedside table.

Into the room bustled Maria with my breakfast on a tray. Setting it down on the bedside table, she went over to thrust open the shutters. As sunlight flooded the room, I was astonished to see an immense bouquet of russet-bronze and deep-gold dahlias before the mirror on the dresser. The double image of those large, unruly blooms, cinnamon and amber, filled the chilly room with unexpected radiance. I asked where the flowers had come from. Propping me up on the pillows and setting the tray in my lap, Maria informed me that the flowers had been brought by an errand boy from the tower that morning, along with a demijohn of wine. She had put the flowers on the dresser while I was asleep, so that I might have the pleasurable surprise of discovering them upon waking. Now that I had had this accident the Count seemed to have discovered my existence.

Maria went about tidying the room, chattering to me, retrieving and folding some of the garments shed, I thought, the night before. Instead I learned that I had slept soundly for nearly 36 hours after I had been brought home from the tombs. I sipped my coffee, rather perplexed, while she recounted the story; for I remembered nothing that had happened after she put me to bed.

After carrying me upstairs, the driver had fetched a doctor from the nearby town of Viterbo. Drops of opium and arsenic were prescribed, which Maria somehow managed to make me swallow although I lay half unconscious. By morning my fever was down. Upon returning the next afternoon, the doctor declared the danger was past, and told Maria that I should spend the next ten days in bed, if only to give my sprain a rest. On this second visit the doctor had not come alone, she added. Another gentleman had accompanied him.

"Oh?" I said, presuming he had brought a colleague, or perhaps some young assistant he was training, "And who might that have been?"

"I believe it was the driver's master with him, Signora."

My goodness, I thought with a slight shock and sat up a little straighter on the pillows. The driver's master. That could only be the Count himself.

It was odd to think that I had received the doctor and the Count while asleep and unawares, but I appreciated the Count's courtesy in coming to see how I was. Doubtless I would soon have an opportunity to meet him face to face and apologize, if necessary, for the trouble I had caused. After all, I remembered somewhat sheepishly, my accident had happened while trespassing on his land. Seeing his kindness in sending flowers and wine, I felt doubly embarrassed.

After breakfast I asked for pen and paper to write a note to the Count. I still did not know his full name, so I addressed him formally as *Signor Conte, Tower of Vitorchiano,* as I had done when I first wrote to him asking for permission to photograph the tombs.

I wanted to thank you for your kindness in lending me your cart and driver. I am deeply grateful and I do not know how to repay you. Thank you also for the lovely flowers and the wine, which I have not yet had the pleasure of tasting. I would appreciate it if you would tell me the name of the man who found me down by the tombs, as I promised him a reward for his help and I do not know how to find him."

Here I paused and then added,

Given the piteous condition of the poor man's son, he no doubt could put a small gift to good use.

Yours sincerely,
Harriet Sackett.

I had just entrusted the envelope to my errand boy when I

heard the door bell clang followed by the plodding of Maria's footsteps down the stairs to answer it. When she reappeared, she handed me a brown parcel, saying, "The same fellow as before brought it," and left me to open the package alone.

I undid the knot and opened the rough brown paper. Inside I found my hat, rather squashed but intact and brushed free of mud, my blouse and woollen undershirt, which had been laundered and ironed, and my rucksack, complete with all its contents. The peasant who had rescued me down by the tombs must have gone back to get my things and had delivered them to the Count, who was now returning them to me. A note from the Count accompanied these objects. The handwriting seemed clipped and rushed, with a sharp slant to the left:

Gentile Signora,
   I am returning these objects which I believe belong to you.
   Your Servant,
   Federigo Del Re.

So this was his name, Federigo Del Re: a sonorous, properly aristocratic name. I pronounced it softly to myself, savoring the sound. I inspected my belongings again, realizing, to my chagrin, that there was an item missing. My brassiere! It did not please me now to be reminded that I had been half undressed and handled by a stranger while unconscious. The fall and the sprain were unpleasant enough to remember. My mind filled with uneasy conjectures for I doubted that the peasant's motives in removing my clothes had been entirely altruistic. Still, if he had just left me there under the rain, god knows what the dire consequences might have been, and I grudgingly acknowledged that he deserved the promised reward, despite my ambivalent feelings.

It was also a shame to lose such an expensive piece of underclothing, a new design for sportswomen, purchased at Macy's before I came abroad. I wondered what he might have done with it. Perhaps he had given it to his wife, or to one of the wenches who hang about the station in the evenings. He was vigorous enough to keep such company, although he was not young. Here in the country, where women wear bloomers and camisoles, if they wear any underclothes at all, such an exotic gift would surely be appreciated. Or perhaps he was embarrassed to hand it over to the Count, fearing he might arouse an unseemly curiosity. Whatever, I would have to resign myself to the loss, for I could hardly ask Federigo Del Re to see that it was returned to me!

2

The doctor came again a few days later, a sallow-faced, black-clad gentleman smelling of cheap tobacco, with a grey goatee and a ludicrous stove-pipe hat. After prodding me with his bony yellow fingers, he pronounced me fully recovered and refused payment, saying he had offered his services as a favor to his friend, Federigo Del Re. The doctor was amazed at how quickly my sprain was healing, and kept repeating that I was lucky I had not caught my death of cold. He ordered me to remain house-bound for a little while longer and told me not to hesitate to call for his assistance if I ever needed him again.

Those ten days while I lay in bed recuperating, I half expected the peasant might come knocking at the door to ask for his reward, but no one came round. When I described him to Maria, she only shook her head and frowned, saying that she knew no farm-hands answering to that description, but there were so many men working for the land owners in the area nowadays, especially in the autumn when the grapes and olives were harvested. She did know that the vineyards near the tombs belonged to the tower grounds, and if I had seen the peasant and his son working there, they were probably employed at the tower. This I had already guessed.

As soon as I was able to walk again, I set out traipsing across the fields in a new pair of rubber boots, for I had brought a whole stock with me, on my way to Norchia again. But this time I wasn't planning to visit the tombs. I was looking for that peasant as I intended to honor my promise. Although I went several times to look for the fellow along the road to the tombs, I never found him or his son. In the end, I desisted, thinking that sooner or later I was bound to run into him, if the Count did not inform me of the man's address first. Besides, if the man wanted his reward, he should come forward and ask for it.

Days passed and the Count never replied to my note. I was disappointed, but I was also a bit annoyed. After such a show of concern, calling on me personally and sending wine and flowers, I had imagined he would have visited me again to see how I was. Or at least he could have had the decency to answer my note. Having heard that Federigo Del Re was generally considered unsociable, I concluded he wanted to be left alone, or perhaps he was away. I gathered he was often absent from the tower for long periods, which, I supposed, was why he needed someone to handle his affairs for him. For though he seemed to own a great deal of property in the area, it was administrated by a house agent, Signor Di Rienzo, through whom, in fact, I had rented my own house. The Count, it seemed, wanted little to do with his tenants.

My misadventure had put me off schedule and now that I was quite well again, I was eager to get down to work. I was also anxious to finish putting my house in order for at the time of my accident I was still in the upheaval of settling in. I was renting a quaint old farmhouse along the road to Vitorchiano, a village a few miles from Viterbo and other Etruscan sites of interest. It had long stood abandoned before I moved in, so there was a good deal of cleaning to do. I wanted to make the house comfortable for guests, as I hoped to invite my cousin Stephen and his wife Sarah for a visit, at Christmas time. I had just spent several months in London with them.

Sad circumstances had taken me to London the previous spring to visit my cousin: the death of my uncle James, Stephen's father, who had left me a small inheritance. Since the time of my mother's death, Uncle James had been for me a sort of benefactor from across the ocean, although I had only seen him about six or seven times in my entire life, he was always traveling somewhere, mainly in the Orient. I had not expected to be remembered so generously in his will, for which I was grateful. After my stay in London, I had traveled on to Italy in early August.

The official reason for my coming to Italy was, as I said, to research Etruscan tombs and photograph a few little-known sites for the London Theosophical Society. My patron, a distinguished member of that society, was particularly interested in what Etruscan art could reveal about the Etruscans' concept of the afterlife. He hoped that the documentation I might gather would help shed light on this lost, shadowy race, whom the Romans held in awe for their mastery of the occult sciences.

But I had also more personal reasons for such a long sojourn. I was planning to stay at least two years. I had some wound-licking to do, which I preferred to do in private: A man I had been seeing in London had cut our friendship short, with no justifications, although perhaps the age difference between us provided sufficient explanation. Peter Cranshaw was at least ten years younger, if not more, and I had never seen much future in our friendship. I had always known sooner or later it would have to end. At my age you can't really expect much from romance, not that I ever did, seeking my own romance in travel and history. Still I was hurt by the abruptness of it all.

So it was time to go somewhere, I thought. I didn't want to impose any longer on my cousin Stephen. Old ghosts hindered our relationship, and he had never approved of what I had become, a brash and bumbling American with the nerve to call herself an artist of sorts. The irony of it was that he should have married the dearest person to me on earth. Sarah, dear, lovely Sarah. I couldn't face another winter in a cold place. Moreover, I knew that an old admirer of mine, George Wimbly, would soon be back in London from India, and I wanted to avoid seeing him again just at this time, for fear I might be foolish enough to take his marriage proposal seriously, should he ask me again, which I thought was likely. George had recently been widowed, and I knew from his letters that he still entertained thoughts of our potential union. Dear George. A fine man. Honest, sincere, refined, but a bit too staid for my taste. I hated to disappoint such a dear friend. And not only

Linda Lappin

him, but Stephen and Sarah, whom I suspected of plotting behind my back to get me hitched to Wimbly. I don't know why Stephen should have felt such an overriding duty to poke his nose in my affairs, or how Sarah could ever have expected me to marry Wimbly, knowing me as well as she did.

So when the opportunity to come to Italy had presented itself, I rushed to embrace it.

It was a bizarre coincidence how everything just fell into place. It had all begun with an Etruscan statue at the British Museum. How to explain its extraordinary effect on me? A small figure carved in grey marble depicting a man standing: short, squat, broad-shouldered, pot-bellied, with a squarish face, thin but sensually shaped lips curved in a dreamy half-smile. He was reaching out an arm, perhaps offering a chalice or maybe brandishing a sword. The object in his hand had disappeared long ago; all that remained was the pose with out-stretched arm, the inviting smile. The position of the feet suggested the lilting steps of a dance.

As I gazed at this statue, I fell into a reverie, and stood there, rapt for a quarter of an hour, at least, before the glass case in which it was housed. The figure did not seem to make much of an impression on the other visitors to the museum, I noted, who just glanced once and then passed on to something else. But I could not take my eyes away. It seemed to be drawing me into a unfamiliar state of quiet aliveness, in which I fancied I could almost hear it speak.

The label read 'Etruscan funerary sculpture, sixth century BC, Norchia, Viterbo Italy.'

Yes, I had thought as I pondered that statue, that is where I should go next. I had been to Pompeii, Egypt, and Mexico to photograph majestic ruins, but never to Etruria, which I knew wasn't far from Rome. What was I waiting for? Returning to my cousins' home after visiting the museum, I had begun mulling over plans for a trip to Italy.

The next night I was dragged along to a seance by a friend. I agreed to go along only out of curiosity, and to humor my friend, a young widow, who was a fervent believer in such things. It is

59

amazing how full London is of mediums and palm-readers preying on gullible victims.

I am no student of occult philosophy, although I have attended a few lectures on this subject. I have my reservations about seances and spirit communications, so much in fashion these days, but I do firmly believe that in everyone's lifetime mysterious things happen that neither science nor the rational mind can explain. Sometimes we take fleeting note of these odd occurrences, other times we just turn a blind eye, but they may influence our lives in ways we only dimly suspect, as I was to discover.

I had told my friend briefly of my new interest in the Etruscans, but had not gone into great detail. Most certainly, I had not told her about the statue I had seen at the Museum or my plans to go to Italy, which is all rather uncanny when you consider what happened next.

At the mention of 'Etruscans,' she became very excited and insisted even more ardently that I come with her to the seance that night, for the medium's spirit guide identified himself as a member of that vanished race.

"And does the Etruscan spirit guide speak English?" I asked rather doubtfully.

"Of course not," she replied, "he communicates in universal thought-forms instantaneously translated in the medium's mind as she speaks."

I would have been far more convinced by a spirit guide who spoke Etruscan, but since that language is entirely unknown to us, I suppose the poor fellow had to make do with what he could. In any case, I did not want to belittle my friend's beliefs with my scepticism. I knew how important they were for her, as she had lost her husband only a few months earlier and relied on a medium to maintain contact with him. I also knew she had already tried several.

And as I was a little low in spirits myself – forgive the play on words – I thought why not go along just for the experience? All right, I said, I just might ask the Etruscan what's in store for my future.

That night the scene pathetically complied with clichés. The three-legged table. The folding Chinese screen. Peacock feathers drooping in tarnished copper pots. The cloying smell of patchouli incense and carpet dust. The medium was a dumpy, big-bosomed woman swathed in paisley with a brown velvet turban set askew on her head, and a hint of moustache bristling on her upper lip. She spoke with a heavy Romanian accent and smelled strongly of patchouli and gin. Her assistant or, perhaps, husband was a thin, wan Indian fellow in white cotton pyjamas. He also wore a turban wrapped of white gauze. The lights went off, the spirit lamp was lit, seven of us sat around the table holding hands as the medium began to coax the Etruscan into approaching from his nether world.

"Come, come, come," she moaned. After a few minutes of this formula, uttered in growing crescendo, the window blew open with a chill blast of air, lifting the hairs on the nape of my neck. The spirit lamp flickered out. Twice the table thumped. A dog howled faintly, faraway.

"He's here. He's here!" the medium cried.

The elderly gentleman sitting next to my left pressed my hand tightly. The man on my right allowed his leg to brush mine and I shrank back in my chair.

Wide awake and wide-eyed, I observed my companions. Four women, including the medium, and three men, excluding the Indian, who was not a direct participant in the seance and sat by himself in a corner with his hands folded in his lap and his eyes closed. You could tell by the smell everyone was perspiring profusely. All eyes were shut in ecstatic supplication.

The yearning in their faces was chastening to behold. This was no laughable sight: such a naked longing for knowledge, for comfort, or just for a sign that something does await us on the other side.

The medium was concentrating harder than anyone else, her features squeezed into a tiny mask. Then her face relaxed at one stroke, her jaw dropped open and a deep male voice, cavernous and quite convincing, boomed, "Har-r-iet? Is Harriet here?" in a thick Romanian accent.

I was so astonished that I tittered most inappropriately.

There was a great consternation. I was later told that the spirit guide never took notice of newcomers, and rarely addressed anyone by name. Someone urged me to speak up.

"Yes," I said. "Here I am."

I stared at the medium. She was playing the role for all she was worth. Sweat streamed down her face and an ugly blue vein bulged in her neck. I began to be alarmed for her. Suppose she had a stroke right here?

"Why have you called me back from the dead, Harriet, and disturbed my rest? What do you wish to know?"

I certainly hadn't wished to disturb anyone and had no idea how to respond. So I said, perhaps rather rashly, "Whatever you wish to tell me."

More consternation. "Don't be rude. Otherwise he'll go," whispered the fellow to my right.

"I will write my message, but you beware! " the Etruscan said, obviously piqued.

The Indian now jumped up and pushed a slate and a piece of chalk before the medium who let go the hands of the people sitting next to her and grabbed the chalk in her fist. As she scrawled the Etruscan's message, her arm moved in stiff rapid strokes, the chalk squeaking and tapping glassily across the surface of the slate, but I could not see what she was writing from where I sat. Then abruptly, the scuttling hand came to rest. With a loud groan, the medium collapsed forward, and her head crashed to the table. Someone screamed; the lights snapped on. The medium lay with her head on the slate, seemingly unconscious but with eyes wide open, blood trickling out of her nose. The Indian rushed to assist her, propped her up in the chair, and splashed cold water on her face from a pewter pitcher. A woman produced smelling salts from her purse. Someone gently dislodged the chalk from her fingers and handed me the blood spotted slate where the letters B- R- U- T- I – V were barely legible.

I was unable to make any sense of this, and the others were too busy attending to the medium for me to ask anyone about it.

By now the medium had regained consciousness, thanks to the attentions of the Indian and of a young man who was fanning her with a dried palm leaf. "We have a sceptic in our midst," she sputtered, glaring at me, as soon as she was well enough to speak again. "The first rule is no sceptics are allowed. Next time I may not pull through. The spirits don't like to be toyed with." She rose wobbling from her chair and retired to a dusty green couch behind a folding screen. The seance was over. The young man with the palm leaf and another adept waited their turn for a private consultation with the medium. The rest of us filed into the antechamber where the Indian fellow served us all a glass of port. I took the slate with me to show the others.

"Nothing so dramatic has ever happened before," said the friend who had brought me there as we stood sipping port before a hideous painting of Puck and Titania. "You seem to have been chosen as the privileged one tonight." I showed her the slate, but she too was at a loss in interpreting it.

The silver-haired gentleman who had pressed my hand so urgently came over to have a look at the Etruscan's message.

"Perhaps it's Romanian," I ventured, handing it to him, "I certainly don't understand it. What do you make of it?"

He glanced at me unsmiling, gravely studied the slate, then said, "The Etruscans wrote from right to left, not from left to right as we do. Rather than *BRUTIV,* you should read this *VITURB.*"

"Viturb?" I asked, startled. That reminded me of something. I looked at the slate with keener interest.

"An archaic name for Viterbo, a small town north of Rome, and famous center of Etruscan culture," he explained.

"Yes, of course," I said. "I came across the name just the other day while looking at Etruscan art." A curious connection was being made in my mind.

"You know," he mused, "the Etruscans, like the Egyptians, had an extremely complex idea of the afterlife which they expressed in their funerary art. There are tombs in the area of Viterbo which have never been photographed or even documented. That would be a worthy project for some enterprising soul."

I stared at him wondering who was more telepathic, the medium or this elderly gentleman upon whose dry lips a knowing smile had formed? I had not been formally introduced to any of the people present. No one there knew that I was a photographer, although my friend might have told them something about me before bringing me along. Still it seemed unlikely that this fellow would have known of my recent interest in Etruscans or my plan to photograph Etruscan tombs.

Can such things be mere coincidence? And do mere coincidences exist, or are we pulled along through life by some occult design? Not that I believed for one moment that the messenger was a bonafide Etruscan from the other side. Rather, I thought, the medium had extraordinary skill in seizing upon a fragment of my consciousness, and like a distorted mirror, she had reflected it back to me, warped yet recognizable.

The gentleman introduced himself as a member of the London Theosophical Society and invited me to tea the next day. Within a week I had secured the support of his society as the patron of this project.

And now here I was in Italy, living within miles of where that statue was found. I was eager to explore Norchia, the necropolis from which it had come, to learn something of the culture that had produced such a powerful piece of artwork. It had communicated to me not only deep inner peace but a beguiling invitation.

3

I had found the farmhouse where I was living in Vitorchiano through the help of an Italian acquaintance, Fernanda Di Pilli, a solicitor's widow and an eccentric, aristocratic Florentine. I met her in Rome at a dinner party at the home of Marquis Manfredi, the renowned collector of Etruscan antiquities. Signora Di Pilli, a very buxom woman with hennaed red hair, was quite clever and had a biting wit, typical of all Tuscans. She spoke English marvelously well, better than any of the other Italians I met. Like most Italian aristocrats, she had been raised by an English nanny. I now realize that I warmed to her too readily, given the complicity created by our shared language. It took months for me to discover the viper within.

When she learned that I had come to Italy to do research on the Etruscans, she immediately took it upon herself to assist me in finding a place to live in the heart of Etruria, and I accepted her help with good graces. Signora Di Pilli owned a villa in Bagnaia, not far from Viterbo, where she resided in the summer months, away from the oppressive heat of her native Florence. Bagnaia was far less fashionable than Fiesole, thus less expensive to keep up in the grand style to which she aspired. At the end of August, she had received me at her villa for two weeks and our hunt for a suitable house began.

It rained for the whole time. Day after day, I trotted behind Fernanda Di Pilli and her giant black umbrella, sloshing through open sewers pouring across slick cobblestones.

Wherever we went, despite my mud-spattered cloak and bright red nose, for I had caught a nasty cold, I aroused admiration tainted with scandal thanks to my rubber galoshes and my trousers, which had proved indispensable in those climatic conditions. What a curious sight it must have been for those peasants and provincials to see a woman wearing trousers: unnatural or for some, merely hilarious. I believe we visited every single uninhabited property in the Viterbo area, whose owners were overjoyed at the prospect of having as their tenant a rich if dotty *straniera* in pantaloons who had come to roost in their territory, like some exotic bird.

She had dragged me off to any number of miserable flats and town villas in the dreary town of Viterbo, before I managed to convince her that I did not want to be in town. I wanted something quiet and rustic where I could concentrate on my work. What I needed was a house large and comfortable enough to receive visitors from England and to set up a photographic studio and darkroom, but even a relatively unfurnished structure would do. Chipped gilt furnishings, statue fragments and mildewed damask were not necessary. I was prepared for nun-like simplicity, and in any case I preferred the countryside to the town. She had concluded then that a little house in a village might be the answer, and swept me off to inspect a number of places in sad, grey, damp villages perched atop crumbling peaks, or along the edge of the deep gorges so common in the area where the Etruscans carved their rock tombs.

I had almost abandoned hope of finding something decent, and feared I would have to retrench to Rome, when one damp evening, I stumbled upon the solution. I was returning from the station at Orte after a brief trip to Rome. Signora Di Pilli had sent a driver with a cart to fetch me at the station, as she had taken her motorcar to run up to Florence for the day, and was expected back for dinner. The driver took a detour through the dripping countryside on our way home to Bagnaia. The purpose of our detour was to stop off at the home of some country peasant whose rabbits Pilli – as I had begun to call her, for that was her nickname – found particularly delectable when cooked with vinegar, black olives, and rosemary.

It was not quite twilight. The sky was deepening to a coppery blue, there was a sting of rawness in the air. In the open cart, I pulled my cloak tighter round my throat. I still wasn't over my cold.

We pulled up outside a house set back about 30 yards from the road. The front of the house was partially hidden by the massive trunk of a mulberry tree, not yet denuded of its broad yellow leaves fluttering like banners in the evening wind. A small caretaker's cottage stood nearby and the yard between the cottage and the house was filled with rabbit hutches and chicken pens, scattered litter and prowling cats, but despite this clutter, my eyes were attracted to the main house.

Stalwart and square, three storeys high, it was built of grey stone with a slanting red-tiled roof. On the middle floor gleamed two darkened windows, like two little eyes. On the top floor, a small round window, like a third eye in the center of its forehead, reflected the pinkish wisps of sunset. The front door opened onto a flagstone path lined with waxy evergreen shrubs, leading to a gate and out to the road.

The driver got down, opened the gate, and went over to the adjacent cottage, where a lamp glowed in the window. He knocked loudly on the door. It opened and he was admitted.

While waiting, I examined the house in the fading light. It looked uninhabited, if not abandoned. It was exactly the sort of place I had been looking for: an entity not a mere soulless habitation. I surveyed the surrounding countryside: low lying fields, a hump of purple mountains to the right, a row of oaks dotted on a distant ridge, a tower beyond the bare hills. Yet it was not isolated, I noted three or four other houses not too far away. The road led to a village and I could see the stone archway of the village gate, about half a mile away.

The driver returned with a basket of rabbits, properly skinned and dressed, and we set off.

I turned to stare at the house as we drove away. "Whose house is that? Does it belong to the peasant who lives in the cottage?"

The driver seemed surprised at my question. "Of course not! That house belongs to the Count."

"And does the Count live there?"

"He lived there for awhile but now he lives in that tower beyond the cemetery." He pointed out a row of cypress trees in the distance that I had not noticed.

"And what's the name of that village down the road?" I asked.

"Vitorchiano."

As we clopped home along the country road, I began to form a plan. I was determined to get more information out of Pilli that night at dinner.

"The Count of Vitorchiano?" she had said, looking up from her rabbit stew with a blank frown, as if trying to place him. "Oh, *him*! Yes, of course, I know who you must mean. A perverse individual whose chief enjoyment is rifling tombs. Etruscan ones mainly, but possibly others as well. I wouldn't trust him with mine. He has provided Manfredi with several of his prize pieces unearthed from the tombs around Viterbo. What is it you want to know about him?"

When I told her that I was interested in renting the house I had seen, she was scandalized. "But those boorish peasants are living in the cottage nearby. Who knows if the landlord will agree to send them away?"

"There would be no need to send them away," I said. "I want to rent the house, not the cottage."

"But how could you bear living with such people so close! My dear, think of the smell."

"Perhaps I could get them to move the rabbit hutches around to the back of the house at a more suitable distance."

"There may be no plumbing."

"I can do without, if need be. It wouldn't be the first time."

Pilli sniffed.

"Besides, I believe he lived there himself for a while."

"Who?"

"The owner. The Count. Surely he had plumbing put in."

She shrugged in assent. In the end I convinced her to enquire for me, and a few days later, we drove to Vitorchiano in her motorcar. It was the only sunny day of my visit, a golden September afternoon. I was keen to meet this rifler of Etruscan tombs.

A shabby little man in a brown suit was waiting for us on the front steps.

"Is that the Count of Vitorchiano?" I asked rather disappointed by this meagre figure with a pock-mocked face.

"The Count of Vitorchiano!" she laughed and shook her head. "Hardly," she said, climbing out of the car, and throwing her mauve chiffon scarf round her neck with dash. "This is Signor Di Rienzo, a house agent, who shows the properties and collects the rent for people wishing to let their property."

The man came forward to greet us and together we walked

up to the door. Then I discovered something I had missed that first evening, as it had been too dark, and the mulberry tree had obstructed my view. To the right of the door was a small stone mask portraying a bizarre horned god, a sort of guardian.

I stared at the mask while Di Rienzo prodded a large black iron key into the lock and the door swung open onto a steep staircase of grey stone flecked with black. Light filtered in from a side window at the top, where a silvery flash caught my attention. A mirror hung on the landing above a marble table with curving legs and lion's paws. From behind the paws, another stone mask peered down the steps at us. It was an Etruscan gorgon with fleshy lips and protruding tongue. "Hhmph," said Pilli frowning at it, "Whoever put that there likes looking up the ladies' skirts vicariously as they come up the stairs."

Though the face was both somber and mocking, it did not disturb me, rather I found it intriguing, but Pilli was right, it did have an odd way of peeping at one's legs. Of course, my own legs were encased in trousers, so I didn't give this a thought.

There was a strong smell of dust and mildew and damp. Cobwebs hung from the ceiling. Pilli sneezed and tossed her scarf over her hair. Coming up the stairs, we paused before the mirror on the landing which reflected our figures in full form, blurred by a patina of dust, like a faded daguerreotype. I looked out the window at a small plot of cabbages and a gnarled apple tree laden with fruit. I was charmed by everything I saw. Pilli fussed with her hair in the mirror, complained about the dust and sneezed again.

"If the Signora had not been in such a hurry to see the house, I might have had it cleaned for her visit," said Di Rienzo.

"No matter, no matter, I was so glad the Count agreed to show me the place," I said quickly, wanting to sound appreciative and gracious.

Di Rienzo shot me a puzzled look, raised his eyebrows, but said nothing.

Here on the landing stood a door set in a handsome frame of grey stone. Di Rienzo produced a second key and opened it. We entered the main body of the house.

It was like stepping into a Chinese box of antique red lacquer. A floor of maroon brick tiles, low wooden beams, a few pieces of dark, glossy furniture. On every wall hung a large gilt picture frame covered with a cloth, presumably to keep off the dust. Signor Di Rienzo strode over to the window, opened it with some effort and then began to struggle with the rusted latch of the shutter. At last he burst the shutter open and the warm September sunlight streamed into the room.

I approached one of the frames and peeked behind the cloth. It was not a painting, as I had imagined, but a magnificent mirror. I investigated the other covered frame, this too a mirror. Di Rienzo came over and pulled the cloths away, and I almost cried out at the astonishing effect. From where I stood, the mirrors captured the view from the window: yellowing lindens and oaks in the garden, a stone arch with pergola, all faintly tinged in the mirror's mercurial blue. It was a marvelous illusion, a secret garden in the darkest recess of the house.

A few words popped into my head at that moment, whose meaning I cannot guess. *This is a house where time is not!* And I knew I must have it at all costs.

Within 48 hours I had signed a two-year lease – that should be enough time, I had thought, for the project I had in mind – and I had the keys in hand. That night I wrote to Sarah and Stephen, telling them of my new surroundings, and suggesting they come for a visit at Christmas time.

Cleaning my new house and rendering it habitable was quite an undertaking, for it had long stood empty after the previous occupant, the Count, had moved out to take up residence in the tower. So I asked Signor Di Rienzo to recommend a maid, which is how Maria – all the country women here seemed to be called Maria – had come into my service.

Maria was a mountain of a woman whose weight was chiefly concentrated in her massive bosom, stomach, and huge pink arms. A widow of 35, she looked twenty years older, her sparrow-colored hair streaked with grey, her ruddy face deeply lined by worry. She was originally from a small town south of

Rome. As a young girl, she had married a blacksmith from a village near Viterbo. Her husband had been much older than she, and had died of consumption just three years after their marriage. All alone, working as a housemaid, she had brought up three sons, now away in the army. I took an immediate liking to her, for she was a cheerful and industrious soul and seemed competent enough for the little housekeeping I required. She had excellent references. Her employer of many years, a Viterbo prelate, had recently died and she was in need of a position.

Maria owned two skirts, of coarse wool, one black, the other brown. Over this she wore a blouse of homespun hemp, a grubby apron, and, on her head, a faded floral kerchief. Although her movements were slow and cumbersome, given her great bulk, she was extraordinarily strong, and exigent when it came to cleanliness.

Once we had set to work, we were dismayed to discover that the house was full of scorpions: curled under the pots in the kitchen cupboards, creeping out of cracks in the wall, lurking beneath rugs. Large dead ones dangled overhead from the spider webs, thus I learned that spiders can actually be beneficial creatures.

Maria was superstitious when it came to spiders, and never harmed them unless they were of the poisonous, hairy variety. Otherwise, she was careful not to squash them while sweeping away cobwebs. *"Ragno porta guadagno,"* she would mumble to herself – for in the local imagination, spiders are associated with earning. As she raked the ceiling with a long broom made of twigs, she would gently shake spiders out the window or pretend not to notice when they scuttled to safety in a corner of the ceiling.

But with scorpions she was relentless, stamping them to death with her heavy black boots. We became so used to finding them that by some strange mental projection, nearly any dark stain on a wall or the floor, any ball of dust under the bed immediately took on the form of a scorpion, two pincers and a curling tail. It was curious to observe this process in my mind, to see how predisposed it was to interpret and shape an impression into that very form. The mind truly sees what it is prepared to see. Photographs, however, are far less selective. How many times had I cried out while going through the contents of a drawer or trunk, "Maria, here's another one! Only to discover that my alarm was uncalled for, and the dreaded menace was only an ink spot, or a small wad of dust and hair collected in the corner.

Soon I realized that Maria could not do the job alone and so I encouraged her to call in the daughters of a neighboring peasant to help clean the windows and numerous mirrors, blackened, like everything else in the house, by a layer of soot and grime. The mirrors were perhaps the most striking feature of the house, for there was one on nearly every wall and some were huge. The peasant girls, no less than Maria herself, were amazed to see so many mirrors, and regarded them with a mixture of fear and fascination. They were terrified lest one be broken and bring bad luck upon us all.

Once, checking on the girls' progress as they cleaned, I had found a thin blonde child standing tiptoe atop a dresser in the sitting room, vigorously rubbing the mirror mounted there with a rag soaked in ammonia and vinegar. Her face was turned to the side and her eyes were squeezed shut. I supposed it was the smell of ammonia that had induced this attitude, and fearing that she might topple off the dresser and hurt herself, I asked the girl, not unkindly, how she thought she might clean the mirror with her eyes closed.

Staring at me wide-eyed, she put down her rag, and said simply, "Things move in them mirrors."

The mirrors in the sitting room were placed in such a way that they gave a view of all the doors and corridors in the house, while reflecting the light from the windows. I had supposed that this was the Count's ingenious device not only for controlling the premises, but also for increasing the amount of light, for the sitting room windows were small and faced north, and the red brick floor and dark ceiling beams absorbed most of the sunlight filtering in. A fire flickering in the kitchen hearth, Maria's shadow flitting down the corridor to the kitchen, even a branch waving in the wind outside, all these could be glimpsed as indistinct movements in the mirrors. Sometimes the reflected image of a single candle flame, when placed in the right position, rebounded through the entire house.

I thought that it was these furtive movements that had frightened the girl, so I smiled and said, "What things?"

She looked at me solemnly, picked up her rag, and said, "Things that aren't really there." For her those mirrors were like dangerous portals opening onto an imaginary world.

Maria, too, despite her hardy physique and practical good sense, was just as superstitious as those peasant girls. Around her neck, she always wore a little red horn dangling down into the yellowish cleft between her enormous breasts. She explained to me that this charm protected her from the evil eye and suggested I wear one as well, but I just laughed. Then once, in the process of turning the beds, a little red coral horn just like the one she wore was found beneath the mattress of the master bedroom where I slept. Maria carefully inspected it, dusted it off, and replaced it, saying that indeed was the proper place for it. Later, I wondered if she had put it there herself, or if it had really been left there by one of the previous inhabitants.

When an old horse shoe was found beneath the woodpile in a corner of the kitchen, she insisted on hanging it over the doorway with due ceremony. I said nothing, but found this all very quaint, if harmless enough, and even briefly considered collecting these folk customs and writing a report about them.

I soon learned that the daughters of the local peasants came to her to have the evil eye removed: a special procedure that she performed in the kitchen. Sometimes on Sundays after mass, a girl would knock and be discreetly led into the kitchen, where, from behind the closed doors, I could hear a faint mumbling. I never intruded and let Maria enjoy these moments of privacy. She was, however, very religious and saw no contradiction between these rustic superstitious beliefs and her religious faith. She operated only for good, she told me, and had nothing to do with the devil's work. One night I saw her standing on tiptoe in the yard, holding a silver coin I had given her as part of her monthly wages up to the new moon. When I asked what the meaning of this rite was, she explained she was trying to increase her earnings for the month to come, as she was saving money to buy a few lengths of cloth to sew herself a new dress. I promptly complied with this request and raised her wages, so I suppose it could be said that her little spell had worked.

4

It took three weeks for us to render the house habitable, and when I had my unfortunate accident at the tombs, my studio was not quite ready. As soon as I was well enough to move about easily again, I busied myself with this task. This entailed traveling to the nearest train station and collecting the trunks of books and photographic equipment waiting for me in storage there, shipped weeks ago from London before I came out. I had hired a young boy from the village, Andrea, to run errands and help with the harder work, hauling heavy boxes, putting up shelves, laying in wood for the stove. If he proved to be bright and quick enough, I thought I would make him my assistant and teach him the art of photography. Andrea was a ruddy boy with freckles and coppery hair and a rather lopsided grin. I thought he would do very well.

When at last the studio was ready, I turned my attention to more sedentary tasks. I had several letters of enquiry to write to private collectors of Etruscan artefacts about viewing their collections. I was particularly interested in tomb sculpture found in the area of Norchia. Marquis Manfredi had given me a list of collectors who were likely to collaborate and who would be pleased to have their prize pieces photographed for my report. Federigo Del Re's name did not appear in the list, which I found puzzling, if only because Pilli claimed he was an expert of some renown. But I didn't intend to waste any more time wondering about him or waiting for him to reply to my note. I had other things on my mind.

Twice a week I sent Andrea to collect my mail at the village post office, although I did not expect to receive many letters. Sarah and Stephen were the only people to whom I had given my current address, apart from my patron, the fellow from the Theosophical Society. I had promised to keep in touch with him about how my project was coming along. I didn't really want anyone else to know where I was for awhile.

One morning near the end of October, Andrea brought two letters back for me. I was delighted to see that one was from Sarah for I recognized immediately the pale blue envelope scented with lavender. She rarely wrote letters, just a line or two, although she demanded copious correspondence on my part, but then she knew how much I enjoyed writing to her, especially when traveling abroad. Stephen never wrote, either, except to admonish me or warn me about something or other. His few letters were as tiresome as those from a maiden aunt. I had just written Sarah to tell her I was settling into my new house and had suggested that they both come out for Christmas, if that would suit Stephen. It was rather soon for her to have replied.

Sarah's letter was characteristically brief and made no mention of my recent invitation, so I assumed that at the time she had written it, she had not yet received my letter.

I thought you should know, she wrote, *I have just heard that Peter Cranshaw is now married. He married Eliza Duncan-Pitsworth, that awful woman from Cambridge. I thought you would rather hear it from me than not know at all, or to learn it from a stranger. I suppose it is for the best. Don't be too disappointed. He wasn't really worthy of you.*

I crumpled the letter and threw it into the grate. I could feel the blood stinging in my face. I was astonished that I felt so angry, but at whom? At poor Peter? At Eliza Duncan-Pitsworth? At Sarah? At myself, perhaps. Silly, silly Harriet. Perhaps I should try to become a serious person by marrying George Wimbly, should he ever ask me again, and learn to play bridge and mahjong, or whatever it is older women do to pass the time of day.

I examined the second envelope, made of fine cream-colored

paper, stamped with an Italian postmark. No sender's name appeared and the handwriting was unfamiliar. I thought it was probably a reply to one of the queries I had sent. I opened the envelope and removed a thick piece of pasteboard where the name *Baronessa Elisabetta Colonna* was finely engraved in copperplate. It was an invitation to a dinner party to be given next week in Bagnaia at the Villa Colonna.

Baronessa Elisabetta Colonna. Did I know this woman? Had I met her perhaps in Rome at Marquis Manfredi's or perhaps at Pilli's, seeing as though she too owned a villa in Bagnaia? I could not remember ever meeting anyone by this name, but concluded that Pilli must have had something to do with this invitation. I knew she was eager to introduce me into local society.

I was not surprised, then, when two days later Pilli herself pulled up outside my door in her motorcar, all the way from Florence, where she generally spent the opera season, and called on me unannounced. There were no telephones out here in the country.

I had Maria prepare tea – I had at last taught her how to make a decent pot, although I generally preferred coffee. I knew there was nothing that Pilli loved as much as an exotic English tea, complete with cream biscuits, which I had sent from London in one of my tin trunks, for occasions such as this one, to mollify Anglophiles. In provincial European towns, even Americans are sometimes expected to entertain in British fashion. And after all, though my mother was English, I consider myself a Yankee through and through.

We had our tea in the studio, a bare room with a plank table and two iron chairs. When I moved in, the house was almost void of furniture, which suited me, and I made do with the bits and pieces left behind by the Count. To make the studio a bit more comfortable – as it was the room I intended to spend most time in – I had added a folding teak table, brass oil lamps – there was no electricity in the house – a small Ottoman carpet, and on the mantelpiece above the hearth where I always kept a fire blazing, was my lucky little bronze Buddha, a childhood gift from my

Uncle James. Although she complained of the dust and cold, Pilli found the setting rather Bohemian, and therefore amusing. Being American I was allowed to be odd and to feel at home in primitive settings.

When I showed her the Baronessa's invitation over tea, Pilli shrieked with glee, "Well, you must thank me! I arranged it, as you asked." She devoured another biscuit and brushed the crumbs from the lace frills on her ample bosom.

I asked her to explain.

Patting her wet lips with a napkin, she sputtered, "Federigo Del Re! I have arranged for you to meet him!"

I suppose I frowned, for Pilli quickly added, "I thought you said you wanted to meet him and talk to him about Etruscans."

Actually by this time I had quite forgotten him, yet the mention of his name irked me.

Pilli couldn't wait to fill me in on all the details. Elisabetta Colonna was Federigo Del Re's mistress. Although not a true blue blood, despite her title, she was rich, and aside from her many properties, owned several exclusive ladies' emporiums, including one in Venice and another in Rome, where one could purchase decent silk stockings and hats and sundries from Paris. Pilli had run into the Baronessa at the coiffeur in Viterbo a few days before while having her hair hennaed and crimped, and had seized the opportunity to mention me, her protegee. She had told the Baronessa that I was an English archaeologist, currently staying near the village of Vitorchiano. Having heard that Federigo Del Re was a noted authority on Etruscan matters, I wished to meet him.

I protested that I was neither English nor an archaeologist.

"Well, you are half-English, that must count for something, even though you deny it," she said wrinkling her nose at me. "After all, if I had told her you were an American, she probably wouldn't have invited you. She is a terrible snob."

A party had been arranged to celebrate the publishing of one of Federigo Del Re's books on Etruscan tombs. His mistress had probably paid for having the book printed, Pilli explained, as rumor had it that Federigo del Re was heavily in debt and could never have paid for it himself. No doubt among the guests there would be one or two specialists from the University of Rome, or the Etruscan museum, who would be useful for me to know. Not that these scholars took his publications seriously, she emphasized, but they humored him for he had an almost uncanny knowledge of the tombs, and a knack for discovering sites no one knew about and unearthing valuable objects. It was chiefly this talent that endeared him to the specialists in the field, and it was from this activity that he drew his main source of income, although many of his archaeological investigations and other activities were said to be financed by his patroness and mistress, the Baronessa.

"But you can't go dressed like that, of course," she said pointing to my trousers.

"Of course not. I have some silk Turkish harem pants for special occasions."

Pilli groaned and fluttered her eyelashes, "We're not in Paris, you know, or in Constantinople, either!"

The evening of Elisabetta Colonna's reception, Pilli's driver deposited us at the foot of a long, curving marble stairway flanked by a handsome balustrade, where an alabaster sphere glowed atop every pillar. A fountain bubbled at the base of the stairway, and in the middle of the fountain, a forlorn and dirty Pegasus perched afloat a tiny island crumbling beneath his weight. There at the top of the stairway glittered the villa, in all its baroque pomp and severity, brilliantly illuminated with electric bulbs. It must have been the only building within a radius of five miles that had electric lighting. I could see that the Count's mistress must be a very wealthy woman indeed.

We hurried up the stairs to the villa, where a servant in eighteenth-century livery ushered us inside and removed our wraps. Pilli was dressed in a violet silk frock, with matching slippers and a yellow turban plumed with peacock feathers. I wore my harem trousers of black silk, which I had had made in

Turkey, and a man-tailored jacket of heavy black silk. Pilli
remarked that at least I wasn't wearing my abominable hat. The
room was hot, stuffy, full of smoke, crowded with transpiring
ferns in gaudy Faenza vases, and obtrusive Roman statues with
cracked torsos and broken noses. A gramophone in a corner
scratched out American jazz tunes. My outfit, although admittedly
unusual, would not have been scandalous in Paris, or in some circles
in New York, but as I entered the salon where most of the guests
were gathered, my *pantaloni* created a stir, as Pilli had predicted.
Most of the other women were in full evening dress about twenty
years behind the fashion. 30 pairs of dark eyes, glinting behind
lorgnettes and monocles, turned to inspect me with amazement,
and a lithe, dark woman dressed in a black sheathe spangled with
sequins came mincing forward. Pilli whispered in my ear that this
was the hostess, then introduced us.

Elisabetta Colonna was no longer a young woman, yet she
was extremely attractive. I guessed we were the same age,
although she might have been a year or two older. She possessed
the classic traits of the Mediterranean beauty, thick black hair
coiled into a chignon, olive skin, intense brown eyes with arched
black brows penciled above. She was petite and shapely, and the
close-fitting sheathe did justice to her figure. A fortune in pearls
was knotted around her throat, perhaps to hide her slightly
withered skin, the only sign that betrayed her age. Despite her
beauty, there was something witchlike about her. She reminded
me of a wicked queen in a fairy tale, dazzling but deadly.

The Baronessa welcomed me tepidly, complimented me on my
Italian, and on my unusual 'costume', as she put it. She enquired
politely as to how I found the rustic life and whether I knew so-
and-so in London. Once I had answered these questions, she
steered us towards the buffet where a waiter was serving hors
d'oeuvres and pouring champagne and there she left us. Sipping
champagne, I followed Pilli through the rooms, all decorated
with the same ghastly opulence. Pilli seemed to know nearly
everyone there, and stopped to introduce me to various
personages of rank: a judge, a banker, an officer or two, a couple

of elderly ladies who wanted to know what was in store for the winter theater season in London. Alas, no professors or museum directors seemed to be among the guests. Pilli had probably just told me they would be there so she could convince me to accompany her. I kept looking around for the misanthropic Count.

I imagined him to be in his late 60s, balding perhaps, grave, with a beard and a monocle. Disinclined to society, he would no doubt be sallow, sinewy and Saturnine. We paused outside the French doors of the library. A fire was burning briskly in the hearth, and a small crowd was gathered around a glass case of sculpture fragments, listening to a man who stood with his back to the door. Whatever he was saying had captured their attention. With his back turned to me, I could not see his face, but I recognized the grizzled grey hair. There stood a body I already knew, compact and muscular, barrel-chested, not too tall, radiating a youthful vigor.

"There he is," said Pilli, bursting open the door and tottering into the room on her stubby little legs, "Federigo Del Re."

So this was the man who had rescued me – if rescued is the proper term. The Count himself. How blind, how stupid I had been not to realize it before! Then suddenly remembering the phrase I had added to my note: *Given the piteous condition of the poor man's son, he no doubt could put a small gift to good use.* I understood I had made, as usual, a horrible blunder in being so frank. He could only have found that remark offensive and that was probably why he had not replied. But this was only one cause for my embarrassment for, recalling the missing brassiere which he had removed from me himself, supposedly in my best interests, shame and anger now burned in my cheek. I dreaded being introduced to him, but there was nothing to be done, it was too late to retreat, for Pilli had run up to him, seized him by the arm and was now tugging him in my direction.

"Federigo darling," she fawned, which surprised me, as she had spoken so derogatorily of him before, and I would not have thought she knew him well enough to address him by his first name. "There is someone who is dying to meet you."

Federigo Del Re turned towards me with a quick half twirl on his heels, as agile as a tango dancer. Yes, there was no mistake. It was him all right, yet he was somehow different. Of course, I had previously seen him rain-drenched in mud-spattered clothes, and here he was in a tuxedo, albeit a size too small. But it was not just his formal clothing, or the elegant setting, or the glow of the lamps and firelight. He emanated a certain something that I cannot explain. It piqued my disapproval and yet drew me to him strongly, against my better judgment. He looked me up and down and gave me a crooked little half-smile, and I was instantly charmed, as I have not been in years. Poor Harriet! I strode forward with outstretched hand and felt as though I was teetering on sponges rather than crossing a solid marble floor.

"Ah," he said, "Our intrepid English archaeologist."

He took my hand and lifted it to his lips. Once again I felt the extraordinary warmth of those brown fingers and momentarily recalled the peculiar sensations I had felt while he rubbed my feet and ankles with brandy in the tomb. Before letting go my hand, he pulled me slightly towards him and murmured in a low voice no one else could hear, "I see you are in disguise tonight. Like myself." As he leaned close to my ear, a few tufts of my hair were caught up in his thick grey bush, creating a soft electric cloud that buzzed around my head. He pressed my hand twice, dropped it, and the buzzing stopped. But the timbre of his voice, the warmth of his hands had dislodged a memory and I suspected that he had indeed done more in the tomb than merely rub my feet.

"No, I am afraid there is a mistake," I heard myself saying awkwardly and rather too loudly. As I spoke I had the odd sensation of viewing myself from outside my body, which sometimes happens to me when I am extremely flustered. "I am not an English archaeologist, but an American photographer," I prattled on, "But I am here to take photographs of the tombs."

The Count frowned. I could see he did not like being contradicted.

"No matter," he said, testily, "whatever you are, you are sure to find this interesting," and stepping aside to make room for Pilli and myself, he proceeded with his explanation of the fragments of statues and vases displayed in the case. Pilli listened politely for awhile yawning and tapping her foot. Then she detached herself and wandered out of the room in search of more congenial company. I listened, deeply absorbed, as Federigo Del Re described his recent discovery of an Etruscan site buried in a field on his land. Now and then he stopped in mid-sentence to gaze at me, puzzled and reflective, perhaps to make sure that I was following his meaning, but I confess I hung on every word.

Through the glass doors, I could see Elisabetta Colonna, lounging on a sofa in the adjoining room surrounded by a crowd of admirers. She was flirting with a young officer in full dress uniform, flashing her white teeth as she laughed, and tossing her head, but now and then she turned towards the library with a sudden, gelid frown and jiggled her foot impatiently. At dinner I was placed at the other end of the table, and had no further opportunity to converse with the Count. I caught him glancing once or twice at me abstractedly, as though preoccupied.

I spent the rest of the evening chatting with the two spinsters who had asked me about the London theater season. Elisabetta Colonna did not deign to address me again, but she observed me sharply from time to time, studying me from across the room. Federigo Del Re disappeared into another room to smoke cigars with a group of gentlemen straight after dinner, and there was no other conversation worth listening to. When at last Pilli decided it was time to leave, I felt immensely relieved. The Count reappeared just as we were saying goodbye to the hostess, when he presented Pilli and myself each with a copy of his newly published book, which he pressed warmly into our hands.

"I would be very interested in hearing your opinion of it," he said pointedly to me. Elisabetta Colonna, standing by his side, looked up at me – I was a good head taller than she was – and with an enigmatic smile, remarked that she knew I would find it fascinating.

I smiled cordially, thanked them both, shook hands and said goodbye. I did not know what to make of this strange couple. He was no doubt the most extraordinary man I had ever met, but not handsome, there was something toad-like about him. She was a wealthy merchant's daughter, glacial, but beautiful and rich. I certainly never dreamt she might consider me a possible rival for his affections.

Later that evening, I sat propped up in bed, leafing through the book, entitled *Gli Etruschi in Tuscia*. I suppose I was expecting some marvelous tale of discovery and was disappointed to see that the book was actually an anthology of dry, academic papers on Etruscan findings in the area. Aside from the introduction, only one article was by Federigo Del Re, who was the editor, not the author, of the volume, and his style in both these pieces was so long-winded and flowery in the worst Italian manner that I found them unbearably tedious. I was just about to put the book away, when a piece of paper stuck between the pages fell out on the bed. It was a note from the Count:

Carissima Signora,

Next time you wish to visit such places, you must not go alone. I would be more than happy to accompany you. You need only ask.

Federigo Del Re

5

I did not reply immediately to the Count's message, for although I was intrigued, I was also slightly repulsed by him. Such a hasty and surreptitious manner – slipping that note into a book under the watchful eyes of his mistress – boded no good, I thought. If his intentions were honorable: if he only wished to offer himself as a reliable guide to the area, surely he could have said so in her presence, without any harm being intended. Nonetheless, Elisabetta Colonna was clearly a vain and jealous woman. Maybe she kept him under lock and key. I thought it wise to wait until his intentions were clearer, and as I expected another note arrived a few days later:

Gentile Signora,

You once offered to repay me for a small service I performed for you.

I would be deeply grateful if you would make a photographic portrait of myself and of my son in our home. If you agree, I will send a driver around for you and your equipment.

Your servant
F Del Re

I was secretly very pleased by this request, for I knew it would give me an opportunity to spend some time with him in a neutral way, without having to go out wandering in the woods alone with him. I also found him a noble subject for a portrait. His well-sculpted head was worthy of a late Roman emperor with a jutting brow beneath which smouldered eyes like green coals. The line of his jaw was squarish and defiant, and there was an almost Oriental downward tuck at the corner of his eyelids, a typical Etruscan trait often seen in tomb sculptures. I wrote him back to say that I could come Tuesday the following week, and that morning, I set out for the tower, along with Andrea, my assistant. I preferred to walk, so I had declined the Count's offer to send his driver round. Our equipment, packed in a zinc case, was loaded on a small wagon which we pulled along behind us. It was a brisk sunny day with a chill breeze. The road to the tower was strewn with chestnuts fallen to the ground after a recent storm. The woods were full of children gathering them in baskets.

Federigo Del Re was considered rather odd because he let the grounds around the tower grow wild in a mass of brambles, ivy, and scrub thickets. Although this may have been an ideal game reserve, stocked with pheasants, boar, and deer, it was also a haven for vipers. Luckily now that the days were colder there was little danger from snakes. Looking up through the main gate, I could see a large window had been made in the very top floor of the tower, commanding a view of the countryside. Along the cornice at the very tip, a dozen crows perched all in a row.

The rusted gate creaked as we stepped inside. A muddy path

of about twenty yards led to an untidy rose garden surrounding
the base of the tower. The garden was enclosed by a boxwood
hedge that bordered the woods on one side. Approaching, I was
almost overwhelmed by the nauseating stench of poultry for all
along the gravel paths, chickens and peacocks scratched in
among the rose bushes. Next to the tower, on the other side of the
hedge, lay the ruins of another structure half sunk into the
ground, covered with briars. From the arched gothic windows it
looked as though it might once have been a medieval convent.
Now its dilapidated walls formed the enclosure to a small
cemetery containing an imposing funerary monument in baroque
style, dating perhaps from the 1600s.

The tower was clearly much older, say 1200s, and the door,
painted dark ochre, was fitted with an antique iron lock. On
either side of the entrance stood a pillar, obviously added on for
decoration in the late baroque period. A crumbling coat of arms
hung over the doorway, depicting an oak branch laden with
acorns, sheltering a boar and a porcupine. I was quite attracted
to its heraldic design and studied it a moment before I knocked.

A servant opened, an elderly woman in a faded black dress
with grey hair plaited in a bun. She frowned at me then stepped
aside without a word, as the lady of the house appeared on the
stairs behind her. A sallow, sour-faced woman in her 40s came
forward to meet us. She was unhealthily thin and in her shapeless
brown dress looked rather like a bundle of sticks. Long greying
hair, lusterless and unkempt, hung to her shoulders. I was rather
surprised by this unexpected apparition. Who was this woman?
The Count's wife, a relative, or perhaps his housekeeper?

"What do you want?" she demanded.

I explained that the Count had sent for me to take his
photograph.

She looked at me with a sort of disgust, then shrugged her
shoulders. "You'll find my brother upstairs," she said, tossing her
head in the direction of the staircase. I was relieved to hear this
hag was not his wife, but his sister! With a tired gesture she
signaled to the servant to accompany us and we started up the

steps behind the elderly maid. My assistant carried our equipment up in the zinc case.

It was very dim and dirty on the stairway and smelled of burnt toast and boiled cabbage. The only illumination was the veiled sunlight shining down from an overhead skylight cluttered with leaves, and from the narrow slits in the sides of the wall through which a sharp wind whistled. Grubby candle stubs, unlit, were fastened to the walls in wrought-iron holders, columns of melted candle wax dripped down beneath them forming hardened pools on the floor.

The old woman had to pause every few steps on the way up to get her breath. I felt sorry for her having to exert herself so strenuously on our behalf. On the very top landing, we came to a door guarded by a dusty suit of armor standing in a corner. I was amused to see a filthy mop and broom leaning against its iron glove. The servant opened the door without bothering to knock and announced rudely, "Somebody for you."

Federigo Del Re sat facing the doorway, writing at his desk. A fire blazed in the hearth behind him, the big black dog lay at his feet. Above the mantelpiece hung the trophy of an enormous boar's head, with fierce tusks and glass eyes. As I preceded Andrea into the room, the Count looked up at me and smiled, and the dog pricked up its ears. Even the boar seemed to turn its eyes in my direction. The room was a cross between a scholar's study and a hunting lodge. The walls were lined with bookshelves and glass cases displaying pottery and small statues. Other ornaments were mounted above the mantelpiece near the boar's head, including a sword and several antique firearms. Despite the crackling fire, the room felt chill and draughty, perhaps because of the lofty ceiling. There was no sign of the young man.

"Buon Giorno, Signor Conte," I said. "I have come to take your photograph."

The Count rose to greet us, and the dog leapt up, trotted over to me, and pushed its cold nose into my hand, demanding a caress which I gladly gave. Federigo Del Re examined me through the slits of his eyes: I was dressed as usual in moleskin trousers and a mannish wool jacket, but that day I had yielded to my feminine vanity in choosing a tailored flannel blouse with an unobtrusive lace trim. I suppose I wanted him to know there was a woman in those trousers, after all.

For the occasion, he was wearing a rather old fashioned and formal black suit, handsome and very well-cut, although it pulled a bit across his chest and stomach. It obviously belonged to his younger years and as he reached out to take my hand, I noted that the cuffs of both his jacket and shirt sleeves were soiled and frayed. This time he did not kiss my hand, but only pressed it kindly. In that draughty room, his hands seemed remarkably warm.

"I can see," he said, "today you are yourself again," and I supposed he was referring to my work clothes – he no doubt found women in *pantaloni* very amusing – but his face betrayed no hint of a smile.

"Speaking of disguises," I said, "I have something that belongs to you," and I handed him a package containing his rough woollen shirt, which Maria had laundered, mended, and ironed. I wasn't quite bold enough to ask what had become of my brassiere, however, and he did not take the hint, but only smiled, and put the package away without looking at it. I asked where he wanted to sit for his portrait and he said he wished to be photographed there in his study, surrounded by his precious antique art collection. As Andrea set the camera up on the tripod, Federigo Del Re pointed out to me a few pieces of his collection. They were a mix of Roman, Etruscan, and Egyptian artefacts. Each one was meticulously labeled.

I went over to one of the glass cases to look at the pottery. There were several sacrificial goblets glazed in shiny black *bucchero*, a stone sphinx with a seraphic smile, and a ship modeled in terra cotta with a crowd of tiny human figures. The label read: *la nave della morte*. This was the Etruscan death ship bearing the souls of the dead to the shores of life everlasting. Among the various objects I saw a brown hand made of clay, then a foot, then a tiny arm bent at the elbow, its hand raised in greeting.

The Count stepped up behind me with a brass key and opened

the case. There were several other anatomical pieces: a stomach and intestines, a heart, other parts I could not recognize. They were obviously not dismantled pieces of a statue, but individual sculptures in themselves. I asked him for an explanation.

"These were votive offerings to the god of healing, left by pilgrims. If you were suffering from paralysis of the fingers, for example, you would commission a craftsman to make a model of your hand, and then dedicate it in the temple," and he pointed to the clay hand.

I looked again at the heart and stomach, and then noticed an unfamiliar object, resembling a small, ribbed hot water bottle.

"And this?"

The Count took it out of the case and handed it me. "This is the matrix of life. A human womb. An exact replica in scale. Women no doubt dedicated these in the temple hoping to cure themselves of barrenness or other feminine diseases."

In other circumstances, I might have retorted that for some women childlessness was not a disease, but a choice, but I did not want to annoy him.

I turned the object over examining it. I had never seen the organ in question except in anatomical drawings, and this representation of it seemed rather fanciful to me. Still, it is always thrilling to hold a piece of antique sculpture in your hands, to reflect on who made it and what it signified to its maker. I reckoned this piece was nearly 3000 years old. I was awed not only by its age, but by the yearning it made so completely manifest – for health or fertility – of a woman who lived thousands of years before I was born.

Gently I put it back in the case.

"I'm sure this will interest you, too," he said, and he drew out a small rounded pyramid and held it for a moment between his palms before giving it to me. In those few seconds in which the clay had been in contact with his hands, it had absorbed a surprising quantity of body heat. I had a start when I took it in my hand, for it was almost like holding a warm piece of living human flesh.

I looked at it, then suddenly realizing what it was, blushed and blurted out, "Oh ! A breast."

I could see that my assistant was growing more inquisitive – after all, he was just a young country boy – for whom such things could only titillate his youthful imagination. I wondered if the Count were trying to test me in some way, or perhaps embarrass me with these pieces of female anatomy. The best reply was a good dose of Yankee matter-of-fact-ness. I glanced at the case again and now discovered a whole row of male attributes, much smaller than the other anatomical pieces, and made from more refined materials. These were not shaped of rough clay, but made of smooth porcelain with a shiny glaze. Before the Count had time to put one of *those* in my hand for my inspection, I quickly replaced the breast, and indicated the row of male organs.

"Obviously to protect against impotence or other masculine diseases," I clipped, picking one up and peering closely at it. "From the number you have in this collection, it would seem to have been a widespread concern for Etruscan men." Thinking, but not saying, *if not for yourself.*

The Count nodded. "Perhaps." The corner of his mouth twitched. I could not tell if he were irritated or amused, so I put back the clay object and decided to change the subject.

In the adjacent case there was a large mask of a Gorgon with monstrous lips and protruding tongue. I observed that it was quite similar to the stone mask on the stairway of the house that I was renting from him.

"Yes," he said, "The one in your house was the guardian of a warrior's tomb."

I asked him if he had lived very long in the house I was now occupying. He replied that he and his family had lodged there briefly, while having the roof of the tower repaired. He enquired, in passing, if I found it suitable to my needs. I told him that it was both suitable and comfortable.

"And do you sleep well?" he asked with an odd little half-smile.

"Very well. After my misadventure in the tombs, I am told that I slept for 36 hours."

"I ask because of the mirrors," he said. "They sometimes disturb one's dreams. If they disturb you, I can send over a workman to take them down. Or you may just cover them with a thick cloth."

"No, no need," I said perplexed, "I rather like them. They make the rooms more luminous." I was curious about his reference to dreams, so I said, "I had no idea that mirrors can disturb one's sleep."

"Some people who are extremely sensitive have to cover them with veils at night."

I expected him to elaborate, but he said nothing more on the subject. There was a lull in the conversation, as if he were waiting for me to say something so I admired the sword hanging above the mantelpiece. Pleased that I had noticed it, he took it down and placed it in my hands. I was astonished at how heavy it was and how much physical strength was required to wield it.

"This sword has been in my family for generations," he said. "For all ancient peoples, the sword was not merely a weapon, but a powerful religious symbol of male potency."

If this was intended to be an innuendo of some kind, I simply glided over it. After all, I had seen the stone linghams in Indian temples and wasn't shocked by them.

"Yes, of course," I said, "Many English folk dances derived from the sword dancing of the Celts in connection with fertility rites."

He seemed pleased by my remark and said, "Here such traditions, passed down from the days of the Etruscans, have not completely died out."

My arms shook as I tried to lift it above my head. He took it from me and replaced it on the wall. "Too heavy for a lady," he said, and I bristled at that word.

Andrea was nearly ready, so I asked the Count if we should call his son to have his picture taken.

"No, I am afraid, not today. He is indisposed at the moment," he said. Then he added after a pause, "It's nothing serious."

I enquired if there were any particular objects he wished to include in the picture, and if he wanted the dog to be photographed with him. "A very fine animal," I said, as I stroked its thick black coat. Its eyes shone with keen intelligence.

"Yes," he laughed, caressing the dog's ears. "He's as human as you and me. His name is Nocciola" – which means 'Hazelnut,' and indeed the dog's nose was just the color and shape of an oversized hazelnut. "Nocciola," he said gently to the dog, "Greet the lady," and at this Nocciola trotted over to me, and bracing his two front paws on the floor in front of me, performed a sort of bow. "Now," he said, "Go to your place," and the dog scuttled back under the desk, and collapsed with a groan, looking up at us with soulful eyes, waiting for further instruction.

We began to select a few objects to include in the photograph. The Count had a particular preference for his Egyptian pieces. I asked how he had obtained them.

"My great-grandfather was born in Malta, and spent his youth sailing around world to visit the sacred sites of ancient cultures. He lived awhile in Cairo before retiring to his homeland. I inherited his collection of Egyptian objects, though much was lost in a shipwreck off the North African coast."

"Then your family is not from this area?" I asked, puzzled.

"My father's connection with this region is actually quite recent, within the last 350 years," he said, "But my mother's origins go back to the shadowy days of the Etruscans. This tower belonged to her family. The rest of the castle, which was previously a convent, fell to ruin after she died. She is buried over there, with her ancestors," he gestured toward the window at the burial monument I had noted earlier.

I glanced at the monument. You would have thought that the ruined convent where it was housed had collapsed centuries ago.

The Count pierced me through with a sidelong glance, as if reading my thoughts. "Don't be surprised. I *am* over 2000 years old you know," he said, smiling impishly and touched my hand. I nearly jumped from the jolt of electricity that flickered up my arm.

I thought he was joking about being old and could think of nothing clever to say in reply, so I only nodded and smiled. He grew reflective, scratched his chin, and stared out the window for a long moment, almost seeming to forget that I was there.

My assistant, growing impatient, asked, "Are you ready, Signora?"

I nodded and told the Count to take a seat at his desk.

I studied him through the camera while he stared back into the lens with a purposeful and determined expression. Then before taking the photograph, I looked up from the camera directly into his eyes.

For one brief second the room around me vanished and I was alone with those eyes and the power emanating from them. As I peered deep I had the sudden, overwhelming feeling that it was all true: he was – or part of him was – 2000 years old or even older. He came – part of him came – from a place beyond time. His eyes rolled upwards for a brief moment, severing contact with mine, and in my mind I *saw* the aeons he had crossed, like a wolf across the tundra, in search of something that cannot be named or defined. Perhaps I would have named it *immortality*, if that word had any sense for me. He fixed his eyes on me again. My awareness of the surroundings returned, but the dimensions of the room had changed, the space between us had become elastic; the air seemed filled with an invisible substance tingling like snow on my skin. I knew I was no stranger to his journey, although I also knew that such thoughts were sheer madness, and these two certainties collided in me with such force I could hardly keep my knees from shaking. I wondered if I were being hypnotized or if there were any other plausible physiological explanation for these bizarre sensations and even stranger thoughts. Approaching the change of life, perhaps? But wasn't it a bit too soon?

I gripped the tripod to steady myself. I had broken out in a clammy sweat. I glanced at his hand on the desk, it was a very mortal hand, no mummy's appendage of 2000 years: swarthy, virile, squarish, with tapered fingers, and a cornelian ring. I knew

I would come to love the owner of that hand with a desperation I never imagined possible, yet all the same I felt a foretaste of revulsion.

Federigo Del Re looked back at me, steadily, gravely. Not a muscle moved in his face.

I realized I was engaged in some new battle of the will, a battle I could never win, but must fight all the same.

"Are you ready, Count?" I asked, finding my voice at last.

"I would be honored if you would call me by my name. Federigo."

"Are you ready, Signor Federigo?"

"*Sì*."

There was a blinding flash of magnesium and a smell of singed hair and dust. A green light flared in the boar's glass eyes.

6

When the portrait was ready, I sent Andrea to the tower to deliver it to the Count. He replied with a long note, telling me how pleased he was with the likeness, and inviting me to go with him on a tomb-hunting excursion. He wanted to show me a place called Barbarano, consisting of a ruined medieval church built above an Etruscan necropolis in the woods. The description was certainly engaging, and nothing could have delighted me more. So one Saturday morning in November, we met at the crossroads and set out together for a long walk through the woods. I wore trousers and boots as usual. The Count was dressed in the typical garb of the local hunters, rough brown trousers and a green shooting jacket, a canvas rucksack strapped to his shoulders. He carried no gun, only a walking stick and a wicker basket, which he explained was for gathering mushrooms. He had left both his son and the dog at home.

Federigo Del Re was quite a fast walker, even faster than myself, and I, for once, had to scramble along the forest trail to keep up with him. I was amazed by the speed with which he darted along the path, while hardly seeming to make any effort at all. Despite that stomach, he seemed to be in superb physical condition.

We were not the only visitors to the woods that day. Not far off in among the trees we could hear the hunters hallooing to each other above the frenzied barking of dogs. Once or twice, a shot rang out quite near. The sound of gunshots unnerved me, but the Count did not seem to notice. He hurtled along the trails, with eyes half closed, orienting himself more by instinct than sight it seemed, dashing branches out of the way with one arm. It did not occur to me that he too might be fleeing from the disturbing sound of gunfire.

"What are they hunting?" I asked, after another shot crackled nearby.

"*Cinghiali.* The boar season has just opened." He strode a few paces along the trail, then turned and said, "The boar is the beast of death and November is the death of the boar."

I shuddered. "The beast of death?" I asked as he trotted on.

"For the Etruscans, the boar brought the death of winter, and thus was an agent of transformation."

I could hardly believe that wild boar still roamed these woods as freely as they did in the days of Etruscans, yet their presence was clearly evident. Boar tracks lined the muddy trail, and the ground beneath every oak tree was pitted with holes where these animals had been rutting for acorns and truffles in the night.

"Are boars as dangerous as legend claims?" I asked when we finally sat down to rest on a mossy embankment where pink cyclamen flickered amid the dead leaves.

"Only at night. Especially females with their young." He indicated several tracks in the mud beside us. "A sow with her piglets passed by a few hours ago. Probably this morning before the dawn. She may be asleep with her brood, there in that cave," and he pointed to a small cavern-like recess in some rocks across the trail.

We heard the men shouting again, off through the trees.

"You don't hunt? I asked, remembering the massive boar's head I had seen in his study.

He grimaced. "I don't like the sight of blood. Mine or theirs. I hunt only mushrooms. We will surely find some of those today, up in the chestnut grove," and he reached down to pull me to my feet. The warmth of that brown hand was startling.

As we penetrated deeper into the woods, the sound of shooting died away, and the Count slowed to a more relaxed pace, for which I was grateful. Once in the thick of the trees, he stopped many times to stir the forest floor with his walking stick, looking for mushrooms brought out in abundance by the recent rains. Federigo Del Re was an expert in mushrooms and that morning he taught me to recognize quite a few varieties: the pale yellow and cream parasol of a *prataiolo,* the orange scalloped cap of a *finferla,* or the brown fleshy *porcino* which he immediately picked and dropped into his basket.

"And this," he said bending down to pluck something from the ground, "is a little death trumpet – *La trombetta di morte.*" He held it out to me in the palm of his hand.

It was a small funnel-shaped mushroom covered with a glossy violet sheen.

"Is it terribly poisonous?" I asked, resisting an urge to touch it.

"By no means," he laughed and slipped it into his basket. "This is probably one of the best edible mushrooms in these woods. The name refers merely to the color. The poisonous ones generally look quite innocuous," and he pointed his stick at a white dome-like cap not yet unfurled, thrusting up from beneath a pile of decaying leaves a few feet away.

"Isn't that a *prataiolo* not yet opened?" I asked, going over to study the mushroom.

"Don't touch it," he warned as I squatted down to look at it. "If even a trace should remain on your fingers, you could become very ill. The smallest morsel would kill you in a few hours."

Alarmed, I rose. The Count strode over, uprooted the mushroom with his stick and tossed it aside. He fixed his eyes on me and I noted again those unusual flecks of yellow in the green.

"You see how easy it would be to make a fatal mistake. Never come here to gather mushrooms alone. It takes many years to become acquainted with all the local varieties, to know which ones are edible and which ones are not. Which ones you must boil a while before eating, and which ones inspire special dreams."

"Dreams?" I asked. This was the second time Federigo Del Re had mentioned the subject of dreams and I was even more intrigued.

"Etruscan soothsayers enhanced their visionary powers by consuming special mushrooms." He looked around, then gestured to a nearby tree where the base was encircled by a proliferation of ear-shaped lichen.

"That for example. Boiled ten minutes, the broth will numb all physical pain and give you vivid – some say prophetic – dreams. If boiled too long it becomes a powerful abortive and even a poison, strong enough to kill a horse."

He was silent for a long moment as I stared at the lichen, then said, "I don't suggest you try it."

I laughed, shook my head, and met his eye. "And why should I want to?" I asked.

He took a step closer, staring at me with a slightly perplexed expression. For one wild moment I felt he was about to embrace me. Or perhaps it was I who felt an inexplicable rush to throw myself against his chest, but instead he took my arm gently and steered me back to the trail, saying, "We have almost reached the tombs."

At last the trees thinned and we came to a clearing. Straight before us rose a tumulus, a mound of clay and rock, covered in a mantle of heather. As we walked across the top of the mound, the ground resonated at each step, for the tombs were hollowed out beneath us. A path wound down to the entrance to the tombs which were cut into the slopes of the mound. Descending the trail, we came to three imposing doorways. Outside the entrance to the tumulus, a long groove had been carved in the rocky ground leading straight to the central doorway.

"For the Etruscans burial meant returning to the mother's womb. This groove symbolized the birth canal. The whole complex could be said to represent female genitalia."

He shot me an oblique glance to see if this comment had made any particular impression on me, but I did not lift an eyebrow. Rather I was fascinated by his explanation of an ancient myth.

"Enter with me now into the body of our mother," he commanded in a solemn tone, setting down his stick and basket, then to my amazement, he dropped to his knees and began to crawl down the groove towards the door.

"Follow me," he whispered, "By this posture, you show your humility to the earth."

With some misgivings, I crouched down on my hands and knees and crept behind him into the central chamber, although I could not see where I put my hands and was wary of nettles and spiders. Once inside, he rose to his feet and pulled me up, then took a small lamp from his rucksack, lit it with a match, and lifted it high. We were standing in a dank room twelve feet square. The walls were flanked by tall stone beds spotted green with lichen, like the ones I had seen in Norchia. On either side a doorway opened, framed by a giant T shape, giving into a series of other chambers hollowed out in the mound.

He shone a cone of light into one of the side doorways where chamber upon chamber led into the blackness. I took a few steps forward and my hat brushed against a clump of bats hanging from the ceiling. Rudely disturbed, they flapped their wings in my face and I cried out at the unpleasant surprise.

Federigo Del Re laughed as I waved them away. "Don't be afraid," he said, "They are harmless."

He held the lamp higher to illuminate the tunnel. "These subterranean passageways can go on for miles. One day we'll explore them all, like a pair of old moles."

"I should like that," I said, pleased by this prospect of future excursions together.

He raised the lantern to a niche, hollowed in the wall, where the remains of a fresco were barely visible, half-eaten by the moss, but I could clearly discern the outline of a ship. I knew what it was: the ship of death. I had seen the small model of one in his study. "*La nave della morte*," I murmured, pointing to the image. The Count nodded. "Each one of us must prepare his ship," he said, "and load it up with wine and grain and oil, for the long journey home."

Now he shone the light towards the back wall of the tomb where an even larger doorway stood. Approaching it, I saw that it was not a real door at all, but merely an image sculpted in the wall. I asked if the builder had meant to add another chamber.

"No," he said. "That is the door of the soul through which the dead exited our world and sailed beyond time. Sometimes you find such doors carved in the rock, other times only painted."

I reached out to run my hand across the chill stone surface. The tomb wall was beaded with cold drops of moisture, and my hand left a greasy streak upon the stone. "What did they envision on the other side?" I asked.

The Count set the lantern down at the base of the carved doorway. The flame flared high and our shadows danced, huge, then merged on the tomb wall. He took a step toward me and intoned in a low voice, "Beyond that door lies an unknown world, where men and women . . . " here he paused like a skillful actor for dramatic effect. His face glowed orange in the lamplight, ". . . where even you and I . . . can become immortal, if we choose."

I shivered at his words, although I knew these histrionics were intended to impress me. Who knows how many women he had taken to these tombs and what he had done to them there? Still I was fascinated with his knowledge of the Etruscans, and moreover, I had never felt so drawn to any man or woman. Every nerve in my spinal column was alive to the warmth of his presence and I could feel the hair prickling on the nape of my neck. He stood very close to me now, and although he spoke softly, the timbre of his voice created a faint buzzing resonance in the tomb. Our eyes locked for one long moment and I thought I would jump out of my skin, so impatient was I for him to touch me. Such raw feelings quite astonished me. I usually manage to keep such instincts in check until I am sure where I stand with a person. With him there was no knowing but I was certain he was winding up to something. But instead, he said, "There are other things I wish to show you," and whirling round on his heels, he sauntered out of the tomb, leaving the lamp flickering at the base of the door. I noted that no special posture was required in exiting the tombs and hurried out behind him.

Once outside, it took a moment for my eyes to adjust to the light. We were midway down the mound. From here the trail followed a gentle wooded slope down to a small stream.

"On this side lay the realm of the dead," said Federigo Del Re, motioning to the tombs around us. "On that side," he pointed across the stream, "the realm of the living. A city flourished there from the days of the Etruscans until late medieval times. The ruined church of San Giuliano is just beyond that ridge." Taking up his basket and walking stick that he had left outside the tomb entrance, he led me down the hill.

The Count took my hand as we crossed the stream at its narrowest spot, tottering across the slippery stones. I clung to those fingers that seemed to be emanating sparks, but he let go as soon as we had safely reached the other side. As we followed the stream for some distance, he walked briskly ahead of me, and seemed withdrawn into his thoughts. I mocked myself for misinterpreting what I had vainly imagined were advances. Perhaps I had misread him entirely.

The stream meandered through a willow thicket, then broadened out into a clearing strewn with immense boulders thickly furred with dark green moss. A few stunted thorn trees grew here, sprouting up out of piles of stones. Jutting out into the water was a large flat rock that looked as though it had been carved for some special purpose. I asked him if this was where the peasant women came to pound and wash their laundry, but he shook his head, almost in irritation at my question.

"This is sacred ground," he growled and a distant look came into his eyes. "That rock was a sacrificial altar dedicated to the gods of the stream. The *genii loci*."

Sacred ground or not, the Count left me briefly to answer a

call of nature in the bushes, his back turned to me in full view, while I sat on the flat rock, staring down into the stream, so as not to have to watch him urinating against a tree. Red and brown pebbles glistened at the bottom, magnified by the ripples washing over them in endless succession. After a few moments, I had to avert my gaze, as I began to feel dizzy and the kaleidoscopic patterns of the pebbles made my eyes water. For relief I looked up at the trees on the slope above the stream where I noticed a deformed tree, its trunk twisted in a loop at the base. I decided to investigate it, so I got up from the rock and climbed toward the tree.

Coming closer I saw that this freakish formation consisted of two different trees springing from the same spot in the ground: an old, crooked hawthorn tree and a much younger fig with smooth grey bark. The two trunks were knotted together at the base and the fig had grafted onto the hawthorn in several spots so that you could hardly tell where one ended and the other began. Around the base of the hawthorn there grew a thick ring of that yellowish ear-shaped lichen the Count had pointed out to me earlier that morning. As I bent down to study the lichen, I was immediately overcome by a very unsettling sensation.

It was as if a barrier, invisible yet as resilient as a rubber wall, had thrust itself between me and the tree, and I was tossed off my balance. I heard a roaring in my ears and felt myself falling, but somehow managed to regain my footing by grabbing hold of a branch. When my full senses returned, I found myself gasping for breath, clinging to a branch with one hand, my whole body clammy with cold sweat.

A twigged snapped behind me. The leaves rustled. "Signora?" said the Count, coming up stealthily beside me. "H-a-r-r-i- e -t," he drawled, and put that warm hand on my shoulder.

He had never called me by my first name before. The aspirated H and rolled R's sounded almost ludicrous, and in other circumstances I might have laughed at his attempt to pronounce such a difficult English name, but at the moment I felt much too ill.

"Are you all right?" he asked, eyeing me with concern.

"I must have had a dizzy spell," I said.

"Perhaps we were unwise to venture so far after your recent accident."

"No," I said, "I'm sure that has nothing to do with it."

"Have you had dizzy spells like this before?" he asked, gazing at me thoughtfully and stroking his chin.

"No, never," I said, then remembered that I had nearly fainted the day I took his photograph. I did not mention this, of course.

"The ruin I want to show you isn't far," he said, gesturing up through the trees with his walking stick. "We can rest there for awhile and have something to eat. Perhaps that will give you strength."

He offered me his arm and we made our way up the ridge through the trees. After my bout of dizziness, the electric attraction to him I had experienced in the tomb had subsided and I was relieved to feel once again in control of my feelings and sensations. I was also tired and hungry, and glad that we would be stopping for a rest soon. Emerging from the woods we saw the ruin before us.

There was nothing left of the main church, only a crumbling apse and a low wall covered by a dense growth of briars. Three mossy pillars still stood upright in the cloister, others lay broken on the ground. The capitals were carved with curious figures that had not entirely eroded away. The Count pointed out a puffy round moon face with drooping eyelids, "That is you," he said simply, and then indicated another figure – a fierce bearded sun with flames of fire for a mane, "And that is me."

Off the cloister a small chapel stood intact. The iron gate creaked as he pushed it open and we stepped inside. The warped wooden pews were coated with dust. Snail shells had collected at the base of the altar, swallows' nests hung from the rafters. We walked down the aisle and stopped before the altar where a shriveled bouquet of wild flowers lay amid brown rose petals and the withered bodies of dead bees. Behind the altar, several dates, initials and names were scratched in the wall. One inscription read *Del Re*, followed by a series of dates: *1650, 1789, 1833, 1900*. With each date, the writing style changed.

"Ancestors of yours?" I asked, pointing out the list of dates.

He smiled strangely and nodded.

I wrote my own initials with my finger in the dust on the altar. *H.S. 1922.* Then after a moment's hesitation I added the Count's initials.

He glanced down at our initials in the dust. Feeling him standing so near me sent metallic shivers down my spine and I leaned back against his chest, waiting to be embraced at last, but instead, he cleared his throat, wheeled round and marched back out to the cloister.

I followed him outside and sat down straddling a fallen pillar. I was becoming annoyed with his games. His aloofness was maddening and no doubt studied to sharpen my interest.

Such coyness was ridiculous at our age and I resolved not to let him go on making a fool of me. He sat across from me on a stone ledge, his legs stretched out, his back leaning against the cloister wall. He asked if I was hungry and when I nodded, he took a packet out of his rucksack and unwrapped it. He had brought a hunk of bread, some hard-boiled eggs, and a small flask of wine. He lifted an egg to the sun, balancing it delicately between his thumb and forefinger like a precious object, and said, "Harriet, I give you eternity."

In that half reclining position, holding up a translucent egg gilded with sunlight, Federigo Del Re might have been a sculpted figure on an Etruscan sarcophagus, which often portrayed reclining figures in a similar attitude, holding an egg or a chalice. He surely knew that I had seen pictures of those sculptures and I guessed that he had struck that well-documented pose for my benefit. I made no comment, however. I simply plucked the egg from his hand, peeled it, and ate it, saltless, as it was. He nodded gravely as I ate, watching me with sly approval as I swallowed the last bits and removed a fragment of eggshell from the tip of my tongue. Then he tore the bread in half and offered me my share, took a sip from the flask and held it out to me.

I ate the bread and drank the red wine, astringent and sharp. It was a meagre feast, but I would not have asked for anything more satisfying than this simple meal, shared with him, like that. After we had finished the last drop of wine, he drew a small fruit out of his rucksack. It was a pomegranate with a mottled husk, ruby and gold. Slipping a knife from his pocket, he slit the fruit in two, and handed me half. The purple grains glittered in the light. He watched as I picked out a few grains and crushed them against my palate, savoring their tartness, then spit out the seeds into the cup of my hand.

"You cannot taste the flavor by picking at it like a sparrow," he said gruffly. "Don't be afraid. Swallowing the seeds won't harm you." Lifting his half of the pomegranate to his mouth, he bit straight through the rind, swallowing a chunk of fruit, seeds and all, as the red juice spattered his fingers. I did likewise, filling my mouth with the tang of the juice and the sharp bitterness of the rind. He seemed pleased. "For the Etruscans, the pomegranate was a sacrament."

"Of what sort?" I asked, again intrigued, and took another bite.

He evaded my question. "For them everything was a sacrament: eating, drinking, dancing – sex, of course, and dying. Not like nowadays," he added with scorn.

He fell silent, then took out a cigarette case and offered me a smoke, which I accepted. We smoked in silence, and a brooding vagueness settled over his face again, as though he were deep in thought. Rousing himself, he peered at me, and said, "I've seen women dressed like you in Paris. I can't say I liked them. But oddly enough, trousers seem to suit you."

I suppose I blushed despite myself. I could very well imagine what sort of women in trousers he had seen in Paris and what he thought of them. I thought I should speak up to clear up any doubts he might have about me on that account.

"I dress like this not to deny that I am a woman," I said, "but simply because it's practical and more comfortable for working and for travel. Men's jackets, for example, have so many more pockets. Trousers are better for strenuous physical activity."

He nodded and agreed that trousers were an excellent modern invention, much warmer than robes or skirts. We sat in silence again, then with a sweep of his arm embracing the cloister, the church, the surrounding meadow, he said, "I can remember when this church was still all in one piece and barefooted monks shuffled through this cloister in tattered brown robes."

"When was that?" I asked doubtfully. The place must have been in ruin for centuries.

"Oh," he laughed, and closed his eyes, "Long ago, before you were born. I'm an old, old man, as I told you, and much older than you think. Close your eyes and listen. Can't you hear them muttering their prayers in corrupt Latin?"

Again, I thought this was some sort of joke. To humor him I shut my eyes, but heard nothing but the wind in the grass. Then suddenly his mouth brushed mine, but it was such a fleeting sensation I wondered if I had imagined it – or perhaps a moth had alighted on my lips and then flown away. I opened my eyes and was startled to see him gazing fixedly at me. He rose now abruptly, picked up his things, and reached down to pull me up, saying, "There is one last place to see in this journey through the centuries. I have loved it ever since I was a child."

This time he did not drop my hand, but clasped it firmly and led me down a hill, waist high in dry weeds. We came to a gate in the hillside. Through the rusted bars, I saw a flight of stairs disappearing into the gloom of a subterranean archway.

"The gate wasn't here years ago. It was only a hole in the hill, covered by a few dogroses and blackberry vines. The local peasants avoided it, out of superstition. They thought it was the door to the underworld."

We opened the gate and descended a slick flight of mossy steps where water dripped from the ceiling and ferns sprouted from cracks in the walls tickling our faces. Coming out into the light again, we found ourselves on a terrace extending over a canyon. High up, across the canyon, a row of oaks stood along the rim, their russet leaves tossing in the wind. The sound reminded me of a rising sea.

In one corner of the terrace, a large square pool was carved. The spring feeding the pool had dried up ages ago, although you could clearly see the crevice from which it once gushed. Now the pool was full of stagnant rainwater, covered by a scum of algae, where dead leaves floated. This was what was left of the ancient thermal bath.

The terrace had a south-westerly exposure, well-protected from the north wind. At this hour of the afternoon, the rock walls were still quite warm to touch, despite the chilly air.

He sat down on a sunny ledge and tugged me down by the hand. "I come here," he said, "to quiet the turbulence in my mind. So many voices; so many echoes." He closed his eyes and leaned against the tepid wall, and seemed to fall asleep for he breathed deeply, made a snuffling noise, and then, to my amazement, began to snore very distinctly.

Amused, I studied his face.

Federigo Del Re seemed older in the scrutiny of sunlight. A stubble of white beard sprouted on his chin where the skin beneath was no longer firm and taut, and yet hardly a wrinkle was etched in his face. His features were an odd composite of contrasts: the thin lips of an aesthete, the jutting forehead of a brooder, the full cheeks of a sensualist. With his eyes closed, the energy and light had drained away from him. He looked grey and sad, quite different from the bronze mask blazing in the lamplight that I had glimpsed earlier in the tomb. This unexpected vulnerability in him moved me and I reached out hesitantly to touch his face. As he did not wake, I grew bolder and let my fingers travel across his eyelids, his lips, tracing the whorls of his ears where thick down grew, almost like fur. Unaware of my caresses, his face remained impassive, as void of expression as a blank slate of stone. Then with no warning, a nostril flared. He stirred, opened his eyes wide, and shot me through with an arrow of a glance. Although startled, I did not take my hand away. Nor did he move, but only smiled faintly, then groaned, "Harriet, *amor mio*," and fell against me with his whole weight. His head dropped heavily into my lap and in an instant he was fast asleep again.

I do not know how long we sat there, my arms cradling his head, as he snuffled intermittently, an hour or perhaps, two. How was it possible that I had conceived such a passion for this boarlike hulk snoring in my arms? I knew my feelings were unwise, and yet I could not deny them. I gazed across the canyon at the crows flapping in the treetops, and ran my fingers through his thick grizzled hair. It grew late and I began to feel cold, for the sun had begun to sink between the ragged oaks on the cliffs and the wind had risen. With his weight leaning on me like that, I was quite uncomfortable, but I did not want to disturb him. At last he coughed, sat up and disentangled himself from my arms. Springing to his feet, he grabbed his things and announced, "I must go." With no further explanation, he bounded up the steps and out through the gate in the hillside. What could I do but follow?

He rushed on ahead along the trail. I tried to keep in step and was soon so exhausted that I cried out begging him to stop and let me rest. The sun was about to set and we had come upon an olive grove where the olives hanging from the branches glistened in the fading light. I leaned against one of those twisted olive trunks to get my breath and gazed at the sun. Federigo gripped my hand and bent close, his lips almost touching my ear as he murmured, "The world turns, but we stand still in the flux of time."

With those words, something happened that I cannot explain. The moment froze. There is no other way to describe it. I clearly perceived the swaying of the grass in the wind, the shivering of the olive leaves. I could feel the pounding of my pulse and the heat of his hand burning into mine. And yet the sun did not move. It hung there in the very same spot for what seemed like hours, motionless above the horizon. I stared at it, I expected it to move, I *willed* it to move, and yet it would not budge. It occurred to me that I was being hypnotized. As my mind seized on this thought, slowly, imperceptibly, the sun began to move again, and slipped behind the hill.

Federigo eased his grip and the luminosity in which I had been plunged for that long moment drained away. He dropped my hand and coughed, or perhaps, chuckled. I looked at him bewildered.

He patted my arm fondly. "*Mia cara signora,*" he said, "You are a natural!"

"I beg your pardon. A natural what?"

"A sibyl," he replied, leaning over to touch his lips to mine, then pulled away. His tone turned serious. "I am convinced that you are a natural born dowser."

He gave me no time to take stock of the fact that he had kissed me.

"You mean a water witch?" I laughed, "You must be joking."

"I suspected it at first, but now I am sure. That is why you grow dizzy in certain spots in the woods. You are unconsciously susceptible to underground springs. This became apparent to me when you fainted by the stream."

I laughed again, and stepped towards him, expecting another kiss.

But instead of embracing me, Federigo Del Re cleared his throat loudly and began to instruct me on the subject of dowsing.

"Dowsers can find other things besides water," he said, "They can find precious metals or buried tombs or simply discontinuations in the geological strata. It is an ancient art and very scientific. Today, as we visited places from different eras, you were exposed to various influences, but you showed the greatest reaction to underground water. Your body is a finely tuned instrument."

Indeed it was, but not perhaps in the sense he meant. By this point I was completely exasperated by his behavior, for he was keeping me at bay with a stream of words.

"Deformed trees often indicate the presence of underground springs. That is why you felt sick when you approached that misshapen tree. A typical dowser's reaction."

I could see he was speaking in earnest. I shook my head. I thought it was quite unlikely and ascribed my dizzy spells to more physical causes. I had no doubt that other people, like him, had such occult gifts, but certainly not me. Yet I was flattered that he thought I was endowed with some mysterious talent. This offered a crumb of consolation for my romantic disappointment.

"Perhaps we should try some more experiments," he continued. "Tomorrow afternoon I will be drilling for water on my land, and have called in a dowser, one of the best of the old timers. You might find it amusing to come along and try his willow wand."

I said I would come, eager to spend another afternoon with him, I wanted nothing more than to be with him, but did not know what to make of his advances and retreats. What held him back? Discretion? Timidity? I stood waiting for him to kiss me again, although the moment for that had clearly passed. I looked down at the ground and tapped a stone with my toe. I must have sighed audibly for he frowned at me. Tucking a straying lock of hair beneath my hat, he said, "It will be night soon. I'm sorry, but I must go." Then he turned and walked off at a determined pace. No man had ever made me feel so furious.

At last I managed to catch up with him. We walked briskly, without speaking, through the dusk as an early moon, not quite full, yearning, pinkish, crept up behind the hills. Soon we were in sight of the iron cross marking the fork in the road where we had met that morning to set out on our excursion.

The road to the left led to the tower, the one to the right, to the village and to my own little house on the outskirts. I did not want our walk to end. I did not want to part from him, to be left at the crossroads without another kiss, without some confirmation of the intimacy that had sprung up between us and then withered in an instant. I would have dawdled to look at the moon but he would not relent.

The road was bordered by a thick hedge of laurel where I heard sparrows scratching in the twilight. After the rustling had accompanied us persistently for a few yards, I realized someone must be running alongside us on the other side of the hedge, but Federigo seemed to have noticed nothing. Through a gap in the bushes I glimpsed a furry black paw, then a plumed black tail. Nocciola was trotting along there on the other side. Federigo's son was sure to be close by.

When we reached the crossroads the Count suddenly slung down his basket and lunged at me, seized me in his arms, and bent down to fold his lips over mine, crushing the brim of my hat against my face. Although I wanted nothing more than to feel his body pressed against me, I pushed away with all my strength, for I sensed that his son was watching us and would not be pleased to see his father kissing a strange woman in trousers. And indeed, as Federigo pulled me tighter to his chest, there came a wild shout from the bushes and both dog and boy leapt out of the hedge.

For Nocciola it was just a game, he pranced about us barking, but the boy launched a furious battle, pummeling us with his fists. When I managed to break free from the Count's arms, the boy flew at me, pulled my hat off, and yanked out a handful of my hair.

I managed to defend myself as he swung punches in my face, until at last the Federigo subdued him and I stumbled back, gasping. He gathered the boy to him and stroked his dark hair while Nocciola sat whimpering by the roadside.

Federigo was aghast. He held the boy's head against his chest, tilting his own face up toward the sky, eyes shut in supplication. "It's all right," he repeated. "Never again."

I stood there awkwardly, not knowing what to do, until Federigo, aware once again of my presence, opened one eye and shot me a pitiful look. With a wave of his hand, he indicated that I should be on my way without further ado, and so I picked up my hat and ran off. Ten minutes later, I looked back and saw them still there, father and son, embracing, rocking slowly from side to side, at the foot of the iron cross.

7

Before I even opened my eyes, I heard the sound of rain pelting against the shutters. I shrank deeper beneath the eiderdown, remembering snatches of an unquiet dream.

"There is a message for you, Signora," announced Maria as

she set down my breakfast tray on the dresser and threw the shutters open to the dreary morning.

I sat up. The room was chilly. I shivered and reached for the cashmere shawl left draped over the foot of the bed. Maria passed me the tray with coffee, toast and boiled egg. A small, cream-colored envelope was slipped beneath the saucer of my coffee cup. The envelope was wet and wrinkled, the familiar handwriting blurred. It could only be a message from Federigo Del Re. Today we were to conduct our dowsing experiment, but considering the weather, I supposed – with some disappointment – it had been put off. Before reading the note, I took a sip of coffee. It was cold and metallic tasting, and Maria had forgotten to add sugar.

"The dog brought it," Maria said bustling about with a feather duster, obviously anxious for me to be gone so that she could tidy the room.

I examined the envelope and smiled as I noted a semi-circular imprint of tooth marks where the dog must have carried the letter in its mouth.

The note read:

Carissima Signora,
I am very sorry for yesterday's incident. I have been called away for a few days on business. Please keep this token for me until I return to reclaim it.
Your Federigo.

Puzzled, I searched the envelope. There was nothing else inside. What token did he mean?

"Was there anything besides this envelope?" I asked Maria as she dusted off the dresser.

"A basket of mushrooms and a porcupine."

"A porcupine?"

"Makes a delicious stew."

I must have made an unappreciative grimace.

"You'll see, Signora, when you taste it."

"And the dog brought a basket with those things to the house?"

"No, a boy brought those. The dog brought the note. It won't go away. I shook the broom at it, but it wouldn't budge. It's still out there, in the rain." She pointed out the window with her duster.

I got out of bed and looked out the window. Nocciola sat in the garden under the shelter of an apple tree, looking up at the sky. He wagged his tail at me and barked a greeting.

Please keep this token until I return to reclaim it.

Federigo could not expect to reclaim either the porcupine or the mushrooms. Perhaps he meant the dog.

"Let him come inside," I said.

"Who?" she asked.

"The dog, of course."

"Signora! A wet dog in the house?"

"Please do as I say."

In reply, Maria grumbled something about dogs carrying disease, vehemently stripped off the covers on the bed, and began to shake them vigorously, as if the feared contagion had already crept in.

"Nonsense," I said, "If a dog is clean and well-cared for, there is no reason to keep him out of the house."

It was clear that I would have to let the dog in myself, so I went in search of an old blanket to dry him off with. Passing through the sitting room, I saw that the shutters and windows were still closed. Last night's ashes had not yet been removed from the hearth and no new fire had been lit. The room smelled heavily of old, cold, pungent ash. I stepped into the kitchen. No fire had been built in the kitchen hearth, either, and the stove had gone out. That explained why the coffee was cold. Maria must have made it hours ago and left it on the extinguished stove. I wondered what she could have been doing all this time.

Then I saw Federigo's gift. There on the marble table before the hearth was a large wicker basket of freshly picked mushrooms: cream, orange, violet and brown – *prataioli, finferle, porcini, trombette di morte*. I could smell the scent of humus and rain on them. I marveled that he had found the time to pick them before the heavy rain had started falling, but perhaps he had sent one of his farmhands out early. In another basket was a porcupine with all its quills, curled up as though asleep, and a black branch with three dark ruby pomegranates.

I touched the porcupine and pricked my finger on a quill, which was surprisingly sharp. Then I put the branch of pomegranates in a vase, carried it back into the sitting room, and set it on an oak dresser by one of the mirrors where I studied it for a few moments. This gnarled branch with gleaming fruit was a worthy subject for a Japanese scroll. Federigo Del Re had the eye of an artist and this intrigued me all the more.

With a sigh, I opened the shutters and leaned out, gazing though the dripping trees in the garden at the distant tower. Fog was swirling up from below and would quickly blot out the entire view. Where had he gone? And for how long? I frowned as I remembered the episode with his son along the road and wondered if Federigo's absence were connected with that incident. Perhaps the boy had had a seizure of some sort and required immediate treatment.

I flinched thinking of the dank tower with its smell of mildew and boiled cabbage where he and his son lived with that old battleaxe. As for the Count's mistress, Elisabetta Colonna, I had completely erased her from my mind. I closed the window. Turning back to the room, I caught a glimpse of myself in the mirror above the hearth. I looked sallow in the pale morning light, my figure rather dumpy in my loose flannel nightdress, my face creased from the pillows, bluish shadows under my eyes. I brushed my cropped hair away from my temples, peered closer into the glass and spied a few white glints in among the blonde. I plucked out three white hairs and dropped them into the fireplace. "And please, Maria, take those old ashes away and light the fire."

I found an old piece of woollen cloth in the bottom drawer of a dresser. Then I went down the stairs, opened to the chill morning, and whistled for Nocciola. He came dashing to the door, and leapt up to lick my face with wild joy. I swaddled him in the rag, wrestling to keep him still, patted him dry and led him upstairs as he left muddy tracks on the stone steps. In the meantime, Maria had lit a cozy fire. The dog claimed his spot on the hearthrug, and there he lay deep asleep for the rest of the morning, opening a yellow eye now and again to peer at Maria as she went about her chores, and growling very faintly if she came too near.

It was quite a busy day in the kitchen. In addition to the usual baking and pasta-making there were the mushrooms to prepare and the porcupine to pluck and dress. Maria performed these tasks with her usual efficiency.

She was quite impressed with Federigo's gift, and told me that the mushrooms would have brought a pretty penny at the local market. I sat in the kitchen and watched as she sorted through them, dividing them into piles. Some were for the pasta sauce, some were to be pickled, and others to be dried in wicker trays on the stove top. The great caps of the *porcini* and *prataioli* would be roasted on a grill, smaller ones would be preserved in olive oil. She examined each mushroom carefully, turning it over in the light, studying the pleated underside of the caps, flicking off bruises from the stems with a knife. A few did not meet her approval and she set them aside. When she had finished sorting all the mushrooms in the basket, she took a coin and touched it to the caps of the discarded ones. "The coin turns black if the mushrooms are bad," she explained. We waited, staring at the coin, but nothing happened.

"There then, it's all right. It's just that they are old. But can't be too careful," and she threw them away.

"Do you think they would have made me ill if I had eaten them?" I asked, indicating the discarded mushrooms.

"No, not ill, Signora, maybe they might give you a headache if they aren't really fresh. But there's no need to worry – I checked them all and only kept the good ones. Whoever picked them knows how to recognize the very best kinds."

Next she turned her attention to the porcupine which she stewed with wild fennel and onions. The smell was quite agreeable. Later, I went into the kitchen and peeked into the pot. With the quills removed, the porcupine looked rather like a suckling pig.

At dinner, Maria brought me a dish of stewed meat and a plate of roasted mushrooms and set them down triumphantly. The meat was quite edible, and not at all disgusting, but it had a strong flavor, like all game, and no doubt was an acquired taste. The mushrooms instead, seasoned with garlic, olive oil, and parsley, were superb, and if I had any misgivings about eating wild mushrooms, they dissolved at that instant.

After dinner, the three of us sat by the fire. I brushed Nocciola's coat and picked it free of burrs, while Maria darned an old pair of stockings and muttered about strange foreign customs, and keeping dogs in houses. I did not usually sit with her in the evenings. She generally retired to the kitchen, where she received her visitors: one of the local peasant girls or sometimes an old widower to whom she offered a glass of the Count's wine. I did not mind that she helped herself freely. There was far more than I could have ever drunk. But that night it was so cold and rainy, and devoid of comfort, I did not mind her company. My thoughts were full of the Count and his gifts and as to when he would return. As I tugged the steel teeth of the brush through the thick ruff around Nocciola's neck, I felt something attached to his collar, and looking closer I saw something glinting, gold and orange, half hidden in his black mane. It was the Count's cornelian ring.

Please keep this token until I return to claim it.

Surreptitiously, for I did not want Maria to notice, I undid the dog's collar, removed the ring, which was fastened on with a twist of wire, and slipped it in my pocket. Then I buckled the collar back on, stroked the dog's head and stared into the flames.

Seeing me musing like this, Maria looked up from her mending to admonish me sharply, "Never look straight into the flames, Signora."

If only I had been wise enough to heed this simple peasant woman's advice.

Nocciola kept me company for that long rainy period while Federigo was away. He was a silent, friendly, watchful companion, although he and Maria only barely tolerated each other. I let him sleep on the floor by my bed, my hand dangling down over the edge of the mattress to play with a tuft of fur. I had many things to do to keep my mind occupied, and I tried to discipline my days. I was writing a report of the tombs I had seen so far, but I had taken no photographs yet.

I had decided to wait for the cold, dry spells of late winter when the muddy ground would be hard, and less slick, and when the exuberant vegetation would have partially died back offering a more unencumbered view. I tried reading the book Federigo had given me at the Baronessa's dinner party, hoping to find useful information about the local tombs for my research, but I simply could not make headway, and finally just set it aside.

Although I had invited Sarah and Stephen for Christmas, I wrote to them now, begging them to put off their visit until spring, explaining that the house wasn't comfortable or warm enough yet, given Sarah's delicate health. Moreover, the autumn had been unusually damp.

I was concerned about Sarah of course, but my real reason for delaying their visit was that I wanted no engagements of any kind to interfere with my growing intimacy with Federigo Del Re. For I expected he would return shortly to claim a good deal of my time and attention.

Furthermore, I had much work to do, and did not want to be distracted. In these weeks before Christmas I intended to familiarize myself with a few more areas, if the weather permitted, and if not, to research what information could be found in the local archives and museums, which I had quite neglected since I had made the Count's acquaintance. I also needed to tend to my correspondence, for I had received several letters from various Etruscan art collectors in reply to my request for permission to photograph and catalogue their more important items, which I planned to do later in the spring.

In the morning when it was not raining heavily, I rose very early and took the dog for a walk, just as the sun was coming up, around 7.00. Together we explored the ridges, thickets, and hills that lay between my house and the tower, to which I was naturally drawn, hoping, I suppose, to catch a glimpse of Federigo Del Re as soon as he returned.

One morning, I found a path through the forest leading up to a high ridge from where I could see into the Count's garden behind the tower, where his peacocks screeched and his roosters crowed at all hours of the day. Every morning I would stop to see if there was any sign of life in the tower. Occasionally there were wisps of smoke, and once I saw the Count's sister scuttling through the garden with a bundle of twigs in her arms, coming in from the woods where she must have been gathering kindling.

High on the ridge one could smell the stink of sulphur, and following the smell, Nocciola and I came to a small sulphur spring bubbling out of the earth in a clearing, where it formed a milky greenish pool, surrounded by yellowish pinnacles of sulphur incrustations. There are a dozen such springs in the area of Viterbo, and the local people swear that bathing in or even drinking this foul-smelling yellow water will cure any ailment. So here now I went in the mornings early before the woods filled up with hunters or mushroom pickers, and bathed naked in that steaming pool while the dog sat on the edge and kept guard. It was lovely to loll in the water, half sunk in yellow ooze, the cold wind on my face and shoulders, the rest of my body soaking in water well over 100 degrees.

Beyond the sulphur pool stood a circle of giant, deformed chestnut trees, with crippled branches and gaping hollows in their trunks. The placement of the trees and their great age gave the spot an eerie feeling, and not far off lay a pile of massive stones, which did not seem to be a natural formation, but was probably some kind of primitive tomb, perhaps pre-dating even the Etruscans themselves. Doubtless another sacred spot that would well be worth a photograph. After bathing in the hot water, I would dress quickly, exhilarated by the contrasting sensations of cold air and warm skin, and sit for awhile on the stones, staring up at those enormous trees, which in my imagination seemed to totter around me in a dance.

Nocciola knew the path quite well and quickly adapted to my habits. Every morning he led me straight to the pool. One morning we had set out even earlier than usual, as I wanted to watch the sunrise in the chestnut grove. It was damp and cold at that hour before dawn, and from the ridge I could see a dense vapor rising from the pool, drifting up in among the trees. As we headed for the spring, the dog, instead of prancing down the path in his usual manner, halted in his tracks and began to whine. I grabbed his collar, wondering what the cause of his excitement might be. Perhaps a fox or maybe a boar still roaming about at this late hour, for these nocturnal animals usually retire to their dens just before sunrise. I had not forgotten Federigo's warning that females with their young could be dangerous. I cautiously advanced a few steps, pulling the reluctant dog by his collar, fearing he might break loose and dash off through the woods. Then I saw that someone had preceded us to the pool. A naked man stood knee-high in the water, facing us. The wind stirred the vapor from his face and I saw who it was – Federigo Del Re.

I was amazed, embarrassed. He was only a few yards away, gazing in our direction. I froze, not knowing whether to come forward and apologize for our intrusion, or perhaps call out and give him time to hide his nakedness, or simply slink away. The dog's reaction perplexed me, for instead of rushing towards his master, Nocciola crouched low, tail down, refusing either to proceed or retreat. For a moment I wondered if the Count had ill-treated the dog, which might explain Nocciola's strange behavior, but such a thing seemed out of character. I had seen how fond he was of his dog.

Federigo Del Re could not have missed us, we were right in front of him and he was staring straight at us, yet he did not seem to have even noticed us. I took a few steps towards him and then realized that he was staring not at us, but *through* us, as in a trance.

He stood motionless, his eyes fixed on something *beyond* us, his face expressionless, his eyes open yet blank. He squatted down, splashed water on his chest, then rose again, and climbed out of the pool. Standing in the damp yellow sand, he opened his

117

arms wide in the direction of the rising sun and began to make curious gesticulations, as I have seen elderly Chinese men do at dawn, while breathing audibly in an unnatural manner. Boldly, I took another step forward, and dragged the dog along. Nocciola yelped once, but it made no difference, Federigo did not, *could* not hear. It occurred to me that he was walking in his sleep.

Convinced that in this altered state, he could take no note of us, I approached quite near, and sat down on a stone to observe him. Nocciola, very ill at ease in the sleeper's presence, squirmed to escape my control, but I held on firmly.

Federigo was not a young man, he was at least twelve years older than myself, if not more, but he had the body of a man in his prime, in terms of musculature and vigor. His only flaw, as far as I was concerned, but I was a biased viewer, was the heavy paunch of late middle age, deriving from too much good food and slow digestion. He had a powerful chest, broad shoulders and muscular arms, sculpted with large, knotty veins. His whole body was covered with a thick coat of hair, very dark on the limbs, and like grizzled wool on his chest. Other women might have been repulsed by such hirsutism, but I was not. His legs were too short in proportion to his massive torso and he did not meet Anglo-Saxon standards of male beauty by any means. There was something of the toad about his face and something of the porcupine; and as I have previously noted, something of the boar in his physique. Yet he moved that bulk of flesh with a suppleness and grace that were quite extraordinary.

He had left his clothes on a stone near the pool, and when he had finished performing a series of genuflections, he went over to where they were piled. Among his things I now noticed a sword. He picked it up and without bothering to put on his clothes, made his way toward the circle of chestnut trees. Nocciola and I followed at a cautious distance.

Facing east to the sun rising in between the trees, he held the sword up towards the sky in both hands, in a gesture of offering. A dance began – not unlike the sword dances of the Mandarins. The steel blade cut through the air with a low quiver as he twirled in ponderous movements, striking out against an invisible adversary. Through all this, the blank expression on his face never changed. He saw and heard nothing. It was though his eyes were coated with lead.

The dog, increasingly agitated by this spectacle, at last broke free and bounded towards his naked master, barking loudly. Helpless, I prepared to be discovered, and was anxious as to how the Count would react, for as superstition holds everywhere, it can be dangerous, even fatal, to wake a sleepwalker. But Nocciola abruptly dropped to his haunches, whining pitifully, just a few feet away from the spot where Federigo Del Re continued his dance unperturbed, as though enveloped by an impenetrable sphere. At last he came to rest, once again offered his sword to the sun, and returned to the stone where he had left his clothes. Although he strode right past me, he took no notice of me. I watched him pull his clothes on. Then sword in hand, he disappeared down a path in the woods. The dog and I followed him for quite a distance, until we came to a fork in the path. There I paused wondering whether I should go any further.

•◆•

Mrs Parsons felt her head nodding and leaned back against the lumpy pillows piled in an unfamiliar bed. Hardly had she slipped into sleep's sweet abandon, strange images appeared behind her eyelids. The shadowy figures of boars and porcupines scuttled towards her out of a dark railway tunnel and she snapped awake again. She found herself staring at a little green book lying in her lap. She shook herself and took note of her surroundings – a chilly, bare white room with a low ceiling paneled in dark wood – and remembered with a shudder that she was far away from the comfort of her little room with pink wallpaper and chintz curtains just off Russell Square. She was somewhere in the Italian countryside, where she had come to look after poor Miss Harriet. She had sat up reading till way past midnight and had dozed off with this odd little notebook propped up on her knees.

The lamp beside her began to gutter; the oil had nearly all burned away. She put the notebook on the bedside table, blew out the lamp and lay there in the dark, brooding over the queer impressions flickering through her head. She really couldn't make much sense of the notebook, and the handwriting was so difficult to read. She was even a little unsure what she had read and what she had dreamt she was reading while sitting up in bed. It had been an unsettling thing to read at such a late hour, and parts were truly indecent. That naked man dancing with a sword and keeping a collection of private parts modeled in clay! Just imagine what it would have been like to have to dust those disgusting things everyday. She would've broken them every one, she would, had she been the housekeeper.

As far as she could see, Miss Harriet's diary, if that was what it was, though it seemed very fanciful indeed, shed no light at all on those bloody sheets, and really reminded her more of an old story told at the fireside. She wondered whether she should make the effort to finish reading it as it was such a strain for her eyes. She also wondered if she should give it to the Hamptons when they came, or perhaps just put it back in the drawer where she had found it. That was probably the wisest thing. She would not want them to suspect that she had been snooping in Miss Harriet's personal papers. Mrs Hampton would never stand for that. Besides, her employers should be the ones to find the diary and puzzle it out, if they thought it was important.

A cock crowed faraway in the night. The sun would soon be up. She groaned and crept deeper beneath the covers, hoping to snatch another hour's sleep or two before rising at 6.00.

The coming day would be a busy one, for she intended to give the house a thorough cleaning. The first thing she'd do would be to throw out all those jars of pickled toadstools in the kitchen. Lord knows if Harriet hadn't managed to poison herself with them, on top of everything else.

Didn't she realize that those things could be deadly? Mrs Parsons decided she must tell the Hamptons about the mushrooms she had found, since it was clear from what Miss Harriet had written that she had been eating them. That was something they ought to know, and there would be no harm in her telling them.

She yawned, closed her eyes again, and as images of huge orange toadstools with white spots dissolved before her eyelids, she sank into the blackness and was soon snoring away.

CHAPTER FOUR

The clock ticked loudly. Sarah looked up from the notebook she was reading and rubbed her eyes. The dense, cramped script covering those pages had begun to blur. It was nearly 5.00.

She had been sitting here in Harriet's sitting room for two hours, reading a sort of diary that they had found among Harriet's things. Deep misgivings had nagged Sarah's conscience as she had rushed on across those ink-stained pages. She was ashamed of violating Harriet's privacy, yet with what morbid excitement had she followed her friend's bizarre narration. Now she had to stop and pull herself free from its dizzying spell.

She glanced towards the room where Harriet lay asleep, under the watchful care of Mrs Parsons. Since their arrival almost a week ago, Harriet had lain half-unconscious, battling off a fever. In her rare moments of dazed waking, she had shown no sign of recognizing any of them: Sarah, Stephen, Wimbly, who had accompanied them from England, or even Mrs Parsons who had found her in this pitiful state over a fortnight ago. Parsons had told them that at first Harriet had been very weak, but lucid, and seemed to be suffering from some abdominal complaint, for which she had called in the local doctor. Despite his treatment, her fever had worsened, and Harriet had quickly slipped into delirium.

How grateful Sarah was now that Stephen had thought of sending Parsons over to Italy to check on Harriet, although she had firmly disapproved of this plan at first, and had been angry with Stephen for meddling again in Harriet's private life. But then by March, when Harriet's letters had ceased to arrive, she had posed no further objections to Stephens's plan. Mrs Parsons' telegram had confirmed her worst fears. Harriet had fallen gravely ill.

By coincidence, the doctor had returned to see his patient the evening of their arrival from England, and Stephen had questioned the man. He had diagnosed a serious case of liver inflammation, possibly due to the ingestion of toxic substances. Wary of country doctors, Stephen had looked up an English doctor through the help of the British Consul, and arranged for the physician to be driven over from Rome the very next day. After a thorough examination, the English doctor had announced that Harriet was suffering from a severe case of peritonitis, most likely caused by a very recent and poorly done abortion. Internal puncturing with an unclean instrument – those were the chilling words whispered behind closed doors, out of earshot of Wimbly and Mrs Parsons.

This dismaying news had been a great blow to Sarah, who was now trying to discover how Harriet had found herself in such unfortunate circumstances. She was anxious that Wimbly should not be told the truth about Harriet's condition. Not that this unseemly fact would lower her in his esteem; Wimbly would probably only pity her. But it was too private and delicate a matter for anyone else to know.

Rain battered the windows and the wind moaned in the chimney. Sarah shivered in the draughty room and pulled her shawl tighter around her shoulders. She would have to call Parsons and have her rake up the fire. Sarah had always imagined Italy as a sun-drenched land, instead it had been raining now for days. If it wasn't the rain, then it was the fog: a thick clinging fog, chilling one to the bone. Such an unseasonably cold spring was not helping Harriet's recovery.

She looked around the dreary room, which did not in the least correspond to the charming country hermitage Harriet had described in her letters to them in the early fall. The place was more rough than rustic. Plaster peeling from the walls; crevices in the dark floor-tiles packed with dirt, a table made of bare, unsanded planks which nicked one's fingers with splinters. Rats rustled in the walls at night. The mattresses and bedclothes stank of mildew. One of the first things they had done was have Mrs Parsons launder all the sheets with boiling water and lye. The roof leaked and when it rained, water dripped down with a metallic *ping* into the rusted enamel basins and chamber pots set in all the corners. Then there was the indescribable water closet located out on the steps to the garden, where roaches – or worse, scorpions – scuttled out whenever one opened the door.

Only the stone mask in the entryway and the mirrors with their massive, chipped gilt frames bore any resemblance to Harriet's romantic portrait of the house and its furnishings. Hanging on nearly every wall, the mirrors mocked one's movement, often deforming body and face. Perhaps in her loneliness those many doubles of herself made Harriet feel that the house was full of human presences. But Sarah found it unnerving how they expanded the space around her, rooms giving onto nonexistent rooms. Whenever she opened a door, she had the uneasy feeling that another door was being opened right behind her, and the hair on her neck tingled slightly, as if teased by a sudden draught. The mirrors disturbed her sleep at night, and she had draped shawls over the ones in the room where she and Stephen slept, since on their first night, awaking from a confused dream, she had caught a glimpse of her own figure sitting up in bed and had frightened herself.

Sarah opened the notebook again and leafed through it. She had read quickly through parts of it the day before, and now had begun to read it more methodically, pondering over details. There was a break of several blank pages in the middle, then the text resumed again, and the first long entry after the break bore reference to January. She read a few lines, turned the page, frowned. Harriet had made no mention at all of their visit at Christmas when they had met near Florence at the home of Sir William Petrie in Fiesole and she had told Sarah about her count. This was one of the many perplexing things about Harriet's diary. As the narrative progressed, the outer world shrank away. A distorted piece of fantasy, Stephen had called it and had tossed it aside after a cursory examination, leaving it to Sarah to decipher Harriet's scrawl.

Sarah was convinced that Harriet's passion for her "secret sun" – the man she had mentioned to her as they parted at the Florence station, the man called Federigo Del Re in her notebook, was indeed the root of her present crisis. She hoped the diary might help her understand Harriet's unhappy situation. That morning, at her insistence, she had sent Stephen and Wimbly to see the Prefect of Viterbo, to try to discover something about the enigmatic Count. She had also given them a list of names appearing in the first few pages of Harriet's diary, to see if any of those people could be traced.

She looked up at the mantelpiece where Harriet's fat little bronze Buddha smiled in the shadows. Somehow it did not seem out of place in this bare room, with dark red floors, low wooden beams, and sputtering oil lamps. That small statue had been a childhood gift from Harriet's uncle, James Hampton, Stephen's father, who had been very fond of Harriet. Sarah could remember seeing it years ago, on the shelf above Harriet's bed in the dormitory of the boarding school in Chicago where they had met as young girls. Harriet took her Buddha with her everywhere, as her good luck charm. From Paris to Vienna, across India and into the Hindu Kush, it had traveled packed in with her photographic equipment. She loved his smile, she always used to say, the smile of one who knows.

"Who knows what?" Sarah had asked her once, years ago. Sarah was sixteen then, Harriet, her idol, four years older.

126

"That life is a fleeting illusion," Harriet had replied with a wan smile. And indeed Harriet had dedicated her life to capturing fleeting illusions and vanishing moments in her photographs.

Among the objects arranged randomly on the mantelpiece – a shriveled, brown pomegranate, a jar of porcupine quills, a blue delft vase – was a photograph of Harriet and a large black dog, perhaps the same dog described in Harriet's notebook. Harriet was dressed in her work clothes: heavy wool trousers, a plaid shirt, and a man's jacket; her short blonde hair held back from her face by a floppy-brimmed fedora pulled low on her forehead. The photograph appeared to have been taken on the front steps of her house, where Harriet was bending over in the doorway, both hands placed on the dog's back, as if to keep the animal from bounding away. The dog was peering into the camera with a peculiar, knowing expression, almost human, were it not for the vitreous gleam in its hungry eyes. It must have been Harriet's companion for quite a while, for the claw marks on the doors and furniture did indeed suggest that some rather large domestic animal had been given the run of the house, but where was it now? What could have happened to it? Beside the hearth, a worn black leather collar with tarnished steel studs dangled from a nail.

The bell rang downstairs. Mrs Parsons went to answer. The voices of Stephen and Wimbly echoed up the stairway as they came in.

"I expected you back sooner," said Sarah as the two men entered the room.

"After our visit to the Prefect of Viterbo, we went to have a look at that tower near the cemetery," said Stephen, "the one where that count supposedly lives."

Wimbly looked anxiously at the door of Harriet's room. "How's Harriet?" he asked, "Any change?"

Sarah shook her head. She rang a little brass bell to summon Mrs Parsons and ordered tea, while Stephen teased the fire with Harriet's rusty poker. "This wood makes such a stink and fills the house with smoke," he said, slumping into one of Harriet's iron chairs near the hearth. Sarah could see he was in one of his blackest moods.

"What have you discovered?" she asked.

"Not much. Tower all shut up and locked with chains," said Wimbly, going over to warm his hands by the fire.

Stephen said, "There was no one around to ask, except for a peasant boy who could not understand us, nor we him. So we took a look around the place, but all we found was a cigar stub and an empty bottle of brandy tossed on the ground."

"Fine French cognac," Wimbly corrected him, "Expensive stuff."

Not something a peasant would drink, Sarah was about to point out, but refrained. She reflected that in Harriet's diary, at their first meeting in the tombs after her accident, the Count had revived her with brandy from a flask.

"What did the Prefect tell you?"

"First we waited an hour for the Prefect to come back from having his coffee. Then we waited an hour for his interpreter to come back from having *his* coffee. By then it was nearly lunch time, and they hadn't much time to spare. It was difficult to make them understand what we wanted. That we were not there to report a crime or a missing person, but to track down a mysterious personage whose real name we don't even know. For indeed there is no record of any Federigo Del Re ever having lived in this area."

"Harriet's count probably doesn't exist, at least not by that name," said Wimbly.

"We then visited the property registry office to see what we could find out about that tower. It seems it has recently been sold to a Roman solicitor who has not yet taken possession of it. Its former owner was a Florentine banker who occasionally leased it out as a hunting lodge in the boar season."

Sarah arched an eyebrow at the word 'boar'.

"It hasn't really been inhabited by anyone on a continuing basis for over 50 years, and most certainly not by any count. And indeed, there is no record of any 'Count of Vitorchiano'.

"Then who does this house belong to?"

"It would appear to be the property of the Bank of Monti dei Paschi, in Siena. It was previously owned by one Aldo Di Rienzo, who lost it through a gambling debt."

"But perhaps that's the man! In Harriet's diary that was the name of Federigo Del Re's house agent."

"He has apparently moved away."

"And Baronessa Colonna, Signora Di Pilli? The villas in Baganaia!"

"I asked the Prefect about them too. The Colonnas are an aristocratic family in Rome, of princes, not barons. There is no official record of any Baronessa Elisabetta Colonna in this area, or in Rome either. Nor does the name Di Pilli appear in any local registry. But he did tell us that there is only one villa of note in Bagnaia, which belongs a noble family by the name of Orsini. It has been shut up for over a year, undergoing repair."

"And the Marquis Manfredi?"

"It turns out that he is a friend of the Prefect's, but at the moment is away visiting the Pyramids."

"And the maid? Harriet's errand boy?"

Stephen shrugged. "I doubt if they ever existed."

"Somebody took that picture," said Sarah pointing to the mantelpiece. She got up, went to the fireplace and picked up the photograph to examine it. Turning it over, she saw that Harriet had labeled it in pencil: *Vitorchiano, 1922*. She set it back in its place and sat down on the hearthstone with her back to the fire.

"Anyone might have done that, if Harriet had set up her camera for them and explained to them what to do," said Wimbly.

"So we don't know anything, really, do we? About the Count. About what happened to Harriet. So nothing she describes in her notebook is *real*."

"I was firmly convinced of that from the start, as I told you," said Stephen grimly, "I only went along to the Prefect to humour you! Managing, I might add, to make a laughing stock of myself in the process."

"Is that your opinion, also?" Sarah appealed to Wimbly.

"Don't know," he sighed. "Tired out now. Must have a rest."

"But we haven't had tea yet. Wouldn't you like a cup?" said Sarah.

"Yes, indeed," said Stephen, "What is Parsons thinking of to take so long?"

"No tea for me, please," said Wimbly, "Must rest," and he shuffled out of the room.

It pained Sarah to see George looking so old and worn out. "George has become so moody. Do you think he'll ever resign himself?"

"Resign himself? My dear, just between the two of us, I think he is lucky not to have put his neck in the noose, after all this nonsense."

When Mrs Parsons finally arrived with the tea, Stephen frowned, said nothing, but followed the old woman's movements with glowering scrutiny.

"I am sorry for the tea being late, Miss Harriet has kept me quite busy today," Mrs Parsons said, putting down the tray.

"That's all right," said Sarah, dismissing the housekeeper and getting up to pour her husband a cup. She poured some for herself and sat down in an armchair. The warmth of the cup in her hands and the tang of the strong bitter brew restored her energies.

"You shouldn't be rude to Mrs Parsons. We owe so much to her. Harriet might have died without her help."

"I wasn't rude to her. I didn't say a word to her."

"It's your manner, Stephen. I suppose sometimes you just don't realize the impact you have on people."

Stephen did not reply and sipped his tea in silence. Then noticing Harriet's notebook lying on the floor beside Sarah's chair, he asked, "Still reading that rubbish ?"

She leaned over towards her husband, reached out her hand and placed a finger across his lips, saying softly, "No, Stephen, please . . . don't. Haven't we had enough?"

"When you've finally done with it, I'll throw it into the fire," he grumbled.

"You wouldn't dare destroy something belonging to Harriet."

They sat in silence again.

"I was thinking," Sarah began, hoping to mollify her husband's mood. "Perhaps you are right that it is not all meant to be – taken literally –"

"Taken literally? A count who claims to be 2000 years old and descends from the Etruscan race and runs around the woods naked with a sword?"

"So you have read it then!"

"I read a couple of pages – and when I read that I stopped. You're wasting time if you are hoping to find any sort of facts or evidence in it."

"Maybe it's like an allegory –" she mused. "Or a record of her dreams."

"A record of delusion. Believe me Sarah, there is no count. There is no Federigo Del Re. He exists only in Harriet's diseased fantasy."

"She might have given him a false name and circumstances to cover his identity."

Stephen groaned and shook his head.

"But if she had to have a doctor do *that* to her," said Sarah, referring to the botched abortion that was the cause of Harriet's fever "– and so badly that she has developed peritonitis, then there had to have been *some* man, Stephen, even if his name isn't Federigo Del Re, and even if he doesn't live in a tower."

Stephen rose from his chair and began to pace in front of the fire. "Might have been anyone. She may have been carrying on with one of the local peasants or even with Sir William's chauffeur in Fiesole!"

The strangled emotion in his voice shocked Sarah even before the meaning of his insinuation sank in. Then when she had absorbed it, she was astounded by the import of such a suggestion. She had assumed that Harriet's unfortunate pregnancy had derived from her affair with the man who so obsessed her, the man she had named Federigo Del Re. That it could have happened in other circumstances had never crossed Sarah's mind. Now she made a quick mental count of the months since Harriet's visit to Fiesole and was struck by a thought so astonishing she could hardly bear to maintain it long in her consciousness. The image of Wimbly and Harriet laughing in the snow popped into her mind, then of the lantern burning in the window of the *limonaia*. And if George had been the father? She refused to pursue this thought any further. Observing her husband now, she wondered if he had also considered this possibility.

"What are you implying, Stephen?" she asked, her voice strangely quiet.

Stephen knocked his fist against the wall and growled, "If I find the man who has done this to her, I shall make him pay for it."

"Don't you think she knows that? Don't you think she'd go to any lengths to conceal the man's identity from you, from all of us, if she thought you strongly disapproved? There might be some reason she would want to protect him from revelation. Especially if she is in love with him."

"In love?" sneered Stephen, seizing the poker again and jabbing at the fire. "What has love got to do with any of this?"

A moan came from Harriet's room. Sarah looked up at her husband, but he pretended not to have heard, and continued poking the fire. She approached the doorway of Harriet's room and stared at the shrunken yellow figure beneath its mound of covers. Harriet stirred, moaned again and for the first time in days, her eyes fluttered open. Darting to the bedside, Sarah touched her friend's forehead, and was relieved to feel it quite damp and cool. The sheets bunched around her body were drenched. The fever was breaking.

"Harriet, can you hear me? It's Sarah."

"Sarah?" she blinked and closed her eyes again. "Don't go."

"I'm here."

Harriet dozed off and began murmuring in Italian. "*Amore. . . Non andare. Ti prego. Non così. Mi fai male.*" She gasped faintly and Sarah, alarmed, took her hand. Harriet opened her eyes again, focused on Sarah's face and pronounced with effort, "Sarah."

"Darling."

Harriet tried to sit up, but was too weak. Sarah gently eased her down again and plumped the pillows around her head.

"Has he really gone?"

"Who, my dear, has gone?"

"Nobody . . . I must have been dreaming . . ." Now she took note of the room. "I'm not in England, am I?"

"No, we are in Italy, in your house. You have been ill for over a fortnight. Mrs Parsons telegraphed us that you were ill, and so we all rushed, Stephen, Wimbly and I, to be with you."

"Mrs Parsons?"

"Yes, Stephen thought you might need some extra . . . assistance, so he sent her on to you to help you here around the house. Apparently you didn't receive either the letter or the telegram announcing her arrival. She found you . . . ill and in need of care." She caressed Harriet's waxen hand.

"Yes, now I remember, dear Mrs Parsons."

"But don't talk now. Save your strength. As soon as you're well again, we're taking you back to London."

Harriet sat bolt upright with a surprising burst of energy. "Don't you dare try to take me away from here," she hissed, jerking her hand away with such force that one of her fingernails scratched Sarah's palm.

Sarah winced at the fleeting pain. Dismayed by such vehemence and anxious to spare Harriet further strain, she sat down on the bed and tried to soothe her by smoothing her matted hair away from her forehead.

Harriet grimaced at her touch. "Leave me," she croaked, her voice muffled by a pillow.

Sarah desisted. It was vital that she not add to Harriet's agitation. "Harriet, darling," she crooned, "No one is going to force you to do anything against your will." The words left an unpleasant aftertaste in her mouth, for she had never intentionally lied to Harriet before.

In reply Harriet only closed her eyes and turned her face to the wall.

That night, Sarah, Stephen, and Wimbly dined off trays by the fireside. Somehow Mrs Parsons had managed a steak and kidney pie, which they washed down with the rich red wine they had found in Harriet's cellar. After dinner, Stephen sat reading a book by the hearth, uncomfortably perched on a folding camp chair. Sarah sat beside him, half sunk in the only cozy armchair in Harriet's house, a battered antique with worn leather upholstery, the armrests scratched by some cat or dog, and the horsehair stuffing pulled out underneath. She sat so still, a cool compress across her eyes and forehead, that Stephen could not tell whether she was awake or dozing.

The many sleepless nights at Harriet's bedside had exhausted his wife.

Wimbly stood by the fire in a bemused mood, swirling the wine in his glass. Mrs Parsons came in to clear away the dinner things and began piling the dirty plates and cutlery on one of the trays. Suddenly, she straightened up and put the tray back down. Bundling her stubby fingers into a knot, she prepared herself to make an announcement.

"There's something I wanted to tell you, sir," she said. Stephen looked up briefly as she went on, "Maybe I should have said something before, but I have been so busy with Miss Harriet and the house, there's never been a minute . . ."

He peered at her impatiently through his spectacles. "Well, what is it?"

For a moment the old woman seemed to lose courage, her shoulders hunched forward slightly, her whole body appeared to deflate. Then she drew in a sharp breath and blurted out, "I think Miss Harriet has been poisoning herself." She picked up the tray again, and held it close to her full bosom, as if to shield herself with the objects on it. "She has been poisoning herself on toadstools."

"Whatever are you going on about, Parsons?"

Mrs Parsons was obliged to repeat herself in an even louder voice, waking Sarah who suddenly stirred in the armchair.

"Did I hear someone mention toadstools?" she murmured removing the compress with long pale fingers, and staring blankly at the housekeeper, "Or was I dreaming? Was it you, Mrs Parsons?"

"In the kitchen Missis, I found rows and rows of pickled toadstools in jars. Who could eat such things? She did sir, I believe, she ate nothing but toadstools and bread. Some were orange and some were purple, they looked deadly poisonous to me and I threw most of them away, those jars. But she had a taste for even stranger things. A porcupine sir. One night, she asked me to stew her a porcupine."

Stephen's lip curled in disgust and irritation. "Thank you, Parsons, that's enough, you may go."

Sarah stared at their housekeeper, remembering the Count's gift to Harriet.

As Mrs Parsons turned and stepped towards the door, Stephen cleared his voice and said, "And another thing, Mrs Parsons, I should keep away from that wine in the kitchen. It seems to have had an adverse effect on you."

A rush of scarlet flooded the housekeeper's face. She looked as though she were about to drop the tray.

"No, wait," said Wimbly, feeling sorry for her and curious to know more. "Mrs Parsons, please tell me more about these toadstools." He turned to Stephen, "Every clue may be valid. Improper sealing methods can cause near fatal food poisoning, and hence liver inflammation."

Sarah glanced at her husband, and he looked away. She was glad Wimbly did not suspect the real cause of Harriet's illness.

"Did you throw them all away, those jars of toadstools?" asked Wimbly.

"All but one sir, which I kept as evidence. Shall I bring it here?"

"No, I'll come with you to the kitchen."

Wimbly followed to the dark kitchen where he opened the door of the woodstove, threw in a log then took a seat at the marble table as Mrs Parsons piled the dirty dishes in the stone sink.

"Sit down, Mrs Parsons. You can do the washing up later." Then he noticed the half-empty wine flask on the table, and a glass with the bottom stained red with the dregs.

135

"I know what you're thinking, sir," said Mrs Parsons, sitting down across from him. "But I only have a tiny drop at night after dinner. If you don't believe me about the porcupine, look there! That's what's left of him," and she pointed to a basket in a dark corner by the hearth. Peering closer, he saw a bundle of sharp brown and white quills, and his eyebrows shot up in surprise.

"Wasn't fibbing about that, now was I? Miss Harriet did tell me to stew it. A man brought it to the house the night before you all came, and made me understand it was for Miss Harriet. He sat in the kitchen doorway and plucked the quills out. I think he wanted to see Miss Harriet, but I shooed him away. When I told Miss Harriet someone had brought a porcupine, she told me to stew it with onions and herbs. Then she gave a queer laugh, and her mind began to wander. I threw the thing out and the dogs got after it. But there are the quills to prove it, whatever Mr Hampton thinks."

"You must forgive Mr Hampton. He is very worried about Miss Harriet."

"If it wasn't for Missis Sarah, I would never have lasted these long years. I love the Mistress and Miss Harriet as if they were mine own girls."

Tears welled up in the old woman's eyes and he patted her hand. "I'm sure you do," he said. "The Hamptons are very grateful for what you have done. You know that of course." He leaned back in his chair, waiting for her to compose herself.

"Only my duty, Mr Wimbly," she sniffed and drew herself up. "Anybody would have done the same."

"Care to tell me now, about those toadstools, or whatever else you think relevant?" he asked kindly.

She looked down at her wrinkled hands clasped in her lap and sighed. "I had such a bad feeling when that driver brought me to this house. I was sure it couldn't be the right place. And then when Miss Harriet came to the door, I took such a fright. She looked so ill. While I was waiting for the driver to come back with the doctor, I went through the house. There's no describing how dirty and untidy everything was, especially in the kitchen. While looking through the cupboard, I found the toadstools."

She stood up, went to a cupboard, took out a jar and handed it to Wimbly.

He turned it over, inspecting it in the lamplight: brownish chunks floated in an oily liquid dotted with bits of herbs and peppercorns. He unscrewed the lid; it clicked as the air rushed in; it seemed properly sealed. He lifted it to his nostrils and sniffed.

Through his years of training as a tea merchant, he had learned to distinguish even the slightest taint of fungus or mould. He inhaled the rich, earthy fragrance of the mushrooms, then poked a finger into the jar, and under the horrified gaze of Mrs Parsons popped a chunk into his mouth.

"Exquisite," he said, savoring it, "A *Boletus edulis*. In other words, a noble *porcino*." He smacked his lips and ate another morsel. "What a shame you threw the others away. Were they all like this?"

"Some were brown like this. Others were orange, and some were purple."

"I don't think this poisoned Harriet," he said, setting down the jar and patting her on the shoulder, "But thank you all the same for everything you have done."

Pausing in the kitchen doorway on his way out, he asked, "The man who brought the porcupine for Miss Harriet. Could you describe him?"

Mrs Parsons thought a moment and said, "Stout he was. With bushy grey hair. Perhaps about 55 years. Peculiar eyes, sir. Green they were. Like ice, but with bits of yellow."

"Nothing else?" he prodded, intrigued. It seemed to him she was about to say more, but the Hamptons' bell clanged in the sitting room down the hall.

"No sir," she clipped, and bustled out of the kitchen

After his little chat with Mrs Parsons, Wimbly took a candle and went off to bed. A cot had been set up for him in a narrow room across from Harriet's studio, which Harriet must have used as a storage space, as it was full of trunks and boxes. A packing case pushed next to the cot served as a bedside table where Wimbly set his candle. The only other furnishing was a washstand above which hung another of those ornate gilt mirrors, whose opulence contrasted with the monk-like setting. Modestly averting his eyes from his own reflection, Wimbly undressed, hung his clothes on a hook behind the door, dashed a bit of icy water on his face from the pitcher on the washstand, and crawled into bed. He lay staring up at a black spot on the wall above the window, wondering if it was a scorpion or only a black mark on the plaster, all the while musing over Mrs Parson's bizarre account of the porcupine. The idea of Harriet dining on porcupines was not all that preposterous. Wimbly had been obliged to eat even more alien foods on his business journeys to the East to please his native hosts: sheep eyes, filets of snake, and monkey brains, although he had baulked at the fried locusts once served him in Ceylon, which had turned out to be as tasty as toasted almonds.

The important thing was that a man had brought it to the house. Here was a clue, here was a connection between Harriet and the outside world, something which had maddeningly eluded them all till now. He had not yet read the diary – Sarah seemed to feel it was too private to share with him, but she had read him the Count's description. The man who had brought Harriet her unusual gastronomic treat very possibly might have been Federigo Del Re. Mrs Parson's description corresponded in several details – particularly the hair and eyes, thus it would seem to offer corroboration that a man answering to Harriet's physical description of the Count did exist. But how reliable was Mrs Parsons? Wimbly wondered if she knew more about Harriet's count than she cared to say. That indeed was the impression he had received at the end of their conversation. Or perhaps she had read Harriet's diary and been influenced by it, or Harriet herself might have revealed something to her. She may also have been tippling at the wine flasks in the kitchen, as Stephen believed, not a very advisable habit for a woman of her age. Yet generally she seemed to be sober enough, and in full possession of her faculties. Perhaps she did only have a drop or two for a nightcap. Certainly there was no reason for her to lie to him about the man's visit to the house. The porcupine quills were there in the kitchen, whatever that proved.

He rolled over with a sigh as he thought of Harriet lying half dead in the room down the hall. If Mrs Parsons had actually seen Federigo Del Re, if Harriet's caddish lover could be identified as a real individual in flesh and blood having access to Harriet's house, and, presumably, her bed, it would bring him an immense relief. Not because he doubted Harriet's mental stability but rather because Wimbly feared that if no evidence of any other man should surface, he might be forced to consider himself the cause of Harriet's current crisis. This horrible prospect – that he might have brought harm to her in any way had tormented him since his arrival in Italy.

Stephen had been frank with him about the causes of Harriet's illness, but had also begged him not to let Sarah suspect that he knew about Harriet's abortion. Of course, he had acted with a gentleman's discretion, although he was the one who had not been frank with them. Indeed he could not be, for he half suspected that *he* might be the father of Harriet's aborted child, for there in Fiesole four months ago, they had shared a moment of passion in Sir William's *limonaia* – an experience he now regarded as one of the most dreadful mistakes of his entire life. Yet if there were proof of Harriet's having been involved with a man in Italy, with her so-called Count, then he might well unburden himself of this enormous responsibility.

Such was the prayer that formed in his mind. He blew out the candle and soon fell asleep.

CHAPTER FIVE

Wimbly had gone to bed. Sarah was sitting out the early part of the night in Harriet's room, giving Mrs Parsons a rest. Stephen, not at all sleepy, decided to occupy himself with some small task and went into Harriet's studio with a lantern. He wanted to have a look through Harriet's negatives again, though he was not sure what it was he hoped to find. He pulled out a box and began rummaging through it. There were a few plates of tombs, several ones of a dog, and a few scenes of village architecture. No people. No count. No tower. Another three boxes all had similar content. No portraits to be found. A smaller box was pushed into a corner, with a few books and newspapers piled on top of it. He moved aside the books and papers and picked up the box. This one weighed so little he thought it was empty. Opening it, he found only one plate with a chipped corner and a handful of broken shards rattling in the bottom.

Lifting the plate to the lantern to illuminate it from behind, he thought at first that it was the photograph of a statue, but looking closer he saw that it was one of the portraits of his wife dressed up as a winter goddess which Harriet had taken in

December. He studied it now with a clinical eye. He disliked the way people looked in negatives, with that strange transposition of the skin, in which dark and light change places and eyes look like burnt-out embers. There was something vulgar and also, uncanny about it all. He sometimes wondered if that was how the dead would appear to us if only one could see them. Sarah looked alien in the negative, a figure plucked from another world, put down in the wrong place. The costume looked even shabbier and more ridiculous to him in the negative than it had in real life. What had she been thinking of?

Women had become so irrational lately. Of course, they had always been so. But now they were always talking about freedom and art. As if they could do anything useful with their freedom; as if they knew anything about art! Harriet was an excellent example of such ill-guided energies and aspirations, and his own father had encouraged them in her.

He was glad that they had found no prints of Sarah's photograph anywhere in Harriet's house. No one would ever need to see it. He would be spared that embarrassment. There was a tool box on Harriet's worktable. He opened it, dug through it, and pulled out a small hammer. He lay the plate on a piece of paper, and without a moment's hesitation, tapped it twice with the hammer. The plate cracked into three large pieces. He brought the hammer down again and smashed it to bits.

Next he shook the fragments he had found in the bottom of the box out into a heap on the worktable. One by one, he held the larger pieces up to the lantern, and tried to construe them into a pattern. A hand. A sleeve. A frizz of hair. A man's chest in a tight-fitting suit. A fragment of a boar's head trophy, several pistols and a sword. The boar's glass eyes had caught the light with an eerie flash. Stephen remembered the Prefect telling him that the tower had been rented as a hunting lodge. Could this have been taken in the tower? It was impossible to reconstruct the man's face, for the other shards were too damaged to make anything out of. He doubted that this squat figure could be

Harriet's count. It might be anyone at all, one of the local peasants or even a tavern keeper whose face had caught Harriet's fancy. She enjoyed taking photographs of the lower classes, of laborers and such like, claiming that they had interesting faces, ennobled by manual labor or exposure to the sun. This plate merely proved that she had taken a picture of a man, whose face, however, remained unrecognizable. That meant nothing, nothing at all.

There was a dustpan in a corner. He picked it up and with his hand swept all the shards into it, including the ones of Sarah's photograph, then carried them out of the studio and over to the dying fire in the sitting room. He poked the coals, blew them into a flame, and emptied the contents of the dustpan into the fire, watching with satisfaction as the fragments began to blacken. They mustn't waste any more time here in Italy. He had to get Harriet back to London as soon as possible. Feeling a strong sense of purpose and relief, he went off to bed.

Two hours later, he lay sleepless in the old iron bed. The rough hemp mattress ticking prickled through the clammy bedclothes. He was propped up on a pile of dampish pillows, staring at the gleam of a candle reflected in the mirror. The mirror was slightly warped, and gave him the odd impression of peering at a younger, gaunter version of himself. Part of the mirror was covered by a maroon velvet shawl Sarah had draped across it. The dark velvet, the glossy black wood of the clothespress, the dim candles, all lent a lugubrious atmosphere to the room. It was by no means a healthy environment for Sarah, he thought, for her nerves were already strained.

The candle sputtered out and he was left in darkness. A faint glimmer of moonlight shone in through the slats of the shutters. He knew it would still be an hour or two before Sarah tiptoed out of Harriet's room and into his arms. His wife spent the early part of every night curled up on a small sofa placed beside Harriet's bed, until Parsons relieved her of her nightly vigil and took her place on the sofa. Night after night Parsons sat there till dawn, wrapped in her shabby plaid dressing gown, nodding off to sleep, one eye open, trained on Harriet.

Stephen sighed. He knew he would never be rid of Mrs Parsons until she died, and she would no doubt live to be a hundred at least, outlasting them all. He had often desired to send her away, but knew he would never dare do so. She was like a family curse one must learn to live with, and if he dismissed her now to lonely old age and isolation, she would surely retaliate in a most grievous manner.

Perhaps he had been unduly cruel this evening when he had laughed at her idea that Harriet had been poisoned by mushrooms, and had insinuated that she had been drinking.

He supposed he ought to make greater effort to be more patient with her. Still, whenever Parsons addressed him directly like that, he bristled as if under attack. She had always had an unnerving effect on him, even as a child, when she had first entered his family's service as a young Irish widow. Plain and pasty-faced, already dour at that early age in her black and white pin-striped dress; her dull reddish hair gathered beneath a shapeless, starched cap, she had seemed ageless to him even then. Her eyes, grey, downcast, and seemingly vacuous had followed him everywhere with disapproval. Although now half-blurred from nearsightedness, those eyes still never missed a thing; though half deaf, she always overheard every word muttered softly behind closed doors. Not that she had ever pried or peered in through keyholes, or rummaged in locked drawers like other servants. There was no need for her to do so. She knew because others came to her to unburden themselves. She was the keeper of his family's ugliest secrets, the soother of its most painful wounds: his mother's illness, his father's infidelity, the illegitimate half brother whisked away years ago lord knows where, and when his father was dying and no one could stand the odor of his disease, it was Parsons who sat there by the bed, held his hand, inserted the catheter, sponged him off, scraped his tongue with a spatula. It was she who had done everything in her power so that others would be spared as much pain and unpleasantness as possible.

He knew he should be grateful, and yet could not be. Now with her here with them in Harriet's house and with Harriet's being so ill and possibly dying, he could barely tolerate the sight of the old woman shuffling about the kitchen. In London Parsons was so much of a household fixture, he hardly noticed her, but here against the background of Harriet's dilapidated farmhouse, she appeared in sharper relief, slipping like a shadow through the corridors at all hours. In these strained circumstances, Parsons brought to mind something long buried, the one thing in his life he was ashamed of, the one thing he would never tell Sarah.

Yet if hadn't been for Sarah that whole business with Harriet would have been forgotten. Harriet would have remained in America where she belonged, without them having to have any further contact. There was, after all, an ocean between him and his cousin, not only materially speaking, but in a thousand other ways as well: their values, beliefs, their background, even though she was the daughter of his father's wayward sister who had run off with an American. But life has a curious way of making one confront one's weaknesses and mistakes, if not face up to them exactly, at least shed upon them some gleam of dignity, which could only be mustered through strictest self-control. That was necessary, he supposed, for the progress of mankind.

Harriet, he believed, had forgiven him, and had probably quite blotted from her mind that unfortunate incident and the period that had followed it. But Parsons, he knew, never forgot a thing. Even now when he felt her dreamy eyes settle upon him while she stood patient and grave in the doorway, waiting to receive his orders, her head bent slightly at an angle, feigning submission, he wondered if she still remembered that afternoon at the lake, nearly 30 years ago, and still judged him for it. That day Parsons had discovered the two of them – Harriet and himself – lying in the hedge. Stephen lay sprawled on top of his cousin while she sobbed unconsolingly, her eyes squeezed tightly shut, one hand clutching a boxwood branch. Desperately he tried to make her quiet, covering her mouth with his and pinning down her arms as he thrust himself into her narrow channel. She had done nothing to push him away.

Intercourse between first cousins is nothing scandalous, and until that summer Harriet had been a distant stranger across the ocean. In any case, he was not completely at fault. Harriet had encouraged him with her unchaste behavior.

She had come to spend the summer with her aunt and uncle in the country, near Bath, while her mother was in London seeing a famous Swiss doctor about her various complaints. No one realized then how ill Harriet's mother was, an illness of the mind, and no doubt Harriet had inherited her own predisposition towards mental instability from her mother. At the time of her visit, Stephen was eighteen, Harriet fourteen, but looked much older, and was, practically speaking, a woman. Stephen had been dazzled by his tall blonde cousin, well-formed and athletic, with her breasts already developed. She was so exuberant and daring compared to the English girls he knew, challenging him to tree-climbing competitions and extenuating hikes. Odd how now it was this very exuberance in her that he detested as an adult, while prizing his wife's docility above all her other feminine charms. But then he was very taken by Harriet, and his school friend Cyril, who had come to spend a few days with them, was also impressed with her, especially when they all went swimming at a secluded beach along the lake, and Harriet dared the two boys to take off their clothes and swim naked. On that occasion, Harriet had behaved like a perfect little savage, but her lithe, white body darting and shining in the water had thrilled him.

Afterwards, as they lay panting and happy on the pebbly shore, their wet skin tingling with delicious cold, Cyril began to show unmistakable intentions in Harriet's regard, and she eagerly welcomed them in return. Stephen had pulled on his clothes and slunk off, jealous, after all, she was *his* cousin. Cyril was a very good-looking, strapping young man, and had no difficulty in keeping up with Harriet's galloping about, unlike himself. Stephen knew, or thought he knew, what Cyril and Harriet had been doing there, entwined on the beach, although he had not stayed to watch.

The next day he caught them kissing in the garden behind a linden tree. Harriet had her blouse open, her camisole was pushed up over one breast. The surprising sight of her dark, stiff nipple protruding from the folds of bunched up white muslin, excited and infuriated him and in a moment he had thrown himself on Cyril and punched him in the face. Cyril had stormed off to the train, without bothering to collect his things, while Harriet ran to her room to weep over his departure, pretending to be ill.

That night Stephen made a proposition to Harriet: either she agree to do with him what she had been doing with Cyril, or he'd tell his father all, and Harriet would doubtless receive suitable punishment. Stoically, Harriet had submitted. He discovered then that Cyril hadn't really gotten very far with her, as she was still a virgin when Stephen deflowered her beneath the boxwood hedge.

His fleeting ecstasy was shattered by the jolt of seeing Mrs Parson's moonish face peering down at him through the branches as she shouted with enraged disgust. With great effort he resisted the arms pulling him away from Harriet's warm, throbbing body as his own body plunged out of control, down into an abyss of urgent sensation. Mrs Parsons managed to wrest them apart just as he was about to collapse in a spasm of relief. That had been his first sexual intercourse with a female and he had played it over a thousand times in his mind since then. Even remembering it now excited rather than shamed him, after all these years.

Confused, he had tried to cover himself, while Harriet got up and ran off, without even rearranging her clothes. There was a blot of blood on the back of her torn white skirt. As he looked up into Mrs Parson's face more grieved than angry, he had a revelation that was to shape his future attitude toward people of her class and of her sex. She was afraid of him, *tout court*. He had never quite understood this before and it opened a whole new realm of possibilities. His confusion hardened to defiance as his eyes blazed into hers. He possessed a new power over her, the power that men of his class may exercise over women, all women, if only they choose to wield it. How easy it had been to say, "I advise you, Parsons, not to say a word . . . if you wish to remain employed." They had maintained that pact, it seemed, for nearly 30 years.

Stephen never learned what repercussions this incident had had on Harriet, for her visit was cut short, owing to other, more serious circumstances. Her mother's condition worsened and Harriet and her mother returned to Chicago before the summer's end. In the hasty preparations for departure, nothing amiss was noted in Harriet's moody behavior. Later that autumn, Harriet's mother committed suicide, and several years passed before Harriet and Stephen were to meet again. That was when Harriet came to London in the company of her schoolfriend, Sarah, invited by his father, who had been Harriet's benefactor since her mother's death. Dark, sweet, wholly innocent yet aglow with a sensual flush at the age of seventeen, Sarah had enchanted him, then a young man of 26. He had escorted his cousin and her friend on all their sightseeing and shopping trips in London, and on their Sunday excursions to the country. Throughout that visit, he had kept a cool but cordial distance from Harriet. Never once were they alone for longer than five minutes, not a word was said, or a glance exchanged that might have recalled their past connection. Harriet had her hands full in any case, with George Wimbly, called on as a fourth for bridge and tennis, who had then pursued her relentlessly across London.

Over the following three years, Stephen's admiration for Sarah had matured to love, even though he had always told himself he did not like American women. Not that he had loved Sarah passionately at first, she had been slow to passion, but he had seen in Sarah the makings of a sweet companion, ready to smooth his rough places, to quell his impatience, to quench his irascibility. For all this he was grateful in ways he could never reveal to her.

He never wanted her to know about that business with

Harriet. Americans were so naive and prudish about certain things. To Sarah's mind this youthful misadventure might appear an incestuous act of violation. Beneath it all, he was convinced, Harriet had been more than willing. He was also convinced she had forgotten all that, after so many years, and he knew that Sarah, sensitive as she was, would be shocked – if she should ever discover this secret he and Harriet shared.

He threw off the covers impatiently and fumbled on the bedside table for his watch, but the moonlight was too faint to illumine the dial. Damn it, where was Sarah? These reminiscences had made him excited. When was she going to come to bed?

Sarah tiptoed into the bedroom with a candle. The light fell on her husband's face and she saw that he was still awake. His eyes glinted in the candlelight.

"Has she finally fallen asleep?" he asked.

"She wakes intermittently, still delirious, calling out in Italian. I'm afraid I gave her a shock this afternoon when I told her we wanted to take her back to England."

Stephen groaned. He prayed that Harriet would be well enough to travel soon.

Sarah blew out the candle, slipped in between the dank sheets and sought the warmth of Stephen's body. As the cold sole of her foot touched his, his leg jerked under the covers. He gathered her to him and kissed her hair.

"Do you think there could be anything in what Mrs Parsons says? About the mushrooms I mean," she asked, nestling in his arms.

"Oh the toadstools!" He laughed. "Parsons probably found a few jars of wild mushrooms in the kitchen. Apparently a common item in the local diet here in the country. She must be thinking of deadly Irish fairy-rings where the men in green cavort. Quite a different matter."

Sarah frowned. "Must you joke about this? Harriet mentions eating wild mushrooms in her diary. And that doctor did say she might have been poisoned by something."

"Harriet was not poisoned by mushrooms. Or if she was, that

is inconsequential. The specialist from Rome was quite clear about what the origins of her illness were. As for that horse doctor Mrs Parsons called in! Hasn't it occurred to you that he is probably to blame for Harriet's state? Of course I cannot prove that, or accuse the man."

Sarah was shocked by this thought, and pondered a moment. It was quite possible the doctor had lied about Harriet's condition to cover his own ineptness. Still, something nagged at her mind. "You are right, but suppose . . . she *had* eaten some toxic mushroom by mistake. Can't some poisonous mushrooms give you . . . strange visions? Put you in a sort of drugged state? And could that explain why –"

"Certainly you don't mean like Alice in the Looking Glass?" he cut her off.

"I am being serious Stephen. Can't some forms of poison affect the mind?"

Stephen pursed his lips, seemed to reflect and then said decidedly, "No, my dear. I'm afraid we must face facts. Despite her outward display of boldness and independence, Harriet, ever since her childhood, and believe me, I know, has always been mentally unstable. Her mother was also unstable. No doubt something has happened to her here in Italy which has caused this process to accelerate, but I don't think it has to do with mushrooms. She has become unhinged, and we must find a way to help her regain her sanity."

Sarah bent her head in resignation.

Stephen sighed, rubbed Sarah's shoulder apologetically and said, "It's my fault, you know. If I had let her have her way with Peter Cranshaw, this might never have happened."

She paused a moment before replying, "Perhaps now you see why it is unwise to meddle at times in other peoples' sentimental affairs."

"So you *do* think I am to blame?" he prickled.

"You mustn't blame yourself. You believed you were acting in her best interests. Peter would have left her anyway, eventually," she recited these words numbly, trying to sound as though she believed them. Putting her hand on his chest to soothe but distance him, she said, "I must get some sleep now, darling."

"Yes, it's beastly of me to try to keep you awake." He folded his hand over hers and squeezed her fingers.

Still clasping her hand, he stared up at the ceiling and said impulsively, "Did Harriet ever mention anything about me to you, I mean, about our childhood?"

"Oh, some things. Why do you ask?"

"I was just wondering. Seeing her like that, these days, so helpless, I suddenly remembered what she looked like as a young girl. Funny how memories pop up from time to time."

"Was there something particular you thought she might have told me?" Sarah pulled back from him. Her eyes searched his face in the moonlight.

"Did she ever mention an old school friend of mine named Cyril?"

"Never. Who was this Cyril?"

"Oh, just a boy she liked when she was fourteen."

"No," said Sarah, surprised, "She never mentioned any boys to me, ever."

"I was jealous, you see," he said, counterfeiting a laugh, "and gave Cyril a black eye."

"You didn't!"

"I did, and it was the first and last time I ever struck anyone."

Sarah wriggled her hand free, sat up abruptly and reached over to the bedside table for her hairbrush. She began to brush her hair with quick, fierce strokes. Sparks crackled in the dark.

"So you had a crush on Harriet! I never would have thought! But she preferred Cyril."

"Precisely. But it's of no consequence now, is it, darling?"

"Consequence?" She put down the brush and stared at him, perplexed.

He threw off the covers and turned to her. Seizing her in his arms, he rolled himself over on top of her and pressed hard against her.

"This ghastly thing you're wearing might suit a wrinkled old grandmother with pendulous breasts."

"It's the only nightdress I have that's warm enough. I found it in Harriet's dresser."

"Take it off." He pressed his lips to her neck.

"Oh, Stephen, please, it's late," she began, but his lips smothered her words.

With a sudden poke, she pushed him away. "Not now I said," she snapped.

Offended, he rolled away from her towards the mirror, and crushed a pillow in his arms. Then he said, "I've been trying to decide about what to do with Harriet."

"It will be quite a task to take her away from here."

"You'll just have to help me see that she obeys."

"Obeys!"

"I'm going to see to it that she will do no further harm."

"And who has she harmed, pray tell?"

"At the moment she seems to have done a great deal of harm to herself."

"Harriet can come and live with us if you think she needs to be looked after for awhile."

"My cousin needs a place where she will receive proper treatment."

"What sort of place?"

"A special . . . sanatorium, of sorts."

"Stephen, you aren't really serious?"

"Harriet is suffering from what are clinically called delusions. I have only read a few pages of that diary of hers, and from what I have seen, it is a classic account of hallucination and derangement which can only have been written by a raving lunatic."

"Nonsense! I think it must be a novel. A gothic novel based on something she has personally experienced."

"A gothic novel! My dear girl!"

Sarah thrust her legs out of the bed, groping for her slippers.

Then she jumped up, reached for her dressing gown and pulled it on, knotting the sash around her waist with defiance.

"What's the matter now?"

"There's something I have to see to."

"Come back to bed."

"I want to be alone for a while."

She lit the candle, picked it up, and opened the door. There at the end of the corridor stood Mrs Parsons. Her moon-like face turned to their room.

"Is everything all right Mrs Parsons?" Sarah said.

"It's Miss Harriet, she woke and asked for something hot. She swallowed three mouthfuls of broth, and I was just on my way back to the kitchen to fetch some fresh water. Do you need anything, Missis Sarah?"

"You can go back to bed now Mrs Parsons, I'll sit with Harriet for another hour or so."

"You need your rest, Missis Sarah."

"I'm not at all sleepy. I think I'll read for awhile."

"I'll fetch you some warm coals in a brazier. It's cold in that room"

Once again, Sarah settled down on the musty green sofa in Harriet's room, a tarnished brazier of coals at her feet, a small lamp lit on an end table beside her. Harriet lay deep asleep, for once in an untroubled dream, a faint smile on her whitish lips. Sarah contemplated the objects on the bedside table: a carafe of water and a glass, phials of pills and dark blue bottles of medicinal drops, the bronze Buddha that Sarah had put there herself earlier that evening, thinking that the sight of some familiar object from her childhood might comfort her friend.

Although Harriet's fever had not returned, and her taking food was a sign of recovery, Sarah was even more anxious for her after Stephen's revelation. She fervently hoped that Harriet would wake up from this nightmare and provide a rational explanation for her illness, for the Count, for this whole bizarre story. She knew too that she would be powerless to oppose her husband's plans concerning Harriet if his mind were really set on sending her to some special *sanatorium*. The very word made her cringe.

Harriet gave a little gasp in her sleep. Her smile faded and suddenly her eyes blinked wide open. She propped herself up and stared at Sarah, then said distinctly, "*Il cinghiale.*"

Sarah wondered if she had understood correctly. She knew that word in Italian, it meant 'boar'. But she had no idea what Harriet wanted to say.

When once again Harriet repeated the word, Sarah realized that Harriet was not really looking at her but was gazing into the mirror hanging above the sofa where she sat. She got up and went to the bedside. Harriet did not move as she approached; her eyes remained fixed on the mirror. Sarah touched Harriet's brow and was relieved to find it still cool. Taking Harriet's head in her arms, she pressed it against her body and stroked her matted hair but Harriet gave no reaction. Although Harriet's eyes were open, Sarah could see that she was deep asleep. Then Harriet coughed, a dry, grating cough. "Try to drink some water, Harriet," Sarah said, releasing Harriet's head, and turning to pour a glass of water from the carafe. She tilted the glass to Harriet's parched lips. Harriet sipped and swallowed. When Sarah tried to ease her back down onto the pillows, she resisted, arching her shoulders against the headboard. "*Il cinghiale,*" she murmured again, still staring at the mirror.

On impulse Sarah decided to cover the mirror. She went over to the dresser, opened the top drawer and rummaged through Harriet's things until she found a black silk shawl she had come across while inspecting Harriet's belongings. She pulled it out and unfurled it with a shake. The delicate chiffon was torn in the middle, and in spots the fabric was smudged with bits of gold paint. Still, it would serve her purpose very well. She folded it in half and draped it over the mirror above the sofa, obscuring Harriet's reflection.

"Is that better Harriet?" she asked. Harriet stared at the swathed mirror for a moment, then allowed herself to be lowered gently to the pillows. Sarah tucked the covers around her. Soon enough Harriet was asleep again, her mouth open, snuffling into the pillow. Sarah observed her, then went back to the sofa and wrapped a blanket around her legs. From the pocket of her dressing gown she took out the green notebook and was soon absorbed in Harriet's strange tale:

The Notebook of Harriet Sackett
Winter 1922

1

Nocciola disappeared the evening of the day we saw Federigo bathing in the sulphur pool. That afternoon I felt very restless, and later, around 4.00, I took the dog out for a walk right before tea time. Maria frowned as I pulled on my rubber boots and donned my woollen rain cape, as if she guessed I intended to wander farther than just the yard around our house. I should have heeded her advice not to go walking in the woods just before nightfall – the local peasants never do. Not from fear of encountering ill-intentioned human beings, or even dangerous animals – some ancestral instinct warns them to avoid that moment of transition, when the trees are alone with themselves.

I suppose I had been waiting all day for a message from Federigo, which had not arrived, and our steps led us, naturally enough, to the tower. I wanted to see if he had come back alone, or with his family. I surmised that upon returning he had found many things requiring his immediate attention and that was why he had not yet sent word to me. Perhaps his son was still ill, or some other problem had prevented him from contacting me.

Recent storms had denuded the surrounding trees of most of their leaves, so as I stood on the ridge, I had a good view of both the tower and the garden. To my surprise, the whole place appeared even more deserted than usual. No smoke curled out of the chimneys, no lights gleamed in the windows. I decided to get a closer look, and Nocciola and I scrambled down the ridge to the garden and peered in through the hedge. The garden was in a state of neglect. The chickens and peacocks were gone and the roses, frost-browned and withered, drooped on the arbor. A pile of half-burnt refuse and dead leaves had been raked into a corner and left there to rot. Propped up against one of the persimmon trees stood a ladder. It looked as though one of the farmhands had been picking the Count's persimmons, but had left the job undone. The branches were still heavily laden with large orange globes. Many had fallen to the ground, splitting open and smearing their bright pulp along the gravel paths. It was a pity to see so much wasted fruit.

We followed the hedge to the front entrance, where the gate was not locked, only half closed, evidence that someone had been at the tower – how long ago it was impossible to say. There might still be someone there. I hesitated, then summoning my courage, decided to go up to knock on the door. At best I would find Federigo, or someone who could tell me where he was. At worst he might be too busy to receive me and send me away. Or there might be no one there at all. Noticing a letterbox nailed to the gatepost, I peeked in and saw a few letters inside — that was certainly a sign that no one was at home. The rusty hinges groaned as I pushed the gate open. As we walked toward the tower, Nocciola whimpered, excited by the familiar smells of the place that had once been his home.

After the late autumn rains, the path had become a bed of mud strewn with spattered leaves and rotten acorns. Two deep ruts running straight down the path indicated that a carriage or cart had recently rolled through the gates, but I did not see Federigo's carriage in the yard.

Here and there along the trail were very fresh boar tracks. It was unlikely that these shy animals would have approached the tower while anyone was staying there as the slightest noise frightens them. This was a further indication that I might find no one at home.

Resolutely I strode up to the door and keeping a firm grip on the dog's collar, knocked once, then twice more boldly. When no reply came, I lay my ear to the peeling wooden door and heard a sound inside. A chair scraping on the floor. Footsteps. A door closing. A cough perhaps. Then I caught a whiff of tobacco. Federigo's tobacco. Whether from inside or somewhere outside I could not tell. I knocked insistently and rang the bell hanging by the door. "Signor Conte," I cried. "Federigo, are you there? Is there anyone home?"

I waited for several minutes, then receiving no answer, entered the garden and sat on a low stone wall, while the dog sniffed about the boxwood bushes. Had I really smelled tobacco, or only a wisp of smoke on the wind? I reflected that the noises I had heard might have been the stirring of a rat or a weasel that had somehow slipped in from the cellar. And yet I was sure that there was someone inside, peering down at me at that very minute from one of the dark windows, for I had seen a shadow move away from the window when I looked up at the top window in the tower. It might have been Federigo's son, or his sister, that grim maid, or even Federigo himself. But why would they refuse to open the door to me? Nocciola came and sat beside me, alert to every odor and creaking twig as I stroked his ears and picked a few burrs out of his soft fur. At that late hour, the western sky was curdled with pink. Twilight gleamed in the puddles along the garden pathways. It would soon be too dark to see. We ought to head for home. I felt saddened at not finding Federigo. Surely he would send word to me soon?

I was jolted from my thoughts when the dog, with no warning, jerked free and bounded away, dashing through an opening in the hedge, and up towards the ridge. I ran after him, thinking that he had probably caught the scent of a rabbit. I had to catch him before he strayed too far, otherwise his chase might last for hours. As I puffed up the ridge, calling his name, I noticed more tracks in the mud: the prints of a man's heavy shoes led out of the Count's garden and up the embankment towards the woods. Crouching down, I touched the mud. The tracks were quite fresh, probably from that very day. Judging by their size, they might have been Federigo's, but then again they might well have been left by a hunter trespassing across the Count's land. There was no time to investigate them, however, I had to find the dog. I straightened up and called his name again. He barked twice from beyond a hazelnut thicket and I ran in that direction. After ten anxious minutes, I heard him bark once more, further away, near where I had seen Federigo disappear into the woods that morning. From in between the trees nearby came the strangled cry of a deer. Nocciola barked a third time, closer now. Then a shot rang out and all was quiet.

I listened, straining to hear a sound in the silence, but the roaring in my ears covered every external noise. I called out again this time to the hunter who had fired the gun.

"Where are you? Please answer!"

The echo of my voice died away as I waited for a reply. A crow squawked and flapped out of the bare branches overhead. A leaf dropped to the forest floor.

"Whoever you are, be careful. My dog is lost!" I shouted.

Then I began to run in the direction of the shot, but by now night was falling. Soon the trails petered out and the woods grew thicker. There were no lights visible beyond the trees by which I could orient myself. Around me I could hear the nocturnal stirrings of the forest: the owls and bats; the squirrels and foxes. Fearing I might lose my way and have to spend the night there in the woods, I tried to retrace my steps, but all I had to guide me was the stink of sulphur coming in gusts on the wind. Stumbling on through the trees, pushing branches and brambles out of my face, I found my way to the sulphur spring and sat down on the edge of the pool. Deep boar tracks riddled the yellow sand round the edge of the pool where Federigo had stood that morning, performing his strange gymnastics.

I had the dreadful feeling that the dog's disappearance was somehow connected to the shot I had heard and to the hunter who had refused to answer my call or identify himself. I felt sick at the idea that Nocciola might have been shot by mistake, and that the hunter had lacked the courage to confess his error. Yet then again, it was hard to judge from how far away the shot had come. Quite possibly it was much further away than I had imagined, and Nocciola was still roaming about the forest, unharmed. In that case, there would be no reason to worry. He was very familiar with all the trails through the woods, and would have no difficulty finding his way back. Still I did not want to go home without him.

As I sat staring into the milky water, I heard a low drumming from the bushes behind me. The ground began to tremble slightly and then to shake. There came a loud rustling of leaves and crackling of branches as a huge boar with white tusks streaked out of the underbrush and galloped through the clearing. Its bristly hulk almost caught me as it sped by and I was so startled I nearly fell backwards into the pool. I watched it disappear in among the trees. My heart was pounding, though more from excitement than from fear as I had never seen a wild boar so close before.

Males, I knew, wandered alone through the forest, but females traveled in small packs with their offspring. No doubt they too came here to the pool at night to enjoy a mud bath, and it would be quite dangerous to meet a mature female with her young. I got up now, called the dog's name one last time, and then set out reluctantly for home. I easily made my way back to the tower. Deeply distraught over Nocciola's disappearance, I resolved to spend the next day searching the woods for the dog if he had not come back by morning.

Glancing at the tower as I hurried along the ridge, I thought I glimpsed a faint light, a candle perhaps, in the top window, in Federigo's study. But it was only a brief impression, and might have merely been the reflection of a star. It was cold that night and the keen air presaged frost. A thick froth of stars swirled above the tower, which looked as though it had been abandoned for 100 years or more.

For three days I combed those woods looking for the dog, all to no avail. At sunset on the third day, brooding that Nocciola was either dead or lost, I gave up my fruitless search. Climbing back up the ridge, I saw smoke coming out of the chimney of the tower. Then gazing down into the garden I saw that the rest of the persimmons had all been picked and the ladder moved away from the tree and propped against a wall. Scrambling down the embankment, I ran up to the door and knocked, but there was no reply. I noted, however, that several bundles of kindling had been carried from a neat stack in the yard, and placed in a more convenient spot near the door. Someone had been there all right, there was no doubt of that.

Early the next morning, after bringing me my breakfast, Maria went out to hang some laundry on a clothesline strung up in the yard near the rabbit hutches. I heard her call out as I was in the kitchen, pouring myself another cup of coffee. "Signora! The dog!" she shouted and I dashed down the stairs. I expected to find Nocciola prancing about and waving his tail, but when I saw the shrunken black form lying near the hutches, I broke out in sobs. Even from that distance I could tell that the poor animal had died in agony.

I ran over and sank to my knees beside him. His fur was all ragged and full of burrs, his bright eyes whitish and vitreous. His tongue protruded from his mouth. The sweet pink tip had turned bluish black. Maria surmised he had been poisoned, a fate not uncommon to dogs in the country here, for the woods are full of poisoned bait left by the peasants to kill off foxes. Or perhaps he had come across some rat poison in a barn. As I stroked the matted ruff around his neck, I saw that his collar was missing. I asked Maria if she had removed it. No she said, surprised, she had not even touched the dog. That I could well imagine, she hardly ever touched him when he was alive. I wouldn't think she would have touched him now that he was dead.

Of course Federigo had to be informed, so I scribbled a message and gave it to my assistant, Andrea, to deliver to the tower. I wondered if whoever was there at the tower would open the door to him, if not to me. Andrea returned an hour later, claiming that there was no one home, but that he had met a peasant on the road back, carrying a load of persimmons to market. The peasant had informed the boy that Federigo Del Re had been away for several weeks and was not expected back until the end of February. That made no sense – for I had seen him only three days before at the sulphur spring. Then I thought perhaps Federigo owned other properties, and might be staying in town, or even, with his mistress, Elisabetta Colonna whom I had so conveniently forgotten. As for the smoke I had seen and the noises I had heard in the tower, the peasant himself could be the explanation for all that. He might very well be the caretaker, in possession of the keys. He might have been instructed not to answer the door, or perhaps he didn't want anyone to know that he had been inside the tower itself.

Nonetheless, the poor dog had to be buried quickly, so we laid him beneath the old apple tree in the garden. Even Maria, not very tender-hearted when it came to dogs, shed a tear as we covered the grave with shovelfuls of black earth.

With Nocciola's death, winter set in. The next morning, looking from my window I saw the yard below bristling under a coat of frost. Snow dusted the hump-backed hills. The shriveled apples on the tree and the cabbages in the garden were all glazed in white. Even with fires blazing in every room, the house never seemed warm enough. I tried to immerse myself in my work, without much success. I missed poor Nocciola dreadfully. Luckily the evenings came quickly and I retired to bed early. At night Orion hung low in the bedroom window, bonfires glowed on the hills. Eagerly I welcomed sleep for I often dreamt of Federigo who sometimes appeared to me as in a negative, his skin gleaming with a metallic patina that emitted an eerie glow, like a fire from within. In one recurring dream Nocciola and I followed him as far as a fork in the path where I paused unsure which way I should go. Then before I could go any further, something always woke me and for the rest of the day I felt oppressed by a heavy anxiety.

One cold December morning my assistant and I visited the

tombs in Barbarano, which were the most accessible of all I had seen, and took a few photographs. In the bright winter glare the tombs had lost their mysterious appeal. They were mere holes carved in a cliff, the walls inside streaked with mould and slime. Old broken bottles, bits of rusted iron, canvas scraps and other refuse lay in heaps in many of them, and we had to carry all that trash out just to take a few decent pictures. As I also wanted to photograph the thermal bath where I had spent that autumn afternoon with Federigo, we left the tombs and pushed on down the hill, carting my equipment.

The oak trees had shed their leaves at last and stood naked in the biting wind. Huge crows perched in the upper branches, cawing at us as we made our way toward the stream. Along the path, I looked for the cyclamens and mushrooms Federigo had shown me, but now with the sharp frosts at night, there were none to be found. Instead there was a thick growth of butcher's broom, with waxy green leaves and bright red berries, reminding me that the holiday season would soon be upon us. Weeks had passed since my walk with Federigo here in these woods, and I had heard not a word from him. What was the reason for his silence? I could not understand it.

At last we reached the stream, but the water level had risen considerably from when I had last been there. The stepping stones were sunk deep in the water and ice had formed along the banks. With my rubber boots, I was equipped to break the ice and go splashing across, but not my assistant, whose worn shoes, several sizes too big, barely offered protection from the rain. He could easily slip while crossing and drop my valuable equipment, and I didn't want to risk such an accident. So we gave up the idea and headed home.

Quite by surprise, for we had taken a different route, I found myself once again passing by the olive grove where I had witnessed that slowing down of the sun, that moment out of time at Federigo's side. I stopped to contemplate the shrunken sun. The grass beneath the trees had been scythed, the olives harvested, and the trees pruned, piles of clipped branches lay near the road, ready for burning. There was no magic to it any longer, it was just a quiet and charming country spot. I felt nothing at all as I observed it. I wondered then if I had really visited that place before with Federigo or if it had all been a dream.

Returning home, I spent the afternoon in my darkroom. I never tire of the development process, and have always been fascinated by the reversal of light and dark in the negative, by the slow emergence in acid of a moment stolen from time. I have learned that in every photograph there is something unexpected, something that escapes your attention the moment the shutter blinked. I was anxious to see what I would find in these photographs, what secrets they would reveal. But this time I was disappointed. The tombs looked flat and uninteresting. They would never do for the purpose I had envisioned. I began to wonder if I was losing the knack.

One afternoon Andrea helped me label and catalogue the plates of my negatives according to site and subject, and pack them away into boxes. In one of those boxes I stored the negatives of more personal photographs I wanted to keep as mementos: a few portraits of Nocciola, of Sarah, and my portrait of Federigo Del Re. I had given Federigo a print of his portrait, and I intended to print one for myself, along with these others, but I had not yet had the time.

Then Andrea, while moving some things in the studio, dropped that very box to the floor, irreparably damaging most of the contents. I was furious. Only one negative of Sarah remained intact, although chipped in one corner. The negative of Federigo's portrait and several ones of Nocciola were smashed into pieces. The boy tried to make up for the damage by quickly sweeping things up with a sheepish smile, but this only made me angrier, and I carefully salvaged the larger fragments, mostly of Federigo's portrait, and placed them back in the box. It was then I decided to send Andrea away. Too clumsy and distracted to ever become a reliable assistant, he was proving to be more trouble than he was worth. I knew his family would be crestfallen. The pittance I paid him was a boon to them. Nevertheless, I could still keep him on to do odd jobs around the house, and help carry my equipment when needed. For the rest, I would have to take care of things by myself.

The days were bright, the ground was frozen hard, yet, as January passed, signs of an early spring abounded. In my little garden, the pink petals of the Japonica bushes burst out of their black stems. From my bedroom window I could see the mimosa trees with their tiny yellow blooms aflame on the hillside. On my walks alone through the countryside, now towards the village, never towards the tower, I broke off branches by the armful and took them home to fill the house. After a few hours the gauzy yellow blossoms shriveled, the leaves curled and drooped despite the water in the vase. But the very moment they began to wither, the perfume grew most intense, pervading the air with the fresh scent of spring and renewal, sweetening the stench of smoke and ash lingering in the house from the winter fires.

In February another invitation arrived in the mail from Elisabetta Colonna, this time to a Carnival ball in fancy dress. It was a shock to read her name in fine, spidery calligraphy engraved on the card delivered that morning, for I had pushed her out of my mind. Now forced to remember Federigo Del Re's mistress, to remember his real life in which I had no part, I found myself wildly jealous.

As I expected, a note from Pilli followed shortly afterwards. I had not heard from her since Christmas, when we had exchanged notes of greeting and baskets of sweets and dried fruit. She had spent most of the winter in Florence. Pilli explained that it would be a grand gala in costume at the villa. I guessed Federigo would be there. The thought of seeing him again filled me with nervous excitement, or was it perhaps a feeling of dread? Pilli offered to come fetch me with her motorcar, and of course I accepted.

For my costume I took a suggestion of Federigo's . . . "That is you," he had said, pointing to a quaint carving of a full moon on a pillar in the ruined cloister of San Giuliano. I decided I would go as the moon. I made myself a mask of silver paper with drooping eyelids and a pouting mouth and for the rest of my costume I wore black silk Turkish trousers and a black jersey tunic with trailing sleeves, silver slippers and silver gloves, a shawl of black silk chiffon with a beaded fringe of pearls and silver drops, and a thick black fox fur which I sometimes draped on the bed at night and stroked, remembering Nocciola. Pilli was got up like a rather stout Marie Antoinette, which suited her perfectly.

The electric lighting at the villa was not used that night. For this occasion, both the exterior and the interior were lit with a hundred red and orange paper lanterns, dangling from the ceiling, strung up outside in the bare branches of the trees, creating an amber glow where distorted shadows flickered. Candles floated in the fountain, even Pegasus wore a Harlequin mask, purple and gold, set slightly askew on his noble equine nostrils. The villa was packed with costumed revelers visible in every window as we climbed up the staircase to the main entrance.

Stepping inside, I hardly recognized the place at all, everything looked so different by lamplight. The rooms stretched on and on, crowded with Roman senators, leopards, mummies, and hooded monks dancing to the music of a small orchestra standing on a platform in the main salon, playing Puccini and American jazz tunes. Even the musicians wore elephant masks, I wondered how they managed to play their instruments. I had trouble distinguishing the servants in livery from the guests in fancy dress, but there was such a chaos it didn't seem to matter who was who.

All the local notables seemed to be present. I believe I recognized the Prefect of Viterbo dressed as Marc Antony. The Director of the archaeological museum, a thin sallow birdlike man, had got himself up like Cleopatra. There were several Marie Antoinettes, and only one Louis, and a score of Pierrots of indeterminate sex. Someone shoved a glass of champagne into my hand, and a birdcage and an enormous carrot twirled me away in a dance, beneath a shower of confetti. I lost track of Pilli, and later saw her lounging on a sofa with the carrot. I kept looking for Federigo. Was that him, the ghoul with the cigar? No, too tall. What about that heavy set man there in the domino? No, for a moment the hood was tossed back revealing a stranger's face. Once I thought I saw a Flamenco dancer scowling at me with black rimmed eyes, her face half hidden by a scarlet fan. Was that Elisabetta Colonna?

I had to keep dancing to keep moving through the rooms in search of Federigo, for if I stopped, I was pushed rudely to the edge, where I could see nothing but a mob of unidentifiable arms and legs and heads. Dancing made me thirsty, but there was no water to drink, only champagne. As I danced, I looked down at my silver slippers in an effort to keep my balance: the marble floors gleamed in lozenge patterns that seemed to shrink or infinitely expand, depending which way I was whirled. At last I collapsed on a couch and enquired of a servant where I might freshen up. He pointed to a stairway.

Leaning heavily on the balustrade I climbed my way up the curving marble stair, under the stern gaze of an array of portly, aristocratic ancestors, who were not really Elisabetta Colonna's forbears, if I were to believe Pilli. I stopped a moment to survey the writhing spectacle below. Laughter came from the upstairs rooms, where small groups had retired for more private entertainment. A few garments had been shed on the dark red carpet in the corridor. Here and there human shapes bulged in the heavy damask drapes, in other shadowy corners couples embraced less discreetly. I believed I recognized Marc Antony and Cleopatra, but I did not care to investigate.

I found my way to the bathroom tiled with tiny pink scallop shells, removed my gloves and mask – by this time quite crumpled – and rinsed my face with cold water. I immediately felt myself again, and was reluctant to go back down into the fray. I had given up hopes of spotting Federigo in the confusion. All I wanted now was to find a quiet place to sit for a few moments, then I would try to go home.

I opened a wrong door and found myself not in the corridor from which I had come, but in a sort of anteroom, leading to a boudoir or dressing room, where a large armoire with a mirror faced the doorway. I saw myself reflected there, full length, and now went forward to adjust the shawl I had wrapped around my tunic like a sash. As I stepped into the room, I saw, sitting on a couch near a fire, a giant boar. That is to say a man wearing tight breeches of powder blue velvet, a white silk shirt and a fabulous boar's mask, with curving tusks, all painted gold. The boar peered at me in the mirror, tilted his head to one side and seemed to smile at me. I recognized that uncanny green of the eyes through the slits, like bits of ice scratched from an arctic sky. Federigo Del Re held his arms out to me, and I dropped onto the sofa beside him.

A hundred things I wanted to tell him rushed into my mind at once: the ring I had found and kept, but which I had not worn that night, for fear of irritating his mistress, the sulphur pool where I had seen him bathing, the dog's disappearance and death, my troubling dreams, my anxiety at not hearing from him. All this vanished as he put his arms around me.

"Are you sufficiently relaxed?" was all he said, his voice muffled by his boar's mask, which he had not removed.

Sinking deeper into the velvet cushions, I sighed and turned my face to the fire. My head was spinning. I could feel the flames on my face. The champagne had gone to my head. I closed my eyes, and felt once again the warmth flowing from his fingers, not only into my body, but into the infinite blackness of my mind. How was it possible to have encountered such feelings only now, so late in life? I yearned for him as I had never yearned for any other human being. I let my hand drop to the floor in a sort of swoon. He felt my pulse, and then lay his arm lengthwise down my body, like a sword on the reclining figure of a mediaeval tomb. I reached up to touch the muscles of his arm beneath his silk sleeve, then slipped my hand under his shirt to feel the hard muscular plate on his protruding paunch, the grey wool on his chest. Then moving my hand upwards I was startled to touch a sort of bandage fastened across the upper part of his torso. When I drew my hand back in surprise, he responded with a shrill, whinnying laugh.

I pushed the shirt up to reveal his bare chest. An odd star-shaped scar was webbed about his navel. I was amazed for I had not noted any scars on his body when I saw him bathing naked in the sulphur pool. I was momentarily disoriented. Was this really Federigo? Then I examined what I had supposed was a bandage and discovered with an even greater shock that he had tied my own brassiere – the one he had removed from me months ago in the tomb – knotted to an extra strip of cloth, around his own nipples. Now threadbare and greyish, it looked as though he had been wearing it for weeks. I must have gasped for he laughed again crazily. I thought he must be very drunk, but he did not smell of alcohol. Yet there was sharp odor, almost feral, about him. I tried to sit up, but he held me down, then thrust his hands under my tunic into my trousers and groped, none too delicately, between my legs.

"Federigo," I said suddenly, coming to my senses. Someone could walk in at any moment and expose us. It was not the place or the time, and certainly not the manner, no matter how much I desired him. "No, not like this," I said, struggling to sit up, "Not here."

"Don't talk," he said in an unfamiliar voice, his words slurred and slightly menacing. He placed his palm lightly over my lips.

"No, please." I protested, and in reply he clamped his hand down over my mouth and I tasted his palm, salty and bitter, then he pawed away the shawl I had wrapped around my waist. The fabric ripped and a rain of silver beads tinkled to the floor. With surprising deftness, he yanked my trousers down and began to undo his own. I could hardly believe what was happening and was not so much afraid as astonished. All I could think was that I was about to be violently sick. One last time I tried to sit up, but he grabbed me by the nape of the neck and pinched very hard. I felt a stabbing pain and then must have lost consciousness, for I remember nothing more after that.

I was falling, falling, tumbling down an icy slope towards a precipice. Wet snow stung my face as I went round and round. I tried to grab hold of something, to brace my hands against the slick, frozen ground, but nothing could stop my momentum. It's only a dream, I said to myself, and gritted my teeth. With great effort, I made myself open my eyes. Pilli was shaking me vigorously by the shoulders. I shivered and sat up on the sofa. My mouth tasted of vomit. I rubbed my face. It was wet. Water had been spilled down the front of my tunic.

"There now, Harriet, You've had too much champagne! It's time to go home," Pilli said, putting down the pitcher of ice water she had been splashing me with.

An empty bottle of champagne lay on the floor amid the scattered shards of a broken wine glass. The fire was out and the room stank of ashes. Federigo was gone. I glanced up at the oval mirror above the mantelpiece where a Flamenco dancer with blurred rings around her eyes was studying me with cold satisfaction. One brown shoulder was bared, the pink ruffles of her bodice torn, her skirt hung askew. Catching my eye in the glass, she arched an eyebrow and fanned her orange lips.

I wobbled to my feet. It did not seem to me that I had drunk an excessive amount, but my head was swimming, and I had to lean on Pilli to walk at all. We hobbled out of the boudoir, into the corridor, and down the stairway, preceded by Elisabetta Colonna. The red Chinese lanterns had all burnt out, and the electric lights were switched on throughout the villa, illuminating the rooms with a tawdry yellowish glare. Everyone seemed to have gone home but us. The servants in livery, deathly tired, scurried about with mops and brooms trying to re-establish order. Empty bottles and broken glass were strewn across the floors and carpets, along with trodden clouds of pink and yellow confetti. The festoons had been torn from the ceiling and the red damask drapes partly pulled down from the tall windows. Pieces of costumes and masks lay on the floor, and I believe I saw Federigo's golden boar mask tossed in a corner, one tusk bent.

Outside, in the bracing cold, I felt well enough to walk on my own. We hurried down the stairs as fast as we could to the car, though I had to stop and lean over the banister a few times resisting the urge to be sick. Burnt out candle stubs floated in the fountain along with a clutter of colored paper and orange peels.

169

Pilli's driver, rudely awakened from some comfortable chair by the stove in the servants' kitchen, was waiting at the wheel, yawning. As he opened the door for us, he caught my eye, leered at me and winked. But perhaps that was only a momentary impression, for the next moment his face was impenetrable and perfectly composed. I glanced at Pilli. She did not seem to have noted anything amiss in her chauffeur's behavior.

It was nearly dawn. A greenish glow had begun to show behind the dull hills – as the sky brightened from rich cobalt to colorless daylight. An anemic sun appeared as we drove along the fields towards the village. I leaned back on the leather cushions. My thighs and calves ached from all that dancing. I was aware of a warm stickiness between my legs, and was vaguely surprised as it was not yet my time of month. As I adjusted the chiffon shawl I had wrapped around my neck to protect my throat from cold, a few pearls from the beaded fringe slipped off into my fingers. I examined the shawl and saw that the fringe was unraveling, then noticed the tear in the fabric. I looked at my hands. There were bits of gold paint beneath my nails. I tried to remember what had happened there with Federigo on the couch by the fire, but could recall nothing after he had placed his hand over my lips. Everything else was just a groggy impression. Had he been drunk, or was he mad? Or perhaps I was mad to be in love with him?

Pilli was lost in her own musings, eyes closed, her head tilted back against the seat, humming snatches of Puccini under her breath, poking at the air with her finger, following the tune. As we turned down the dirt road leading to Vitorchiano, she yawned, opened her eyes and shot me a look of fond but insincere indulgence. I could see she was still quite drunk.

"Poor, poor, poor little Harriet," she said, reaching over to pat my knee. "Whatever shall we do with you? He's not a real count, you know," she went on, Oh, I suppose he has some smattering of blue blood, who doesn't? It was Betta's idea to call him Count, and he played his part so well, the name stuck. It was so long ago some of the local people, mostly peasants really, started believing it. The Count of Vitorchiano!

"She picked him up in Naples, years ago, where he was playing Othello in some provincial playhouse. He does have such swarthy skin. I doubt he was much of an actor on the stage, but in life he doesn't do too badly."

I looked out at the barren fields baked with frost, then hid my face in the sleeve of my fur. I didn't want to hear any more. But Pilli showed no mercy.

"She keeps him, *and* his family, you know. He hasn't got a penny. And that idiot boy needs plenty of care, although there is no cure for epilepsy. She owns it all, the tower, all that. Oh maybe he convinced her to put some of that property in his name, in the end. I wouldn't be surprised. He can be extraordinarily persuasive as you must have experienced this evening."

I stared at her wondering just how much she had witnessed as I lay with Federigo on the couch.

"Don't think you're the only one who's been had. There are quite a few of us! So you're in good company. Whatever he may be, his powers are genuine. It's the rest of him that's fake."

I began to snivel. I fumbled in my bag for a handkerchief, but couldn't find one. Pilli took one out of her coat pocket and handed it to me.

"Surely you didn't believe that he loved you. He doesn't love anyone. He can't. Perhaps it's not his fault. He has no soul. He must have sold it to the devil a long time ago," and she snorted in amusement at her own little joke.

I blew my nose and looked out at the road. Up ahead, I could see the bare branches of the mulberry tree outside my house. We were nearly there.

"You were the perfect target for him. Rich, eccentric, and quite gullible. Goes with being American, I suppose. But we shouldn't have let you go on like that about him." She sighed.

I choked back a sob. Pilli leaned over and peered right into my face. I could smell the liquor on her breath.

"My dear, you're taking this so badly."

The driver pulled over to the side of the road, and was about to get out so that he could open the door for me, but I didn't want him smirking at me again.

"Don't bother," I said to him rudely, "I can open the door by myself."

"That woman, who do you suppose she is, anyway?" Pilli said snidely as I was climbing out of the car.

"You mean Elisabetta Colonna? His mistress, of course."

"Not Betta, the other one, the one at the tower."

"You mean his sister?" I asked blithely.

"Not only his sister, but the mother of his child," and she began to laugh cruelly, unable to control herself.

I slammed the door and the motorcar sped away in a blast, spinning gravel from the back wheels.

I could not find my key, so I tugged the bell. Maria would be awake by now. Looking up, I saw she had already lit the fire and smoke was curling out of the chimney. When she did not come to open the door, it passed through my mind that it was Ash Wednesday and that she might have slipped out to an early morning mass. I hoped I would not have to wait there long before she came back as I felt on the verge of collapse. I rang again and rapped the door knocker, then heard the shutter creak open slightly overhead.

"Maria, please let me in. I have forgotten my key." I said looking up at the window.

She came running down the stairs to open the door, demanding to know why I had come back so late. I brushed her off without meeting her eye and curtly ordered her to prepare a bath and to bring me some coffee, although I still felt slightly sick. I wanted no help undressing, and as I slipped off my tunic, I noticed a few gold smudges where the paint from Federigo's mask had rubbed off on the black jersey. Removing my trousers, I discovered a small painful reddish mark, like a burn or bruise, on my inner thigh and, as I stripped off my underclothes, I saw clearly that I had had intercourse with a man, with Federigo Del Re.

For three days I waited for some message from Federigo, but

none came. On the fourth day I sent Andrea to the tower with a letter, but upon returning he informed me that the gate was locked, and that no one was there, not even the peasant who was employed as custodian. I surmised then that Federigo was staying at his mistress's villa, and felt a pang of jealousy. When I asked Andrea what he had done with the letter, he replied that he had left it in the tin box nailed to the gate post where he had put my previous messages, when there was no one home to answer the door.

I didn't like the boy's manner at all. He seemed to be laughing at me. Irritated, I ordered him to bring up several loads of wood for the stove, although there were already plenty of logs in the kitchen. Then I made him pile it all up into a tidier stack. He grumbled as he went about this task, muttering to himself.

I wondered if I could trust him with my letters. Perhaps he was too lazy to walk all the way to the tower and had simply tossed the envelope into a puddle along the road. Then another more disquieting thought struck me: perhaps Federigo himself had told the boy to say he was not at home. I began to watch Andrea more carefully. Once it seemed to me that some money was missing from an unlocked drawer where I kept small sums to pay the butcher or baker. Maria's honesty was unquestioned, but the boy's?

Then one week after the ball, I wrote another note to Federigo, brief and to the point: *I must see you. I must have news of you. It is urgent.* I sealed it in an envelope and handed it to Andrea with instructions that he was to deliver it to the tower.

I was amazed when the boy laughed outright, shaking his head. "There's no use going all the way there, Signora. You won't get any reply. That man has gone away."

I was enraged by this impudence. How dare he refer to Federigo as *"that man?"* I could not tolerate such behavior from anyone, much less a person in my employment.

"Very well," I said. "If you won't deliver it, then I will have to, but in which case, seeing your inability and unwillingness to perform the tasks for which you were hired, you may take the pay coming to you and leave this house immediately."

The boy was somewhat taken aback, as I had never treated him so haughtily before, but I was in no mood to brook any nonsense. I went over to the writing table, opened the drawer, and took out some money. Making a rough calculation, I counted out a few lire and held it out to him.

"All right," he said, and bit his lip, "I'll go."

He picked up the letter that I had left on the table, put on his coat and went out.

Maria was bustling about, dusting. She put down the duster and peered at me.

"You seem rather jumpy, Signora. But Andrea is a good boy. He has no manners, but he meant no harm."

"Perhaps," I said, and wanting to be alone, I went into my studio and closed the door.

As Andrea predicted, Federigo sent no answer. Sometimes I thought of sending a letter to him at his mistress's villa, but knew that would be foolish. I often thought of going to the tower myself to see if he was there, but something stopped me. Partly I felt reluctant to wander those trails where I had often roamed with Nocciola. I am not sure what I dreaded more: finding the tower abandoned, the gate locked, or finding Federigo at home there, with that woman, his sister, or was she his wife?

Not that the idea of incest disgusted me, even if it were true, which it might not be. It didn't strike me that there was any family resemblance between the two of them at all. And then again, there might be some mitigating circumstance. She might only be a half-sister, or an even more distant relative, a cousin, perhaps. Who knows what quirk of destiny had brought them together, perhaps only once, to produce that pale, sickly boy? I knew nothing of Federigo's life. I could not presume to judge him, or her.

Rather I pitied her. Everyone knew that Elisabetta Colonna was his mistress, she too must have known and accepted the fact, waiting alone in that tower, for her husband/brother to return from his visits to his lover. I was not jealous of her as I was of Elisabetta Colonna. Still, this revelation had posed a much more solid obstacle between Federigo and myself, one I had no hope of overcoming.

Certainly I could never have matched Elisabetta Colonna's wealth or beauty. Yet, I knew that if Federigo were drawn to me, and of this there was no doubt, it was precisely because I was so unlike her. To this other woman, however, whose name I did not even know, Federigo was bound by something deeper than passion or pleasure: by guilt, a sense of duty, or by other feelings I could not fathom, and this made him even more inaccessible to me. Their little threesome was inviolable. A world in itself, permitting no intrusions, no change, and no relief.

Never had I dreamt that he could be mine or I his, in a conventional way. I knew that could never be. Still, I had imagined we might come together somehow as free spirits, but I had not guessed before the magnitude of the obstacle between us, and now that I realized it would never be removed, I fell into a bleak depression.

I suffered from insomnia and whenever I managed to drift off to sleep for a few moments I found myself in the same, repetitive, anxious dream where I followed Federigo to the fork in the path, but could never catch up with him. Sometimes he turned to glance back at me, inviting me to follow with a gesture of his hand. Often he vanished through the trees before I could find the trail, and as I hastened after him, something always prevented me from proceeding. A boar streaked toward me out of the underbrush. A viper slid across the path. Sometimes I tripped on a juniper root and woke with a start before I hit the ground. How I yearned to meet him in those dreams, down at the end of the trail.

During the day, I felt exhausted, and spent most of the time in bed, counting and recounting the days on the calendar, fearing I might be pregnant with Federigo's child. There was no question in my mind as to what would have to be done, at my age and in my circumstances. I only hoped that when the time came, I could rely on Pilli to lead me to the right doctor.

Maria observed my depression with worry and suspicion. I

had promised to give her a month's leave in spring so that she could attend a niece's wedding in the south of Italy. The day of her planned departure had almost arrived, but she was reluctant to leave me in such condition, and begged me to send for a doctor, which for the moment I refused to do. I did not want her to know the origins of my malaise, but perhaps it was not hard to guess. To humor her, I allowed her to ply me with homey remedies: broth, gruel, herbal infusions, cataplasms of clay. I made a great effort to snap out of my lethargy, to appear more cheerful, although I hardly had the strength to climb out of the bed and dress before the fire.

Then one morning, after bringing me my coffee, which now left such a bitter taste in my mouth I could not bear to drink it without adding three heaping spoonfuls of sugar, she stood, arms akimbo, at the foot of the bed, and announced that she knew what was wrong with me.

"The evil eye," she said solemnly, nodding with conviction.

"Nonsense!" I laughed, "I don't believe in those superstitions."

But she was so insistent I had to give in. She took me into the kitchen, sat me down before a roaring fire, and began her preparations. From a cupboard by the stove, she removed two bottles: one of water, the other of rich green olive oil, and broke off a handful of olive twigs from a bundle of branches hanging over the fireplace. She poured some water from the bottle into a white dish, dribbled a few drops of oil into it, then stirring it with the olive twigs, held it over my head and mumbled a curious incantation, "*Gesù, Giuseppe, e Maria. Se c'è fattura o stregoneria. Mandatela via!*"

When she had finished, she sighed and said, "I'm afraid it's still there, we had better repeat." Pouring the contents of the bowl down the kitchen sink, she began the procedure again: mixing water and oil in the dish, holding it over my head and stirring it with an olive twig, while mumbling her incantation. Once again, she was not pleased with the results.

"Whoever has put it on you is powerful enough. We have to do it again."

While she performed the rite a third time, I felt a prickling sensation along the nape of my neck and across my scalp.

She stirred slowly, muttering the prayer in a soft but fervent voice, then, after a pause, announced with satisfaction, "It's gone now. See for yourself, Signora," and she showed me the dish where a few globs of oil floated. She crossed herself, poured the contents down the sink and threw the olive twigs into the fire.

"You had it bad, Signora. I was afraid I couldn't take it away, but the Virgin helped me." She crossed herself again.

"But who would have put the evil eye on me?" I was sceptical, but I must admit, I had my own idea as to who might have wanted to do such a thing: Elisabetta Colonna.

Instead, Maria's answer offered a more disturbing solution.

"Even a mother who dotes on her child can put the evil eye on him by taking too much pleasure in looking at him. That's why it is wiser to tell someone you love how ugly he is, rather than how beautiful. Some foolish people can give it to themselves, just by looking too long in the mirror or gazing too long at the fire."

That night she took the train for Lecce. She had arranged for a neighbor to accompany her to the nearest station on an ox-cart. There were tears in her eyes as we said goodbye in the doorway. She squeezed me affectionately in her stout arms and pressed a packet into my hand, saying, "You'll need this, Signora."

Out in the road, the driver jangled his bell and she went out to the ox-cart. I watched as he lifted her trunk, filled, I knew with baskets of nuts and baked goods, rounds of cheese and gifts of sausages and other food for her relatives in the South. Then he helped her climb aboard. For once she was decently dressed, in a dark blue woollen dress and cape she must have made with cloth bought with earnings I had given her, and a ridiculous hat with a dead-looking little blue bird, which no doubt, she felt made her look like a lady of fashion. The hat pleased her so much, I did not dare laugh, and there was a grave dignity about her, as she sat perched in the back of the ox cart, despite it. I waved in forced merriment as they drove off, and when they had rounded the bend I felt unexpectedly sad and alone. It was a mild, cloudy

177

evening. I could hear sheep bells tinkling in a nearby field and the sound of children shouting somewhere. I wanted to go walking across a meadow but didn't have the strength. I looked up at the house. For a moment it seemed to me a prison.

I went back inside and opened the packet: it contained a tiny horn of red coral threaded on a string. I smiled for I understood she hoped to protect me by this means. I took it into the bedroom and hung it on a nail by the bed.

Spring 1923

1

There was nothing I craved more than solitude, so I also sent Andrea away back to his parents, promising him double wages upon his return. For the period of Maria's absence, I had arranged for a peasant girl to come in a couple of hours in the mornings to light the stove, boil some water and cook me a simple meal, soup mostly, made of potatoes and beans to which I generously added Federigo's dried and pickled mushrooms, when I was hungry. But I did not really have much of an appetite, and a cup of tea, a boiled egg, a piece of toast often were enough to keep me going for the whole day. I was still troubled by a persistent nausea, though the dizziness had lessened slightly. I had promised myself I would try to return to some kind of work routine, despite my physical and mental malaise. I wanted to put Federigo Del Re out of my mind. I could not understand why he had not written to me. Had he really abandoned me after that night? Could he be so despicable, so cruel? Then I remembered the sight of my own brassiere strapped to his chest, his snickering laugh, and I thought he must be mad.

The peasant girl wasn't very reliable, and tended to be more a bother than a help. I often ended up having to light the stove myself, although I wasn't very expert at it. The right sort of twigs were needed to get the fire started. Too much paper smothered the flame. Now that Andrea was gone, and I never went out to the woods anymore, my supply of kindling was quickly running out.

One morning I had risen earlier than usual and was in the kitchen, trying, unsuccessfully, to light the stove. The girl had not come for a couple of days, and I thought perhaps she was down with a bad cold. There had been reports of influenza in the village and I wasn't feeling very well myself. I wanted to get the stove lit and to boil myself some water for tea, I couldn't stand the taste of coffee any longer, but there was no kindling left, only a few huge logs. Those were no good, unless the stove was already blazing, and I did not have the energy to go down to the yard to see if there were any small pieces of wood left in the woodpile.

I heard a motorcar pull up outside the house and blow its horn. Usually there wasn't much traffic along that quiet road, except an occasional ox cart, or a delivery boy on his bicycle, or sometimes a peasant loping along on a donkey to the village. Moreover, the autumn rains and winter frosts had transformed it to a muddy track riddled with pits. Motor vehicles entering the village approached from the new road, wider and more evenly paved.

I was still in my nightdress. Since Maria and Andrea had gone away, I didn't bother to get dressed properly in the mornings. There didn't seem to be any need to, as I rarely went out of the house. I was kneeling on the dirty floor by the stove, my face thrust into the stove door, poking at the logs, trying to coax a small flicker into a flame. When the horn blew again, I didn't get up from the floor.

I assumed it was Pilli and did not intend to answer. Not that I was really upset with her; perhaps she had done me a good service by telling me the truth about Federigo Del Re. She had come several times since the night of the ball to pound on the door, begging, I suppose, my forgiveness, but I had not even put my nose out the window. I had nothing at all to say to her, either in anger or pardon. I knew, however, I might need her help soon enough, but for the moment I refused to think about that until it was absolutely necessary.

Two loud blows from the brass knocker rang through the house. Then the bell jangled, and a man's voice boomed impatiently, "Signora! Signora! Are you home?"

Who could this be? Perhaps it was Signor Di Rienzo come to collect the rent. It occurred to me that I hadn't yet paid it for the current month and it was nearly the end of March.

Reluctantly I went to the window, opened the shutter just a crack and peeped out for the first time in days, astonished to see that we were well into spring. The Judas trees along the road had burst into flower. A gleaming black motorcar was parked on the side of the road, beneath the mulberry tree, now covered in thick green shoots.

Under my window stood a stout man with very broad shoulders in a grey overcoat. His hat shielded his face from view. He was twirling a cigar between his fingers and the smell nearly sickened me.

"What do you want?" I called from the window

The man looked up at me and frowned. It was Federigo Del Re.

I ran down the stairs in a frenzy to open to him, nearly tripping in my long nightdress the hem of which had come unstitched. I hadn't bathed in days, and as I was undoing the bolt, I caught sight of myself in a mirror near the door: hair unkempt, soot smudged on my cheek, the sleeve of my nightdress streaked with ash. Still, I could not have cared less about how I looked. All I wanted was to throw myself into his arms but when I actually pulled the door open, I felt a jarring blast of cold air which checked me from rushing forward as effectively as a brick wall might have done.

Federigo Del Re stood before me, but I hardly recognized the man in the jaunty hat and elegant dove-grey overcoat with a silver-headed cane tucked under his arm. His body gave off a clean but unfamiliar scent of oranges and cloves mixed with tobacco and he looked and smelled as impeccable as a Parisian gentleman on a Sunday outing.

Suddenly realizing how I must appear to him, I shrank back into the doorway, and said simply, "Signor . . . Conte." I did not offer him my hand. He frowned at me and seemed uneasy. His eyes glanced furtively left and right, as though he were checking the place out for spies.

"Are you ill?" he asked and stepped into the doorway.

"No, it's nothing. I was trying to light the stove."

I did not know what to say to him. I certainly couldn't ask him in, with my dirty face and bare feet. I folded my arms across my chest to conceal the shape of my breasts beneath my worn flannel nightdress. "To what do I owe the honor of this visit?" I enquired.

He reached out and touched my face, then tucked a lock of straying hair behind my ear. His hand was cold. I turned my face away from the nauseating odor of cigar smoke that clung to his fingers.

"I wanted to take you for a drive in my new automobile," he smiled, and pointed with his cigar to the car parked under the tree.

While I dressed and tried to make myself presentable, he waited for me outside, leaning against the mulberry tree, smoking. He smiled to encourage me as I came out of the house, and held the door open as I climbed into the car. He said he was just learning how to drive, and I could see he was not comfortable with the mechanisms of the car. The motor sputtered and jerked to a halt several times before he got it rolling. "I'm used to carriages and carts," he explained, "My mind goes blank, and I don't know what to do with my feet."

We drove toward the village, bumping over holes and rocks, dispersing a small flock of geese, and nearly killing a poor peasant pushing a cartload of cabbages, who managed to jump out of our way just in time. Approaching the village gates, Federigo accelerated too quickly. The motorcar tipped dangerously around the curve, and a few men sitting on benches in the square, enjoying the tepid sunshine, shouted out at us in alarm, as the car swerved right past them, nearly grazing a corner of a new bronze monument honoring the war dead.

Federigo giggled, struggling to keep the car under control, as I urged him to slow down. We turned off the road leading away from the village, out into the country, where a few peach groves were still in bloom. I had no idea where we were going, if anywhere. When I recognized the church of Tuscania in the distance, it occurred to me that we were on the road to the sea, and soon enough, a leaden glimmer became visible beyond the hills.

The road was quite deserted, and with no houses, vehicles, animals, or other obstacles, except for an occasional cypress tree along the roadside, Federigo relaxed and began prattling away, describing the car and how it had come into his possession. I listened perplexed, *for some reason he did not seem himself.* It was not only the new clothes, or the motorcar, or his manner, all clearly those of an impostor. It was not the perfectly manicured nails, his smoothly shaved cheeks shining with cologne, or the fur in his ears neatly clipped. What unsettled me most was the hollowness of his voice and the way his eyes flit back and forth as he stared out at the road stretching on before us.

As we headed for the sea, Federigo told me that he had been away since the month of November and had sold some properties and settled some business, hence the new car, and had only just returned.

I stared at him and said, "But you were here for Baronessa Colonna's Carnival ball in February."

He shot me a quick look out of the corner of his eye. His eyebrow quivered.

"No," he said, "You are mistaken. I spent Carnival night in Naples."

"But I saw you. I spoke with you. You . . . embraced me. And even more. Do you deny it?"

Federigo gave a funny little laugh. "It must have been my shadow," he chuckled. "It gets up to all sorts of tricks." He grabbed my hand and brought it to his lips. His fingers were clammy, his lips dry. The motorcar swerved towards a cypress tree.

"You fool," I said, jerking my hand away, "Keep your hands on the steering wheel."

I was aghast. How could he have thought such an abominable joke was amusing? I decided to bolt out of the car as soon as we slowed down. I hated him at that moment and the intensity of my hatred shocked me.

Perhaps he read my mind, because he said, "It's useless to run away," and sighed.

We drove in silence, then he said, "If you need any medical assistance, you can trust my friend, the doctor, to be efficient and discreet."

At last I managed to find my voice. "Federigo, have you no feelings for me at all?"

Federigo said nothing, but seized my hand again and pressed it firmly against his thigh. I felt the weave of his trousers. They were made of the finest wool.

We had almost reached the sea. An expanse of dunes covered in tall, yellow grass and juniper bushes separated the road from the water. We left the car by the dunes and walked waist high in weeds down towards the shore. Not far away, we could see the port of Civitavecchia, with ships lying in, and steamers in arrival.

For a moment I remembered our first meeting in the tombs, our walk at Barbarano, watching the sunset in the olive grove, that long moment torn from the flux of time. That distant dream had nothing to do with the solid-looking gentleman in the grey overcoat who stood beside me now, smelling of cigars and cologne. A man I knew nothing about. I felt a deep mental distress. I must have stumbled on a juniper root protruding from the ground, I don't know, but suddenly he embraced me, and the rightness of feeling him so close and warm returned, blotting out every doubt and fear.

With one cheek crushed against his coat, I looked out at the sea. "Come with me to America," I whispered.

He said nothing but only held me tighter.

"If it is your son, we can send for him." I looked up at his face. He smiled faintly and shook his head.

"Your sister? We can send for her too . . . if you wish. In America I have enough 'money' to provide for the three of you."

At the word money, he disengaged himself from me, held me at arms' length and peered ruefully into my face. Perhaps he was considering the prospect. Then he caressed my hair and shook his head.

"I don't mind if she comes," I blurted out, " I know who she is . . ."

He laid his hand gently on my lips to silence me.

"I have come to say goodbye," he said.

"You're not going away!" I said.

"There's no need for you to worry."

"But when will I see you again?"

He shook his head again, smiled and gazed out to sea.

"I can't bear to part from you." I cried and kissed his fingers. "I love you more than I have ever loved any human being on this earth."

Tilting his head back, he laughed at the milky grey sky. I noticed how small and white his teeth were, more like the teeth of a child or even a doll.

"Why do you laugh at me?" I snapped.

"I'm not laughing at you, Harriet," he said, and patted my hand affectionately. "With you I feel oddly at peace, as if I could close my eyes and sleep a century or two, and wake up at last, refreshed for once. But I cannot follow you to America. This is an old, old land, Harriet, and my roots go deep. I cannot stray too far from here, from the lands where my ancestors are buried. I will be joining them soon enough."

"Don't talk of such things."

He shrugged and looked away. We walked without speaking along the beach, our arms around each other. The sun, the warmish wind in my hair, the solidity of his body beside me almost made me feel well again. The beach was strewn with driftwood and the trunks of pines brought high onto the shore after a recent storm. There was a strong smell of brine and rotting fish. My heavy shoes sank deep into the sand, but his barely left an impress. When I told him I was tired of walking and wanted to sit down, he said he would take me to a place where we could rest for awhile.

It was then I saw the inn, which apparently had been our destination all along, a little run down building, faded pink, set back among the dunes. The dark green shutters were chipped and peeling from the salt air, and the windows on the ground floor were boarded up. Over the entrance hung a warped wooden sign showing a forlorn moon face with drooping eyelids, reading: *Le Lune*. Federigo went up to the door and knocked.

The place looked so abandoned I was startled when the door opened and out peeped a plump woman in a brown velvet dress, with parched yellow hair like straw. She must have been at least 60, but her lips were painted cherry red and there were dark smudges of kohl around her eyes.

"Signor . . . Del Re, come in, " she simpered, batting her eyes and holding the door open wide. Then, noticing me, her face crinkled to a frown as I followed him inside. The place smelled of stale tobacco and spilled wine. There was a filthy red carpet on the stairway, pink frosted lamps hung from the ceiling. I knew what sort of place it was and what we had come there for.

Federigo pushed something into the old woman's hand and she gave him a key. Taking my hand, he led me up the stairs. On the first landing, a door half-opened. Someone peered out at us and laughed, then shut the door again. As we walked down the corridor, indistinct sounds came from other rooms.

Although the doors, all identical, were unnumbered, he seemed to know exactly which one he wanted, for he stopped unhesitatingly outside one, slid the key in, unlocked it, and smilingly invited me to precede him inside. It was a squalid little room with a large bed, a wash stand, a basin on a low stool, and a musty green sofa by the window, where through the gauze curtains,

I could see the water glinting beyond the dunes. A full length oval mirror in a brass frame stood in one corner, tilted slightly towards the bed. Every free surface in the room was covered by crude lace doilies. It might have been the bedroom of an aging spinster school teacher, were it not the wrong sort of place.

Federigo took off his hat and coat and tossed them on the sofa. I saw then that his hair had been cut and tamed into a more modern fashion. He sat down on the bed, unpinned his collar stud, saying, "With your permission, Signora," and proceeded to remove his jacket, vest, and shirt. Then he peeled off his undershirt, revealing the grizzled grey hair on his chest and the ugly scar round his navel. It gave me quite a shock to see that scar again. Suddenly everything I felt for him welled up inside me and all I wanted was to press my warm mouth against that scar. I went over to the bed, knelt down, and laid my head on his knees.

"Here, Harriet," he said, unbuttoning his trousers, and he took my hand and placed it on him. "Take me in your hands if it gives you pleasure."

He was coldly passive and detached, even, perhaps, I thought, bored. He certainly didn't seem to feel any desire. "Believe me," he sighed, "Whatever we do with these rags of ours makes little difference. Stuff for the cemetery, little more. Lord knows I'm tired of it all."

From where I knelt by the bed, I could just glimpse the sea through the window. I had never felt so lonely in my entire life. Then Federigo Del Re raised me from the floor, folded me to him and kissed my hair.

All night long I heard the sound of waves battering the shore line. Towards dawn a dog began to howl. I woke fully dressed, lying alone in that unfamiliar bed. Someone was pounding on the door. Even before I reached for him, I knew that Federigo was gone. I sat up with a start. A woman's voice squawked behind the door, "Signora, the driver's ready. You must go."

I ran down the stairs out into the broad daylight, expecting to find Federigo, instead I found a cart hitched to a pair of emaciated mules and a little unshaven man waiting for me along the road. He helped me climb into the cart with a rude push, and while we rattled back toward the countryside, he leered at me from one side of his mouth. I had no idea where Federigo had gone, and I never saw him again.

2

I heard shooting that morning up in the hills. The hunters were out again, despite the fog. I opened the window and looked out. Fires were blazing on the mountainside. There was an overpowering stench of burning leaves in the air and the wild barking of dogs. A boar hunt was on, although the season was long over. They were trying to flush some poor creature out of its den.

I was determined to go that morning and have a look at the tower, but the hunters made me uneasy. Still, I put on my boots, tossed my cloak over my shoulders, threw my rucksack over my shoulder and went out into the fog.

It had been days since I had ventured far from the house, and months since I had gone to the tower and the way was longer than I remembered. As I approached the crossroads, a figure came stumbling out of the hedge and nearly collided with me. For a moment I thought it was the Count himself, but it was only a hunter, traipsing home alone across the fields, looking for a lost dog perhaps, a gun slung over his shoulder. I pulled my hat low and stuck my chin in my collar, mumbled a greeting, and passed on. He eyed me suspiciously, but did not pause, and strode on by without a word.

I encountered the hunting party and their dogs not far from the cemetery. The men were dragging along an old cart, where the huge, blood-spattered carcass of a boar was tied. Its eyes were still open in amazement. Blood dripped down from its wounds through the planks of the cart and onto the road. The dogs pranced behind yapping, some stopped to lick the blood. The hunters must have spent the night in the forest, waiting to see the boar return to its den at dawn, and then they had struck. They were so drunk and exultant over their prey they paid no attention to me and I was glad to slink past unobserved. As I hurried toward the tower, the fog thinned out and by the time I reached the gate, it had lifted entirely.

The gate stood open. The path leading to the tower was overgrown with nettles. The letter box mounted on the gatepost had rusted. Peeking inside, I saw it was stuffed with old letters and dead leaves. Among the many envelopes, I recognized some of my own letters to the Count. I opened one at random and read,

Dear Sir,

I am writing to enquire whether you will grant me permission to visit the tombs on your property in Norchia in order to photograph them for an official project sponsored by the London Theosophical Society. Please reply at the address below.

Yours Sincerely,
Harriet Sackett.

I tore open another envelope. This too was a note I had written. It read: *I must see you. I must have news of you. It is urgent.* I didn't bother to open the others.

I must have heard a noise, for I looked up at the garden and saw a figure, a woman in a cape, stealing through the back, out through the gap in the hedge and up toward the woods.

"Wait!" I cried out. The woman froze and stared at me. She had a shawl over her head, so I really couldn't see her face and anyway she was too far away for me to recognize. I thought it might be Federigo's sister, but it might easily have been Elisabetta Colonna, or possibly even the maid.

"Has Federigo Del Re really gone away?" I called out and took a few steps toward her.

Instead of answering, she ran up the ridge and disappeared into the woods. I didn't think there was any point in pursuing her.

I walked up the steps. The door stood ajar. I slipped inside and headed up the stairs, all the way up to the top floor. Nothing remained of the furnishings I had seen that day – on my only visit inside the tower: the swords, the dusty armor, even the wrought-iron candle holders had all vanished, but the melted pools of dirty candle wax were still there on the floor exactly where I remembered them. I opened the door to what had been Federigo's study and went inside. The desk was still there near the fireplace although all the other furnishings, the maps, the books, the statues, the guns had been taken away. The only decoration left was the boar's head, with its fur dull and ratty, its glass eyes cloudy with dust.

On the desk was a small wooden chest. Cautiously I lifted the lid. Inside I found the photograph I had taken of Federigo that day so long ago, here in this very room. I clutched it to my breast. There was a small bundle of women's silk stockings and other undergarments, including my own brassiere, now reduced to a grubby rag. I also found Nocciola's collar, with a few tufts of black fur still clinging to it. I wept to see that. I put the photograph and the collar into my rucksack. At the bottom of the chest was a scroll of paper. Unrolling it, I saw that it was a faded playbill announcing a performance of *Federigo Del Re* in a theater in Naples, in a traveling hypnotist's show. I tore it to shreds.

I ran home through the trees, blindly dashing branches out of my face, hardly knowing which direction to go in. I didn't care if the hunters were near, but now the woods were silent. I heard no shouts or shooting, no sound but the squawking of crows. Half way home, I sat down on a stone, exhausted, and leaned my back against a tree. I sat like that for a while, staring up at the sky through the branches. Getting to my feet again, I noticed a ring of yellowish ear-shaped lichen growing around the base of a nearby tree and I remembered that morning long ago, when Federigo and I had gone walking in the woods around Barbarano. I broke off a few handfuls of lichen and filled my pockets with it. Then I headed home where I managed to light the kitchen stove and put some water to boil. Later that night I resolved to make one last visit to the tombs, if only in my dreams.

CHAPTER SIX

At dawn Stephen woke after only an hour or two's sleep. Sarah had not come back to bed. He went to the window and opened the shutter. A greenish crack glowed behind the hills, slowly warming to a golden pink. The rains had stopped at last and there was promise of a fine spring day. He sniffed circumspectly, then took a deep breath – the vivid air tingled in his nostrils and chest. As he stood yawning and rubbing his eyes, a cock crowed in the distance with raucous joy, waking a blackbird in the oak tree outside the bedroom window. The bird began to chirp a silly little song that seemed to be repeating, *"Do-do-do you? I do, I do."* Then it flew away. In the fields below, green wheat rippled nearly a foot high, and from beyond came the melancholy barking of a dog. From a thicket not far from the house, an old woman with a basket on her head suddenly emerged and began to cross a field, singing softly to herself. The nasal notes of her song drifted up to him through the window. He watched as she stooped down, set the basket aside and began to gather handfuls of leaves from the ground, tossing them into her basket. Some sort of wild salad, perhaps.

Stepping out into the corridor, he heard Parsons bustling about the kitchen, banging the stove door, muttering to herself. He smelled bacon frying. He went to Harriet's room and found his wife asleep on the couch. Harriet, too, lay motionless, her face turned to the wall, her breathing calm and regular. Sarah lay half-propped up, her head thrown back, her face slightly flushed, the blanket sliding from her lap to the floor. She looked so lovely, so inert and abandoned that he was deeply moved. He felt a sudden desire to gather her up and carry her off to bed, but instead he went over to adjust the blanket around her. As he did so, he saw the little green leather volume which had slipped from her grasp. One page had detached itself from the binding and was clutched in her fingers. Deftly, he retrieved the notebook and put it into the pocket of his dressing gown, but just as he was easing the torn page from her hand, she stirred slightly and opened her eyes. By natural reflex, her fingers contracted even tighter upon the page. Stephen furtively drew his hand away and leaned down to kiss her forehead. Still half asleep, Sarah took slight notice of him. Smiling with a voluptuous groan, she snuggled down on the cushions, flung her hand aside out of his reach, and closed her eyes again. Just then, Parsons appeared in the doorway bearing a large clay pitcher. "The hot water's ready, sir," she said, and shuffled on to his room. Looking down at his wife again, he saw that she had tucked her hand beneath a cushion. It wasn't worth waking her and starting a quarrel – he'd just have seize possession of the page some other way. He bent down to kiss his wife a second time, and then followed Parsons down the hall to his room.

After he had washed and shaved, Stephen breakfasted alone in the kitchen. Wimbly was still not up yet, Sarah had wandered back to bed to get another couple of hours' sleep and Parsons was in Harriet's room, giving Harriet her drops and pills. Stephen intended to dedicate the morning to thinking out his plans for Harriet, then he would discuss them with Wimbly, and only after working through all details, would he inform his wife. But not now. When they were back in London. He had heard of a new treatment for dementia that entailed inducing artificial fevers in the patient, which sometimes had a stabilizing effect on deranged minds. He did not know if Harriet was in a sorry enough state to warrant such a cure, but he thought it might be well worth investigating.

Every morning since their arrival in Vitorchiano, rain or shine, Stephen had taken a constitutional down to the village gate and back. Sometimes Wimbly accompanied him, but not always, and this morning he was grateful for a moment's solitude so that he could clear his head after a sleepless night. Before going out, there was something he needed to tend to. Entering the bedroom, he was glad to see Sarah still fast asleep. He looked around to see where he had put that cursed notebook of Harriet's and found it laying on the dresser where he had left it while shaving. He wanted to get rid of it before Sarah woke up. Later he would search through her things for the missing page and eliminate that too. He picked up the notebook and went back to the kitchen, where no one was about. Parsons was still with Harriet. He opened the stove door, tossed the notebook in, pushed it well into the flames with a poker and slammed the stove door shut. There, that was done. The first step had been taken to eradicate this absurd episode from Harriet's mind. Federigo Del Re was only a phantom of Harriet's overwrought, possibly diseased, and most certainly indecent imagination. Surely it would not be hard to annihilate all further trace of him before she recovered, at which time, all this might be nothing but a hazy memory. Nonetheless, he mused, Sarah might be right, in a way. Harriet's diary might be a form of self-justifying fantasy, which she had concocted in order to deaden the shame of having carried on with some rough peasant fellow who had given her a tumble in the tombs. Perhaps now, Stephen supposed, clenching his jaw, she might understand why one must choose one's companions with care.

On his way out again, he passed Mrs Parsons in the corridor, carrying a tray back to the kitchen. She nodded to him coldly and said, "Miss Harriet ate a bite of toast this morning, and finished her tea. She ought to be feeling better today, God willing."

"I do hope so," said Stephen stiffly.

She gazed at him with her blurry grey eyes, mildly perplexed and disapproving.

"Thank you," he found himself saying in a voice that seemed to be stuck in his throat. "Thank you for all that you have done for Miss Harriet and for Mrs Hampton."

"Only my duty, sir" she clipped, and with unexpected grace glided down the hall.

He took his coat and hat from the rack at the top of the stairs, then bending down to tighten the lace of his well-buffed shoe, dutifully polished that morning by Mrs Parsons, he was somewhat startled to find himself face to face with the strange stone mask with protruding tongue, peering out from under the table on the landing. It was one of several old stone carvings strewn about the property Harriet rented, and he had never really paid any attention to it. Struck by the uncanny effect of its blank, lidless eyes, he crouched down to examine it closely, with a professional scrutiny. It was some sort of propitiatory god, he thought, a spirit of the woods or waters, and, from the looks of it, was a genuine piece of antiquity, although he found it an ugly thing, with a mockingly perverse expression. He did not care for Etruscan art in general. The Etruscans were a vicious and cruel people, or so the highest authorities, such as Mommsen claimed, and certainly far less refined than the Ancient Romans.

He had no idea why Harriet had conceived such an interest in their grim civilization, wholly obsessed by death. If the Romans had wiped them out so totally, they must have been an inferior race, and probably deserved it. Harriet's enthusiasm for the Etruscans was perhaps a form of competition with him, with his family, who for generations had distinguished themselves as scholars and collectors of Oriental art. After all, his own father had encouraged Harriet's passion for archaeology and exoticism, and this was where it had all led. Stephen studied the mask again. It was clearly derivative of Greek art, not at all original. With mischievous wit, he reached out to tweak the mask's nose, then stood up, checked his reflection in the tall, gilt mirror and adjusted the angle of his hat. He was looking extraordinarily well, he thought, taking his gloves from his pocket and slipping them on. The country air was indeed salubrious, despite all. From the umbrella stand he took his walking stick mainly used to threaten stray dogs, and hurried down the stairs, whistling a tune. For the first time in many days, he felt rested, cheerful and relieved.

Stepping back into the kitchen, Mrs Parsons saw that the stove had begun to smoke again. Plumes of stinking grey smoke issued from every crevice and fissure in the stove, filling the kitchen with a heavy cloud. That wood of Miss Harriet's was just too green to burn. She opened the window wide, then rushed to the stove, seized the poker, and flung open the door. Peering inside she saw a square object wedged in among the smouldering logs, obstructing the passage of air and smothering the flames, as a dense smoke poured forth. Jabbing it with the poker, she saw, to her great surprise, that the object was a book. She put down the poker, grabbed the tongs, and pulled it out of the stove just as it began to catch fire. She recognized the burning book. It was Miss Harriet's diary!

She dashed it to the floor and stamped out the flames. But who had thrown it into the stove and why? It could only have been Mr Hampton, whom she had just met in the corridor on his way out of the kitchen. Missis Sarah would never have tried to destroy something belonging to Miss Harriet, certainly not without her consent. With the flames safely extinguished, Mrs Parsons opened the volume at random and was glad to see that the writing had not been too damaged, and the content was still legible. She pondered what she should do with the thing. Of course it ought to be returned to Miss Harriet. Seeing that she had written so many pages, it must be important to her, and its importance should be respected. But for the moment, with Miss Harriet in such a state, giving it directly to her was out of the question.

Mrs Parsons lay the diary on the hearth and began mixing some flour, milk, and butter to make scones, then rolled the dough out on a pastry cloth, thinking all the while about the diary. She had read only halfway through it before putting it back in Harriet's drawer, but it was not hard to guess why Mr Hampton had wanted to burn it. The indecencies in it had probably angered him. She herself had found it a disturbing thing to read, especially just before bedtime. Not that she wasn't curious to know how the story continued, but a sort of repugnance had stopped her. In any case, there hadn't really been any time for her to read after that night she had stayed up till dawn, even if she had wanted to. Nursing Harriet and tending to the house had so exhausted her that by the end of the day, she had hardly the strength to wash her face or say a prayer before tumbling into bed. But now that the notebook was back in her hands again, she decided she might just read a few pages more, but only during the daytime.

She did not want Mr Hampton to know she had salvaged it from burning. He might interpret her gesture as an act of insolent disobedience, and if she should give it to Mrs Hampton, Mr Hampton would very likely find it and try to destroy it again. Mrs Parsons wanted to prevent that, if possible. It was a way of protecting Miss Harriet from the cruelties of her cousin, as if that could make up for having failed to protect her when Miss Harriet and Mr Hampton were both youngsters in her charge. After all, if Miss Harriet had grown up to be a bit odd, had never married and slung about in baggy trousers, it was all because of Mr Hampton, of what he had done to her there in the bushes while she was still only a girl. As a young lass, Miss Harriet had been such a sensitive creature, growing up in America without a father, and then being taken advantage of by her own cousin in such a brutal way, pushed down under the hedge with her hair in the dirt and branches scratching her face. Such memories can mar a girl for life, make her take to drink or other vices. Mrs Parsons had heard of far worse stories, of girls becoming twisted in the mind or even losing their wits all together, after being raped by a relative. It was a miracle Miss Harriet hadn't turned out even more peculiar than she was. She was, after all, a perfectly respectable American lady who made her living taking photographs and whose company was appreciated by well-bred persons of good society. Mr Hampton really ought not complain about her.

Of course Mrs Parsons could never have breathed a word to anyone of what she had witnessed there in the bushes so many long years ago. It would have spelled the end of her employment with the Hamptons. Young Mr Hampton would have kept his promise, and brought some false tale to the master's ear, about her pocketing the silver or nipping at the brandy, or something worse, and where would she have gone to find another position, her being a widow and all? Or perhaps Mr Hampton would have been forgiven – the ugly episode forgotten, put down to the mischief that boys get up to when tempted by young girls who do not behave properly. Old Mr Hampton would have been furious with his son, for the old man had doted on Harriet, but then he was always away traveling, months at a time. The unhappy affair might have been hushed up with no consequences, during one of the master's long absences abroad. The mistress would no doubt have defended her son. She had always disliked Miss Harriet and Miss Harriet's mother. So Mrs Parsons had swallowed her secret like a bitter pill, kept it down all these years in the pit of her stomach, where it had soured, ruining her digestion for good. How it had disgusted her to see the young master go unpunished for his crime, while growing daily into an arrogant youth who believed he had the world in his hands. But in many ways, it had to be admitted, Mr Hampton and his sort did indeed hold the world in their hands, and one can only make peace with this state of affairs as Mrs Parsons had learned to do.

She sighed, dusted the flour from her hands, popped the scones in the oven, and picked up the diary again. Soot rubbed off on her fingers as she turned the pages. A queer story it was, with Miss Harriet spying on a naked man at his bath, then watching him dancing with a sword in the woods. That was another reason why Mr Hampton had wanted to burn it! He was jealous of the naked man with the sword. Mrs Parsons doubted that there in Italy nowadays men still danced naked in the woods with swords, as if they were savages in an African jungle. And yet she knew that man existed, for he had brought a porcupine to the house and plucked out its quills on the kitchen steps.

The bell rang downstairs, interrupting her thoughts and Mr Hampton's voice, high-pitched and irritated, called up through the kitchen window. "Open the door, Parsons, I have forgotten my key."

She looked about for a place to hide the diary, then noting the pastry cloth, shook out the flour, wrapped the diary in the cloth, and shoved it in the bread basket. Then wiping her hands on her apron again, she tripped down the stairs to open the door to her master.

Over the next few days, Sarah, assisted by Mrs Parsons, busied herself with packing Harriet's personal belongings and clothes. Wimbly and Stephen would see to her books and photographic equipment. Many things were to be left behind, such as Harriet's stock of Wellingtons, which would be of no use where she was going, besides she could always buy more in London, if needed. Thoughtfully, Sarah set aside a few things for her friend she thought might be important mementos of this period of her life: Harriet's portrait of herself with the dog, the dog's collar, the little Buddha, and made a packet of them. On impulse she plucked a handful of porcupine quills from the jar on the mantelpiece, bound them with a ribbon, and added them to the packet. She was spared the agonizing decision of whether to return Harriet's diary to her or not, for it had vanished from the house. All that was left of the notebook was the very last page, which had come loose from the binding while she was reading the diary one evening in Harriet's room. She had woken to find it crumpled in her fingers, just as Stephen was kissing her good morning. The moment she had opened her eyes, she had the oddest sensation that something was being tugged from her hand, and was quite startled to see her husband leaning over her with curious intent.

Playing a lazy cat still asleep, she had moved her arm away and slipped her hand under a cushion. Then when he had gone, she discovered that the crushed paper in her fingers was a page from Harriet's notebook. She jumped up and searched for the diary, but it was not on the sofa, or between the cushions, or on the floor. Stephen must have taken it from her while she was asleep, but hadn't managed to snatch the last page away before she had awoken. She folded it, hid it in a handkerchief, and tucked it up the sleeve of her nightdress where it would be safe.

Later that morning, after Stephen had gone out, she went through the house, opening boxes, cupboards, and drawers, looking for the diary, but Stephen had probably burned it, as threatened. How could he have done such a thing! That diary belonged to Harriet. There was no use confronting him directly though, he would pretend he knew nothing about it, and they would end up having another quarrel. But surely Harriet would miss it when she was well again, and what explanation would she give?

She was disappointed at not finding it, for she had hoped to read it again, despite the ambivalent feelings it stirred in her. Her initial response to the diary had been puzzlement followed by outrage. Harriet had no right to feel such things for a man who had so utterly debased her. How could she have been taken in by such an unscrupulous person, whose debauched intentions were evident at every turn? But then how much truth did the story contain? Sarah had tried to match Harriet's tale to concrete details she knew were real: the dog's collar, the tower they could see from the studio window, her cornelian ring, the mushrooms Mrs Parsons had found in the kitchen – but Stephen was right, taken together they proved nothing at all.

Yet the diary exerted a strong, sensual fascination on Sarah's imagination, telling of such a blind passion and even devotion, the likes of which Sarah had never felt for any man and certainly not for her husband. Not a human passion at all, but an obsession, somehow connected to tombs and banquets of the dead and dead maidens giving water to fawns, all those eerie Etruscan things

Harriet loved. Sarah had experienced a sickening sort of excitement while reading Harriet's encounters with her count – recalling long snuffed out sensations aroused by the cheap novels she and Harriet had read aloud to each other as girls, sometimes acting out the parts. Sarah wondered if she herself could have resisted such a relentless pursuit, or would she have submitted to the thrill of mindless possession? She shivered thinking of the Count's warm, brown fingers working over Harriet's body as she lay unconscious in the tomb. In a wild moment of rebellion after a quarrel with Stephen she had even imagined herself in Harriet's place, sprawled on the velvet sofa, lax beneath the crushing weight of the man in the boar mask as flames crackled in her face. Such thoughts were probably indecent, but she need share them with no one, and they had brought her satisfaction before falling off to sleep.

In some ways, Harriet's diary made an odd sort of sense. It was probably written in a form of code, which only Harriet could understand. Moreover, it had an odd ring of truth about it – at least to Sarah's ear, and had to have been based on some real experience. Harriet could never have fabricated the emotions she described unless there had truly been some man who had aroused them. And indeed, Harriet had been involved with someone. It little mattered that they had found no proof corroborating the existence of Federigo Del Re – for, after all, they had found no evidence to the contrary. All that could be said was that the names and circumstances Harriet recorded in the diary had not borne out in real life. That did not mean that her secret sun did not exist. Despite his cruelty, Federigo Del Re had been for Harriet a hidden source of dark pleasure and joy, as much as of pain and destruction, and they would never, ever get to the bottom of it. This is what angered Stephen most, Sarah thought, not the damage that the Count had done to Harriet – but the fact that he would never discover the truth about the man called Federigo Del Re, the fact that Harriet had a secret to keep from them all. And not only the secret of the Count's identity, but other far more disturbing secrets as well. What had been in Harriet's mind as she gathered the lichen? To follow the Count in a drugged dream? To destroy herself and the child in her womb? Perhaps Stephen was right in wanting to take the diary away from Harriet, just as he had been right to send Parsons on to Italy. Would it not be devastating for her to read it again once she had recovered? Yet now only a single page of the diary remained and in the name of their many years of exclusive friendship – Sarah felt she must return to Harriet this fragmentary record of her Etruscan adventure. Folding the page into a tiny paper square, she put it into the bundle of porcupine quills, where Stephen would never think to look for it, then locked the trunk, and slipped the key into her bosom.

•◆•

A month later Harriet was on the mend again, although she had lost a great deal of weight and her hair had thinned considerably. Wimbly judged to his regret that she had aged by about ten or twelve years since the previous Christmas. He no longer entertained hopes for their future marriage. Such a thing was impossible, given Harriet's condition. Even if she should recover completely, which he doubted, she would never agree to have him, although now for the first time in her life, she might realize that she needed someone to look after her. Not many men would have been willing to take that on their shoulders before all this had happened. And now her chances of marriage were over – not that Harriet could care less.

The memory of their evening together in the *limonaia* filled him with chagrin. It had been the only time in all those years that Harriet had ever let him approach her. He was still puzzled as to why she had consented. He had seized her in Sir William's garden with one arm, awkwardly balancing the umbrella above their heads to keep off the snow, as he lunged forward to kiss her on the only exposed part of her body, a square inch of chapped skin left uncovered just above her throat where the top button of her cloak was left unfastened. Instead of pushing him away, Harriet had thrown her head back in melancholy acquiescence and when he drew her towards the door of the *limonaia*, to his astonishment, she had complied.

The braziers in the *limonaia* had burnt out, but a small oil lamp still flickered in the window casting a shifting pattern of lemon leaves and branches upon the rough stucco walls. The whole room smelled of lemons and ashes. They lay down on an old musty velvet curtain piled in a corner of a small wooden platform, under the blank eyes of a marble bust of Janus. Harriet's eager lust almost shocked him as they tore off each other's clothes. He threw Harriet's cloak over them to cover their nakedness in the freezing room. Never had he experienced such a range of satisfactions: excitement, passion, tenderness, as that afternoon in Harriet's arms. At the height of their embrace, he felt he had reached through to the hidden core of another human being – something which had never happened with his wife. But then, collapsing against Harriet's breast, he was struck by the withering certainty that his joy was merely an illusion. For though Harriet surrendered herself to him with a savage desperation, she also withdrew herself even as she gave. It is not me she is with at this moment, he thought, as she writhed and grunted beneath him, striving to reach her own pleasure after he had finished. When she cried out in her orgasm at last, it was though from across a void.

Afterwards they lay wrapped in her cloak until the lamp went out. Caressing the long slim line of her flank, he tried to decide whether he was happy or sad. Harriet settled the matter by sitting bolt upright – with her eyes wide as if rudely wakened from a bad dream – and announcing, "This changes nothing, it shouldn't have happened," and then burst into tears. Nothing baffled or infuriated Wimbly more than a weeping woman, but Harriet gave him no time to study the proper tactic of consolation. She jumped up, pulled on her clothes, and ran out, while he stumbled about looking for his trousers and bumped his head on a low ceiling beam. Harriet was wrong – this encounter had changed everything between them.

Wimbly spent the last few days in Vitorchiano sorting through Harriet's books, papers, and plates, and packing them into boxes. Stephen intended to keep only a few of her books and equipment, which were to be sent back to England. Her photographs and sundry papers were to be discarded. This seemed rather heavy handed to Wimbly, but he obliged. He found no letters from the Count, no letters at all in fact, Harriet must have gotten rid all of her personal correspondence. Sarah had told him that the Count had given Harriet a book of archaeological studies he had published, but no book of that description was found in Harriet's studio. The only things of interest Wimbly found while cleaning out the studio was a copy of Harriet's lease for the rental of the house, a hand-drawn map of the area annotated by Harriet with Etruscan sites marked in red ink, and a photograph of a man, which might

very well have been Del Re's portrait, perhaps, given the description of him in Harriet's diary. The photograph had fallen down behind a bookcase in the studio, where it lay propped against the wall. Dusting it off, he held it to the light. It summoned up in him a host of bitter feelings and his first impulse was to tear it to pieces. Then he thought he had no right to do so and felt ashamed. Not handsome by any means, the man in the photograph was burly, slightly wall-eyed, with an unkempt bush of silver hair. There was something womanish in his face, reminding one vaguely of a Caravaggio Bacchus. How had this vulgar, swarthy, pot-bellied Italian managed to enchant Harriet to the point of abandoning all self-esteem? This unsolvable mystery was of little consequence now.

At least this portrait offered Wimbly the proof he required to free his mind from doubt. The father of Harriet's lost child could only be the man in this photograph.

He did not know what to do with the photograph. He did not want Stephen to know that he had found it. He could not give it to Harriet, at least not for the moment, for fear of plunging her anew into a crisis. He did not want to keep it himself. He wrapped it carefully in brown paper and put it in his own trunk, thinking he would decide what to do with it later.

He did show the lease to Stephen, though they had some difficulty in deciphering its antiquated Italian phrasing. It provided no evidence concerning the Count – giving only the rental agency's name, signed with an illegible signature which might easily have been 'Di Rienzo' or 'Di Biagio' – or a dozen other Italian names. Stephen decided to take it to the Thomas Cook's office in Rome and seek their assistance in terminating the contract, intending to leave a large sum at their disposal to pay any outstanding debts Harriet might have run up with the agency.

With her energies replenished, Harriet became her old recalcitrant self, but she was not strong enough to oppose Stephen's plan to take her back to England. Stephen had to call in the doctor from Rome, who prescribed a treatment of bromide and valerian to keep her docile. When that proved insufficient, the doctor prescribed tincture of opium, doled out in what Wimbly judged to be overly generous doses. Out of danger, but heavily sedated, Harriet slept most of the day under Mrs Parson's watchful eye.

One morning, while Stephen and Sarah had gone to Rome with a hired car to arrange their travel plans at the Thomas Cook's office, and Harriet was safely in Mrs Parson's care, Wimbly thought he might take a walk through the countryside and visit some of Harriet's Etruscan tombs. He longed to get a bit of air in his lungs, for he found the house oppressive, with its odors of smoke and ashes and its sickroom smells. He had seen on Harriet's map that there were some Etruscan tombs within a mile or two of her house. This would be his only opportunity to discover something about the vanished culture whose art and myths had absorbed Harriet for so many months. He doubted that he would ever return to this corner of Italy again.

He set out early in the morning, equipped with a rucksack and walking stick, relieved to be out in the open air and the tepid sunshine, following an unpaved road through meadows and olive groves. Spring had advanced across the countryside after the heavy rains of the previous month. The ripening wheat rippled in undulating patterns as the wind blew through the fields. Patches of yellow gorse blazed against the green hills, bright flares of poppies flickered in the tall grass, violets dotted the roadside. He saw the tombs from afar, as he rounded a curve in the gravel road: three giant doorways carved in the steep wall of a ravine, overgrown with ivy and blackberry vines. A sort of goat trail dug in the cliff wound up to the entrance of the largest tomb. He felt a thrill of discovery as he bounded up the path, yet venturing inside, he found the tombs disappointing. Stripped of all their fine decorations, they were merely square dank rooms hollowed out of the rock, full of cobwebs and goat droppings. He sat down on a stone bench, where he supposed Etruscan bodies had once lain, and allowed his eyes to grow accustomed to the dark. He thought of the Etruscan sculptures he had seen back in the British Museum in London, men and women lying together resting quietly, staring ahead, eyes wide open, with a sly, knowing smile. What was the secret of their seraphic repose? He reflected that if he had been an Etruscan, he might have been buried in such a tomb, stretched out beside his wife Dorothy, holding up an egg in the darkness. He took his pipe and tobacco pouch from his pocket, and struck a match. His tiny sphere of light illumined the tomb's back wall, where he was startled to see a huge doorway. The match went out, and he struck another, then got up and went to the door. It was not a real door, but only carved. He lay his hand against the cold stone, feeling its roughness, then knocked twice to see if it were hollow, but it sounded compact and solid. He sighed. This was the barrier beyond which his mind could never travel. He tried to picture Dorothy stepping through the door, wrapped in luminous mist and pink clouds, and he knew that the image of this door unopened would disturb his dreams for the rest of his life.

By the end of June, Harriet was well enough to travel. Mr Hampton had sent their baggage on ahead of them, and had arranged for a hired car to take them to the station in Rome, where they would board an express train for Paris, departing in the evening. Mrs Parsons would stay on for two days, to lock up the house and see that everything was in order. Then she would follow by hired car to Rome, and travel northwards by train to Calais, where she would meet up with the Hamptons, coming from Paris after a brief visit there. All the arrangements had been made with the Cooks people in Rome, and Mr Hampton had left with Mrs Parsons her ticket and a small packet of Italian and French money for the trip, and also the name and address of their hotel in Paris.

Mrs Parsons watched from the kitchen window as Mr Hampton, Mr Wimbly, and the driver carried Harriet, half-drugged as a precautionary measure, out of the house and loaded her into the waiting car, where Mrs Hampton was already settled in the back seat. Distressed to see Miss Harriet bundled about like a pack of old rugs, Mrs Parsons frowned and set her jaw. She did not at all approve of the medicine that the English doctor had given Harriet. As the car pulled out, she raised her withered hand to wave goodbye and uttered a word of prayer.

Then she turned round to contemplate the empty kitchen with its huge extinguished hearth, where bundles of dried herbs and olive branches hung suspended above a row of tarnished copper pots and rusted iron griddles. She was thankful she would be leaving the place soon, relieved she need not struggle with these primitive cooking arrangements for much longer – the cast-iron stove with its enormous cauldrons, the sink hewn of rough grey stone. What labor it had been to produce decent meals and hot water, and other necessities for the Hamptons. She had even had to carry up wood from outside – and her with arthritis and all. It was just like Mr Hampton not to notice she was getting too old to handle such heavy chores. She was glad the Hamptons were gone now but uneasy about spending the next two nights totally alone, and worried about what would happen to Miss Harriet back in England.

She tied on a clean apron and set about her housework, always the best remedy for a troubled mind. She dusted the furniture, scrubbed the floors, and beat out all the rugs, turned the mattresses and piled the blankets in a window to get a bit of sun. Beneath the mattress in Miss Harriet's bedroom, she found a little red coral horn, and though not a believer in old wives' tales, she was reluctant to touch it, for she had read in Miss Harriet's notebook that it was some sort of charm. Later, alone that first night she lay awake till nearly dawn, listening to banging shutters, creaking hinges, and wood worms in the beams. Twice she got up to investigate a noise at the window, which just turned out to be the tapping of a branch against the pane. The next morning she busied herself with the mirrors – it took nearly the whole day to clean them all with ammonia and vinegar. It was very odd how the mirrors enlarged the space of each room, stretching it this way and that, into a series of unending corridors, with doors standing open at the end where she saw her own reflection. More than once she had a start when she thought she saw something moving behind her, but it was only the edge of a curtain blowing in an open window. Throwing the old sheets over them to protect them from dust, she felt as though a battle had ended. The moment the last mirror was covered, the house became oddly quiet, as though it had ceased to breathe. That night to soothe her uneasy nerves, she poured herself an extra glass or two of red wine and slept deeply until dawn.

She had prepared her things for the journey. The little straw valise packed with only the essentials stood ready at the top of the landing – her trunk had been sent on ahead with the Hamptons' luggage. Her grey coat all brushed and tidy hung on the rack beneath her grey felt hat with discreet plumes. There on the gilt table with lion's paws was her black silk purse with silver clasp containing passport, ticket, money, and the keys to the servants' door in Russell Square. Beside the purse was a parcel wrapped in brown butcher's paper: Miss Harriet's diary. It gave her a quiver in her stomach whenever she thought about that diary, now that she had read it through to the end. Poor Miss Harriet, in the clutches of a beast, and she, Ethel Parsons, had seen him in the flesh. Those eyes – she would never forget them – piercing green and yellow in the darkness – sent a chill down her spine. Long ago in her youth, Mrs Parsons had heard of strange tales, in the old days in Ireland – of girls spirited away by less than human lovers and when they returned they were quite out of their heads, as Miss Harriet seemed to be now. Although not unduly superstitious, Mrs Parsons knew that there are some things and some people better left alone, and Miss Harriet's naked man was one of them. It was all to the better Harriet had not brought his offspring into the world, although the poor dear had nearly poisoned herself in preventing such an ill-omened event.

The hired car pulled up as she was pouring a small glass of wine to give her a little strength for her journey. She signaled to the driver from the window, then rinsed the glass and set it upside down on the sink to drain, wondering how many days or weeks or months would pass before anyone set foot in this kitchen again. She untied her apron and hung it on a nail by the stove, then closed the kitchen shutter and window. The house was dark now with all the shutters closed and her footsteps echoed eerily on the brick floor. She went to the coat rack at the top of the landing, slipped on her grey coat, clapped on her hat and put her black silk bag and the packet containing Miss Harriet's notebook under her arm. Reaching for her valise, she met the eyes of the stone mask peering up at her from under the gilt table and gave a little involuntary jump for it seemed to her the thing had moved away from the wall and was staring up at her with an impudent grin. Nonsense, she thought, as she hurried down the stairs. She must have moved it accidentally while dusting, but she looked back at it one last time, just to make sure, before opening the door. Her heart gave a flutter when she thought she saw it flick its tongue at her. Perhaps Mr Hampton was right about the wine, after all, she thought, as she stepped out to the brilliant daylight and banged the door shut – it was much stronger than the stout she was used to. She slipped the key under a flower pot on the steps, as Mr Hampton had instructed her, and ran to the waiting car.

Mr Hampton had booked her a sleeping compartment as far as Calais, which she shared with an untalkative French lady who lay stiff as a board on the lower berth until the lights went out, and then snored and chattered in her sleep all night. Mrs Parsons did not undress and just lay very still on her side on the upper berth, alert to every noise, her face turned away from the door, and her hands firmly clutching her black silk bag. Beneath her pillow she had tucked her prize: the package with Miss Harriet's notebook. As the train rattled through the dark countryside, sweeping her through the northern towns and then across the Alps, she smiled to herself and savored the idea of revenge. For when she delivered the diary back into Miss Harriet's hands, she would have her revenge on Mr Hampton, after all those long years of being bullied. She would have to wait a while perhaps before returning it, until Miss Harried had recovered from her fever, and perhaps even longer after that – when the strange story would be only a memory, like a dream almost forgotten but not quite. When at last the jostling of the carriage lulled her to sleep, she found herself fleeing naked through a forest in winter, pursued by a wild boar.

By the beginning of July, the Hamptons were back in London, where Stephen contacted several doctors to discuss Harriet's case, and finally settled on an institution near Salisbury where she would be well cared for. After the ordeal in Italy, Sarah's nerves were exhausted and she did not come with Stephen and Wimbly to accompany Harriet to the hospital where Stephen had arranged for her to remain for an extended period, a place he still insisted on describing to his wife as a special sort of sanatorium. Stephen and Wimbly drove Harriet there together a week after their return from Italy. She put up no resistance, but increasing doses of tincture of opium were needed to maintain her in such a reasonable state.

The sanatorium was housed in a handsome Georgian building at the end of a long drive lined with well-trimmed shrubs and lilac bushes, surrounded by a pleasant rose garden where patients could stroll. With Harriet propped up between them like a rubber mannequin, Stephen and Wimbly approached the entrance. Wimbly was aghast at her state. Harriet resembled a sleepwalker, with dilated eyes. The tincture of opium had deadened all reaction, the only expression on her face was a vague smile. Stephen chattered to her as they escorted her to the door, describing the private room she was to have, with a view of the rose garden. Harriet bobbed her head to show that she was following – but Wimbly could see her mind was miles away, swathed in an opium mist. Wimbly was repulsed by Stephen's plans to intern Harriet, but seeing her in such a condition, he knew it would be useless to oppose him, unless he himself were willing to fight for Harriet's freedom – given the circumstances, who could blame him for not doing so?

An opulent bouquet of yellow roses and tiger lilies decorated the desk in the cool dark hall where an attractive young nurse in a starched uniform welcomed them and filled out the necessary papers. Harriet's hand shook as she signed the form, then dropped the pen. The nurse put Harriet into the care of two assistants who trundled her in a wheelchair down the corridor to an examination room. Then she showed the two men up to the room Harriet was to occupy, to see if it met their approval. A porter took charge of Harriet's valise and followed them up the stairs. That valise contained only a few clothes and personal effects, mostly toiletry articles and nightdresses, along with the small packet of mementos Sarah had wrapped up for her in Italy, and unknown to Stephen, had slipped into her valise.

A plump bearded doctor with gold-rimmed spectacles and a soft Swiss German accent received them in his study after examining Harriet. He told them he had treated similar cases successfully, but that first she must be cured of her addiction to opium and brought back into a relative state of physical health, before beginning her definitive cure. It would not be without its risks, he warned and it would also take time.

"How much time?" Wimbly asked rather ingenuously.

The doctor's eyebrows shot up, as if to say he did not know.

Stephen nodded solemnly and told the doctor to take all the time he needed, whatever the expense.

Driving back to London, Stephen was disinclined to discuss the subject of Harriet, or even say how long he intended her to undergo treatment in the sanatorium. He only promised Wimbly he would see to it that her stay was not overly long, and that he and Sarah would welcome her into their home the moment she showed signs of improvement. Instead Stephen was eager to speak of his plans for Sarah and himself.

"I have decided to begin adoption proceedings," he announced, to Wimbly's great surprise. "Sarah needs to occupy herself with something, now that this dreadful business is ended." He went on to tell Wimbly about the orphaned son of a distant relative, who now at the age of six, was still at a plausible age for adoption. "All the more to keep Sarah busy, she needs someone on whom to lavish her maternal cares."

211

"Doubtless," said Wimbly, and kept his thoughts to himself.

A few weeks later Wimbly booked his return passage to India. Before sailing out, he paid one last visit to Harriet. The nurse sent him out to the rose garden where Harriet, wearing a plaid dressing gown, sat hunched on a bench, staring at the water splashing in a fountain. He was startled to see that in this short time, her hair had gone completely grey. He called to her as he approached and she turned slowly to look at him without the slightest sign of recognition. The nurse had prepared him for this. Harriet had just recovered from the first bout of induced fever and both her eyesight and memory were temporarily impaired.

"Harriet," he called, "It's me, George Wimbly," and he repeated his name several times.

She squinted in his face as if in pain and then nodded and croaked, "George dear."

"Oh, Harriet," he murmured, and dropped to the bench beside her, clasping both her hands to his chest. Not yet 45, she had become an old woman. He could not bear to meet her eye – the glint of mischievous wit he had loved in her had quite fizzled out. In its place was a furtive vacancy. This was not Harriet. He had been robbed of her. Yet the enormous sense of loss he felt had nothing to do with the unknown, undignified elderly person sitting at his side, with spittle beaded on her lip. To his shame, he felt an overwhelming gratitude that she had never agreed to marry him.

As they sat in the sunny garden watching sparrows picking at the ground, he made an effort to say pleasant things about the place, about her, about their youth, but she could not really follow. After half an hour, he could bear it no more and got up to leave. He promised to come back and visit her the next time he returned to England. Before saying good bye, he thrust a packet into her hands and told her not to open it until after he had gone. He did not really want to see her reaction. She did not even seem mildly curious about it and as she stood up to embrace him, it fell from her lap to the ground.

He picked it up for her, dusted it off, and lay it on the bench where they had been sitting. Then he hugged her again and walked away, his feet crunching on the white gravel. Turning back to wave one last time, he saw that she must have gone back inside through one of the doors giving onto the rose garden, for she was no longer sitting near the fountain. The package he had delivered to her still lay on the bench and he wondered if he should go back to fetch it. Just then, a young nurse emerged from round the hedge in the garden, noticed the packet and retrieved it.

"That belongs to Miss Sackett," he called to the nurse before going out the gate. "Would you be so kind as to make sure it is returned it to her?"

The nurse waved peremptorily to show that he need not concern himself any further. Clutching it to her bosom, she marched inside and Wimbly went out through the gate

This was to be Wimbly's last visit to England, for he died the next autumn, of a liver disease, at the age of 54, while aboard a ship en route to Rangoon, going out to visit one of his sons.

Post Script by Harriet Sackett, December 1945

My liberation came with the end of the war. My cousin Stephen died, then his wife, my dearest friend, Sarah, shortly after him. In October 1945 I stepped somewhat uncertainly through the hospital gates and out into freedom, clutching a small leather valise in my hand. To my great disappointment, Dr Henley had been called away urgently the night before, so she was not there to see me off. At the gate I was met by an efficient young woman, a former army nurse, at the wheel of a silver Bentley, which I was amazed to discover now belonged to me. Liberty, nurse, and car were at my disposal thanks to a provision in Stephen Hampton's will.

I did not look back at that handsome building with the dormer windows and the red door with brass trim where I had spent the last 23 years of my existence. I certainly was not sad to be leaving. Those years had passed swiftly in a blur of deadened sensations with brief flickers of searing physical pain. Had it not been for Dr Henley, who replaced the old director a few years prior to my release, I would no doubt have died under the strain of electroconvulsive therapy, to which I was repeatedly subjected during the last phase of the previous director's reign of terror. Mercifully Dr Henley put an end to the shock treatments and the drugged slumbers and weaned me back to life. To whatever life you may have at my age.

"Harriet," she said, "you are here principally because no one knows what to do with you." After twenty years, I had become a regular fixture around the place. The first ten years had been dedicated to treatments, the following years to recovering from them.

By the time Dr Henley had become director, Stephen was quite ill. Doubtless his conscience devoured him, for he began to make plans for my release. But there was no question of my returning to live with him and Sarah, they were both too ill, and then the war started. The hospital, a bit far from London, was not such a bad place for a lonely old woman to wait out the war. Though the food of course deteriorated.

At the age of 65, I was pushed out into a new life, but my memory had been ravaged by those treatments, and as I walked through that door I hardly knew who I was anymore. I remembered my childhood in Chicago well enough, my mother and father, the friends of my early youth, my career as a photographer, travels to exotic places. Certain objects, places, and sensations I knew belonged to me. But there was a whole piece of myself that had just dropped into the sea. For example, the cornelian ring I wore but could not account for. Who could have given me such a beautiful gift? When I asked Sarah on one of her rare visits, she only sighed and said she did know. I was obsessed with that ring, I would let no one touch it. I knew it was important, but I couldn't say why.

Some things stirred me strangely. The shape of a man's arm or head. Dogs barking. One of the stretcher carriers had a thick scar on his arm. For some reason it fascinated, even aroused me. Good heavens, at my age! These things made me almost think of something that maddeningly escaped me, connected with the missing piece of my life right before I had returned to England.

I knew I had fallen ill in Italy prior to being admitted for treatment of severe opium addiction and hallucinatory dementia. This diagnosis was later altered, I believe, it was found that I suffered from petit mal. Still, Dr Henley never pronounced herself on this subject

The electric shocks jarred sexual memories I was reluctant to own at first. The heat of a man's heavy body on mine. A feral smell. Coarse springy hair. A hand gliding on skin slick with sweat. The thrusting of a tongue and the sucking of breath. Grappling but not wanting to let go. These were sensations that certainly did not belong to the earlier part of my life, but I did not find them unpleasant, on the contrary. I did not know who this man was or what he had to do with me. Sometimes I confused Wimbly with him, sometimes other men, even Stephen. But Stephen was so long ago. That memory came attended by a stabbing pain, the smell of boxwood, a sickening feeling. But this other man was somehow, preposterously, part of me. He was not Stephen or Wimbly or any man I recalled. But I knew him by his smell. The physical reality of this sensation made me feel I was still me, when all the other parts had scattered. But who he might be, I had no idea. Dr Henley tried many tricks to prod my memory, in order to be whole again she said I had to remember.

The day of my release I was driven to a small house in Gower Street converted into flats. Mine consisted of two bedrooms and a sitting room with a gas cooker in one corner. It was not very luxurious and not very clean. This was to be my new home until my future living arrangements were decided. There was a smelly water closet down the hall. The nurse girl would occupy the spare bedroom. That was fine with me, I was glad for the company.

Mr Benson, the Hamptons' solicitor, came in the afternoon and patiently explained my new situation to me. Nearly all my previous assets had gone for payment for those long years of treatment, but I did still own some properties in Chicago whose value had now greatly increased. Mr Benson suggested I sell them. I also had a generous annuity from both Stephen and Sarah, whose heirs, an adopted son and his wife, were only too glad to have me out of that expensive clinic and settled in humbler surroundings – for fear they might have to foot the bill if my money ran out.

Many things needed to be explained to me about what life was like now, though not as many as Mr Benson and the girl assumed. They looked upon me as a sleeper returned from the dead, but I was not as far gone as they imagined. Still I let them prattle on as they would, and bobbed my head and smiled benignly, as people my age and in my condition are expected to do.

Mr Benson said goodbye leaving me as a gift a bottle of cognac and some cigarettes, which I had rarely enjoyed during the years of my treatment, so I was duly grateful. On pretext of getting something for our dinner, I sent the girl out as soon as he was gone. I wanted to taste my liberty once and for all, and to reflect on what I should do now.

I didn't much like the looks of the flat, or the idea of being confined any longer. I wondered if at my age and in my state I could withstand the stress of a journey. For some reason the idea of Italy appealed to me strongly.

I lit a cigarette, inhaled, and looked out at London with its relics of crumbling bricks and shattered glass, its crowds of noisy, swaggering young men, the ubiquitous music and voices of the wireless. And so many cars. What photographs I would have taken if I had had a camera. I would have to arrange to purchase some new equipment.

Suddenly remembering the valise, which I had not yet opened, I put it on the bed and unlocked it. The nurse had packed it for me the night before, on Dr Henley's request. It contained the only clothes and personal necessities I still owned, underclothes and nightdresses, soap and toothbrush, and three packets wrapped in brown paper. I wondered if these were perhaps gifts from the nurses. There was a tiny phial of perfume. I uncorked it, sniffed the odor of Parma violets and thought instantly of Sarah, at the age of sixteen, flushed, with long dark hair. There was a package of her letters too, tied with a faded lavender ribbon. How I had longed for her visits, then for the letters that replaced them. There was a note also from Dr Henley. I fumbled in my jacket pocket for my glasses, opened the envelope and read:

Dear Harriet,

Upon looking through the files for your release, we found note of these belongings of yours put away for safekeeping. I do not know if they are of interest or use to you now, but perhaps they can help you remember something of your past. I am returning them to you with all my best wishes.

Undoing the first packet I found my old lucky Buddha from my childhood, which I was overjoyed to see, for I had quite forgotten its existence until that moment. My uncle James had given it to me as a gift for my sixteenth birthday and for years I carried it with me wherever I went. There were also, inexplicably, a dog's collar, a bundle of porcupine quills tied with a ribbon and an old picture of myself with a dog. There was also note in Sarah's lovely hand reading:

My dearest Harriet,

A few mementos of your time in Italy. May they keep you company.

Sarah.

How poignant it was to receive this gift across time from a dead friend. I brushed away my tears, and studied the picture. It seemed to me I had never looked prettier. God knows where the time goes so quickly. But what house was that? And whose dog? I did not remember having a dog, although I was always fond of them. Written on the back of the photograph was a date *1922* and the name *Vitorchiano*. I repeated the word twice to myself and shook my head. It meant nothing to me. I did not know what to make of the collar or the quills.

Now I undid the other packet. It contained a photograph of a man sitting at a desk, with the same black dog in my old picture, lying at his feet. So that dog somehow connected me to the man, but how I could not fathom. I stared long and hard at the man's face. Not handsome but interesting. I smiled to myself or perhaps at him, and thought, "Now aren't you the very devil of a fellow?" I did not recall his name, but I thought I recognized him from somewhere. His name was there on the tip of my tongue and any moment now I knew I'd remember.

Examining the quills I pricked my finger, for they were quite sharp, and the bundle slipped out of my grasp to the floor. The quills scattered across the floorboards like Chinese pick-up sticks, and there in the middle lay a folded piece of paper. I picked it up and smoothed it out: it was a page torn from a notebook, written in what appeared to be my own handwriting, though even more untidy than usual. I skimmed through it, though I could make no sense of it. It read like a poem, or perhaps a dream I had jotted down. I folded it back up, slipped it into the breast pocket of my shirt, and opened the third packet which was addressed to me care of the hospital and postmarked 1933. It contained a notebook bound in green leather and an envelope addressed to Miss Harriet. The cover of the notebook was charred as if it had been through a fire. Intrigued, I opened the letter and read:

Dear Miss Harriet

I copied your address from a letter of the Missis she had written to you, as I was afraid to ask anyone directly. I wanted to return this to you as it belongs to you and I thought it might be important. I saved it from the stove after Mr Hampton tried to burn it back when you were ill in Italy, and we had all come out to see that you got back to England safely. Please forgive my long delay in returning it. I have had my hands full with the master and mistress. God Bless You, dear Miss Harriet. I hope I have done the right thing in giving this back to you.

Yours Sincerely,
Ethel Parsons.

My heart began to pound as I read through the note. I remembered Mrs Parsons, Stephen and Sarah's housekeeper, a dear old woman who must be long dead. I knew I was about to discover something momentous. I opened the notebook – the pages were sprinkled with ashes and a fine white dust like flour. The ink had faded, but I saw immediately that it was my own handwriting, and that the green-ruled pages with gilt edge matched the page I had found among the quills, which indeed appeared to have been ripped from the very end of the book – where I could see a page had been torn out. I was just settling down in my armchair to inspect the contents of the notebook, when the nurse-girl came back with an armload of fish and chips. Seized by an inexplicable, anxious secrecy, I tucked the book away behind the cushions of the chair, intending to read it all the way through as soon as I had a moment alone.

EPILOGUE

An old peasant woman in rags hobbled down the road to the village gate of Vitorchiano, a basket of onions balanced on her head, on her way to market. Half-deaf, she did not hear the car until it was almost upon her. The silver Bentley roared round the curve behind her, swerved to miss her, honking its furious horn, scattering the chickens that had strayed from a nearby farmyard. She stumbled in the draft of the speeding vehicle, but managed not to totter over. A few onions spilled out of the basket and rolled along the road. With one hand she steadied her load, squatting down to retrieve them as the gleaming motorcar hurtled on toward the village of Vitorchiano. She muttered a curse under her breath and followed it with her eyes. There were so many more cars on the roads nowadays, since the Americans had come. To her surprise, the car made a sharp turn at the crossroads and headed down the old dirt road. They must have taken a wrong turn she thought, for there was nothing there now but the ruins of a tower bombed out in 1943.

The car sped on, down the road full of pits and potholes, which soon petered out into a blackberry thicket. As it went plunging through the briars, leaves flubbed and thorns snagged against the sleek silver sides. The car was finally forced to come to a halt, its progress obstructed by the trunk of a rotting oak lying across the track.

The door to the driver's side opened, and a young blonde woman in khaki trousers stepped out. Maneuvering her way through the thorns, she went round to the passenger's side, and opened the door. An elderly woman climbed out into the narrow space between the car and the cascading wall of briars. She was tall and stooped with cropped grey hair. Like her younger companion she was wearing khaki trousers and tall rubber boots. She had a pasty complexion, as if it had been a long time since she had seen the sun. They contemplated the tree trunk in silence, then the older woman reached into the car to pull out a small square bag, and slung it over her shoulder.

On the other side of the trunk a trail led on through the thicket where there was just enough space for them to slip through single file. Beyond the mass of tangled vegetation they could see the tip of what was left of the tower, a heap of charred stones.

They straddled over the trunk and picked their way through the brambles until they came to a gatepost. In the tall weeds near the post lay a rusted gate wrested from its hinges. The older woman poked about the grass, searching for something, then picked up an object from the ground and showed it to the other. It was a porcupine quill. Smiling, she stuck it behind her ear the way you might stick a pen.

At last they reached the tower, where only one storey remained. The upper floors had been blasted away, and the entire back wall was missing. A crater ten feet across gaped to one side, a growth of scrub sprouted along the rim, and the surrounding terrain was strewn with blackened rubble. The door to the tower stood open and through the doorway they could see nettles growing amid the detritus where the stairway had been.

The older woman crunched across the rocks and broken glass

in her boots and stopped just before the doorway, judging it unwise to go any further, given the remaining structure's dubious stability. She opened her bag and took out a camera. As she snapped a picture of the tower, a chicken waddled out of the doorway, flapped its wings, and clucked at her in consternation, making the women laugh.

Another heap of stones lay beside the tower, this too, overgrown with vines. Here the perimeter of a low wall stuck out among the leaves, and a well-beaten path snaked through the bushes towards what looked like a burial monument which had somehow escaped the bombing.

The older woman now stumbled on through the briars. It must have been a family vault, but no name was carved on the dilapidated door, only a coat of arms showing an oak branch, a boar, and a porcupine. There was a series of dates: *1650, 1789, 1833, 1900, 1922, 1943.* Someone had visited not too long ago, a pile of brown chrysanthemums lay heaped on the tomb. As the old woman ran her finger across the chiseled surface of the stone, flakes of lichen peeled away beneath her touch.

Lifting the camera to her eye and squinting through the viewfinder, she was astonished to find herself peering down a tunnel carved in rock, where lush ferns sprouted from the walls, tickling her face and neck. She shivered as drops of cold moisture dripped down from the tunnel ceiling into her collar. Feeling dizzy, she closed her eyes. Opening them again, she saw a bluish light at the end of the tunnel and now she leapt toward it with amazing agility, although she was standing quite still. In the blinding blue glare, she could just make out the figure of a man, squarely built, not too tall, reaching out his arm to her, brandishing an egg in the sunlight.

When the old woman slumped and collapsed to the ground, her young companion rushed forward and tried in vain to resuscitate her, but her heart had stopped beating. Somehow the girl managed to drag the body back into the car and transport it to a hospital, where the authorities later entrusted to her the deceased woman's personal effects, including a folded piece of writing paper found in the breast pocket of her shirt.

Later, sorting through the effects, the girl flattened out the paper, read down through its contents quickly, hesitated for a moment to touch its edge, before crumpling it in a ball and tossing it aside:

I hesitated there at the fork in the path. Should I return home or follow the Count? Nocciola would go no further, so I decided to send him home. I let go and watched him dash up the ridge and down toward the tower. I knew I would find him later outside my door, waiting for his dinner, pushing his dish along the ground with his nose to show me he was hungry.

I turned down the path where Federigo had gone. Anxiety now gave my feet wings. A muddy trail of boar tracks took me deep into the wood as the wind moaned in the tree tops. A hundred yards down the trail, out stepped Federigo from behind a thicket. His naked body shone red in the sunlight, dazzling my eyes for a moment. He beckoned to me and laughed, and then vanished again through the trees. On I ran till at last I found him sitting cross-legged on a pile of stones beneath a giant oak. Absorbed into himself, he took no notice of me, so I sat down on a stump across from him and waited for him to awaken. After hours it seemed, he opened his eyes and stretched out his arms to me. We sat there together amid the moss and dead leaves, our hands barely touching as our souls poured into each other, filling my veins with a fine black substance studded with sparks and metallic gleams.

It was strange to make love like that, hardly needing a body, except for our hands and eyes. We sat so still, sipping each other's breath, anyone discovering us there might have thought we were statues from a former time. Perhaps such communion comes only once in a thousand years. I knew I would gladly wait for another thousand lifetimes.

＊◆＊

My body is light and has no being. Rising into the blue air, it sails through the wall, floats over the hillside and down to the sea. In a ship tossing on the waves, a row of moon-lit faces, and three tall clay jars of grain, oil and wine. There at the helm stands Federigo Del Re steering his ship to shore.

Finis

Here ends the notebook of Harriet Sackett

＊◆＊

ALSO FROM
WYNKIN deWORDE

AUTUMN 2004
ISBN: 1-904893-01-5

ALSO FROM
WYNKIN deWORDE

GREENE'S
SUMMER

Cafe Bopa

THOMAS E. KENNEDY

AUTUMN 2004
ISBN: 1-904893-02-3